PLANTS vs. ZOMBIES

CONSTRUCTIONARY TALES

Written by **PAUL TOBIN**
Art by **JESSE HAMM**
Colors by **HEATHER BRECKEL**
Letters by **STEVE DUTRO**
Cover by **RON CHAN**

DARK HORSE BOOKS

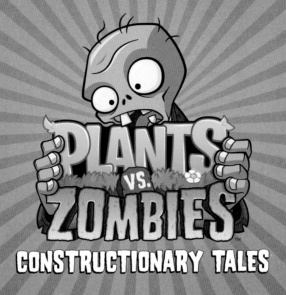

PLANTS VS. ZOMBIES™

CONSTRUCTIONARY TALES

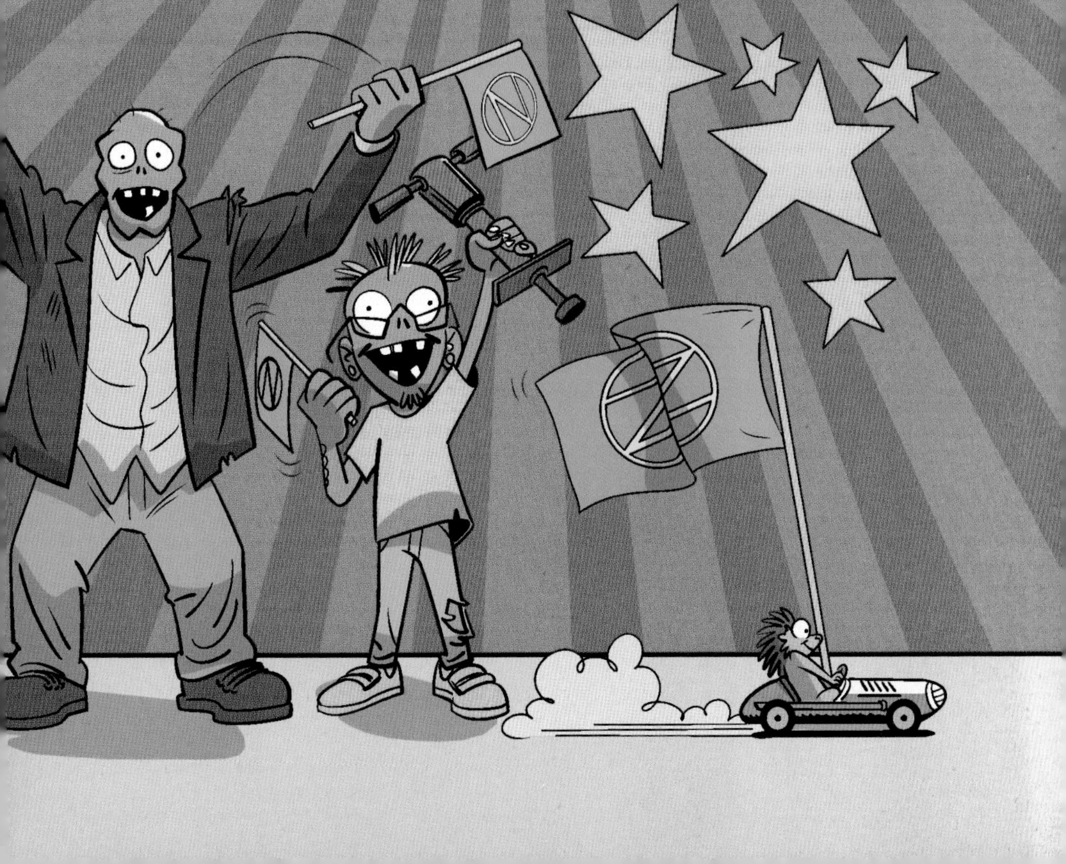

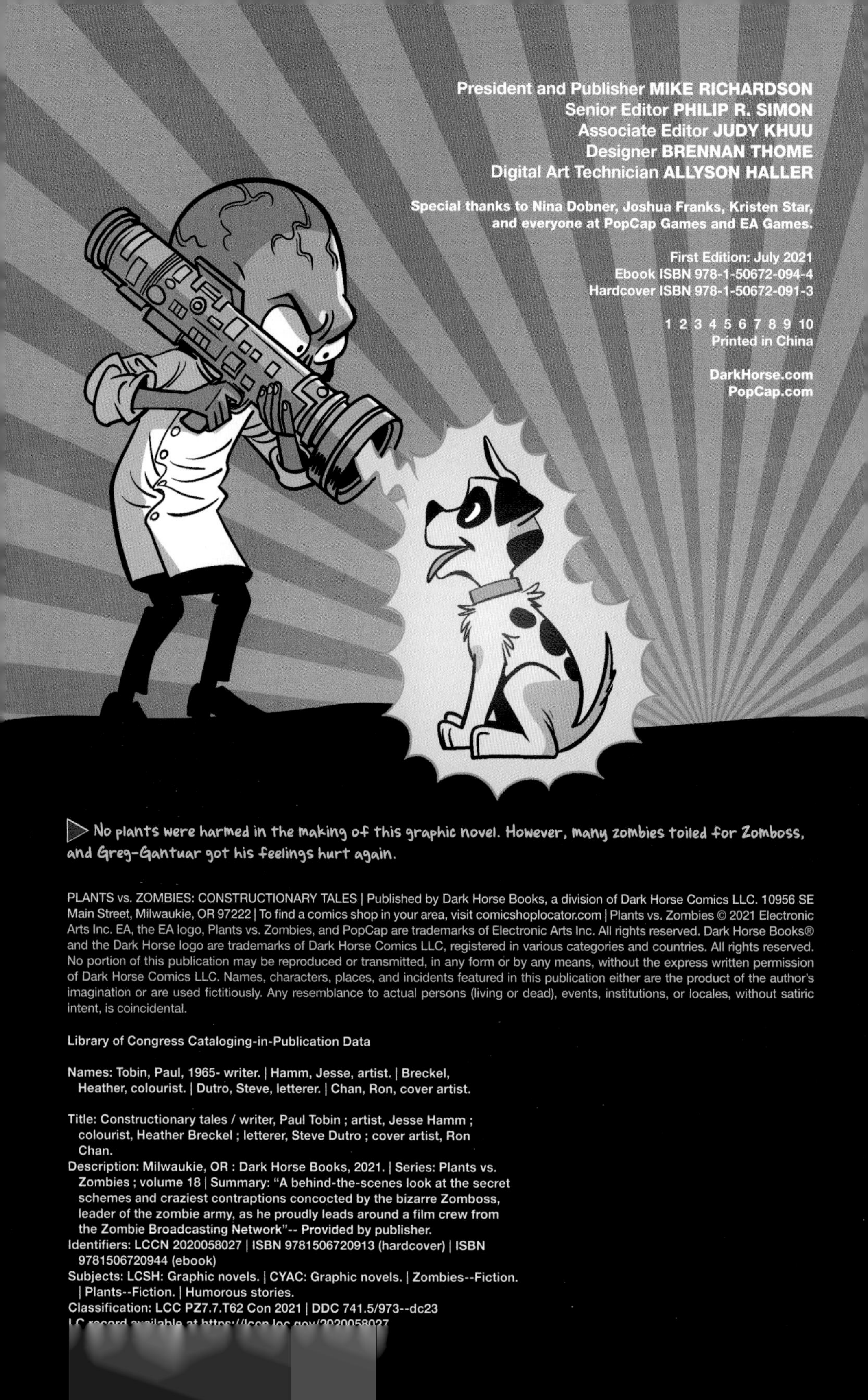

President and Publisher MIKE RICHARDSON
Senior Editor PHILIP R. SIMON
Associate Editor JUDY KHUU
Designer BRENNAN THOME
Digital Art Technician ALLYSON HALLER

Special thanks to Nina Dobner, Joshua Franks, Kristen Star, and everyone at PopCap Games and EA Games.

First Edition: July 2021
Ebook ISBN 978-1-50672-094-4
Hardcover ISBN 978-1-50672-091-3

1 2 3 4 5 6 7 8 9 10
Printed in China

DarkHorse.com
PopCap.com

No plants were harmed in the making of this graphic novel. However, many zombies toiled for Zomboss, and Greg-Gantuar got his feelings hurt again.

PLANTS vs. ZOMBIES: CONSTRUCTIONARY TALES | Published by Dark Horse Books, a division of Dark Horse Comics LLC. 10956 SE Main Street, Milwaukie, OR 97222 | To find a comics shop in your area, visit comicshoplocator.com |

Library of Congress Cataloging-in-Publication Data

Names: Tobin, Paul, 1965- writer. | Hamm, Jesse, artist. | Breckel, Heather, colourist. | Dutro, Steve, letterer. | Chan, Ron, cover artist.

Title: Constructionary tales / writer, Paul Tobin ; artist, Jesse Hamm ; colourist, Heather Breckel ; letterer, Steve Dutro ; cover artist, Ron Chan.
Description: Milwaukie, OR : Dark Horse Books, 2021. | Series: Plants vs. Zombies ; volume 18 | Summary: "A behind-the-scenes look at the secret schemes and craziest contraptions concocted by the bizarre Zomboss, leader of the zombie army, as he proudly leads around a film crew from the Zombie Broadcasting Network"-- Provided by publisher.
Identifiers: LCCN 2020058027 | ISBN 9781506720913 (hardcover) | ISBN 9781506720944 (ebook)
Subjects: LCSH: Graphic novels. | CYAC: Graphic novels. | Zombies--Fiction. | Plants--Fiction. | Humorous stories.
Classification: LCC PZ7.7.T62 Con 2021 | DDC 741.5/973--dc23
LC record available at https://lccn.loc.gov/2020058027

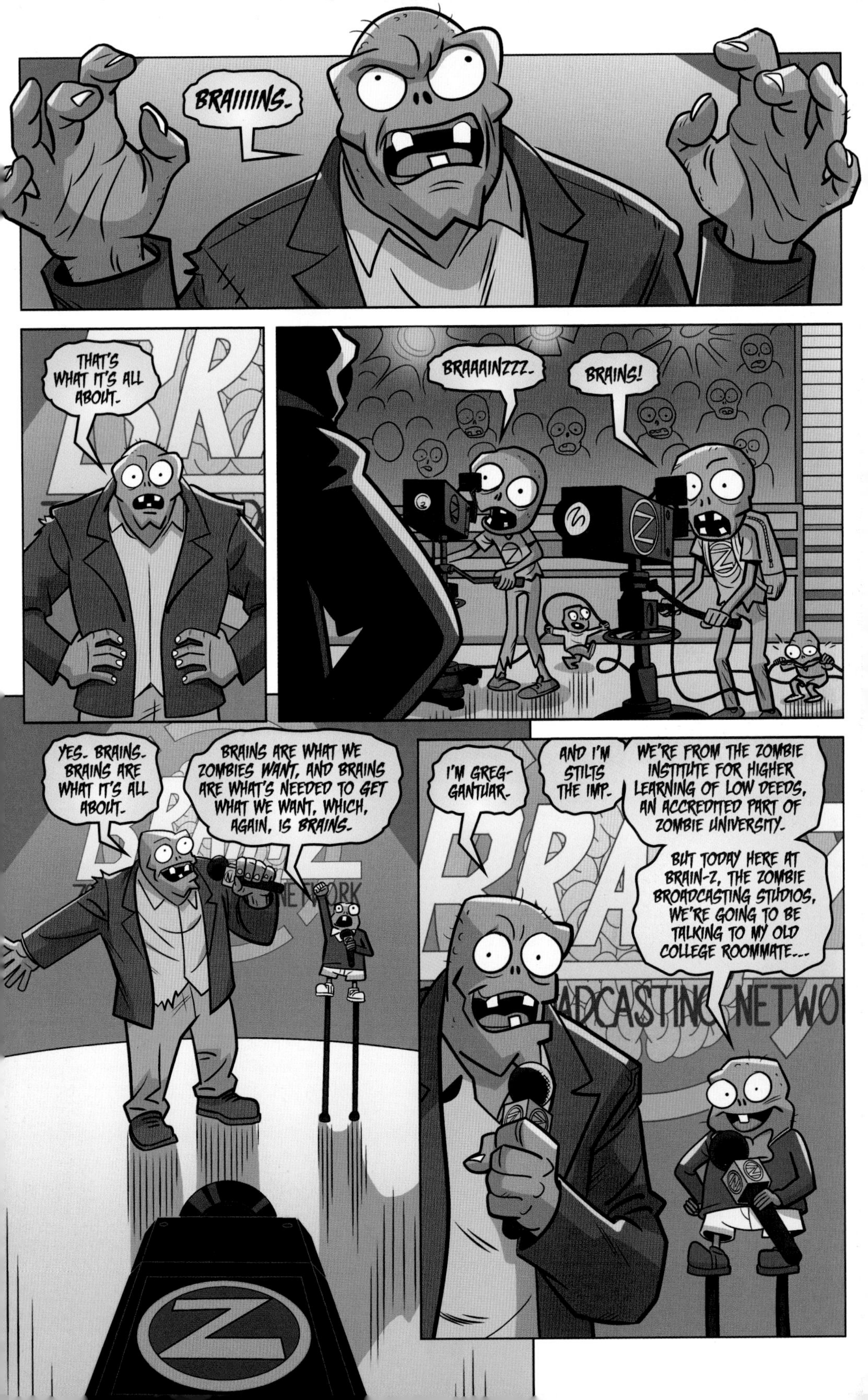

BRAIIIINS.
THAT'S WHAT IT'S ALL ABOUT.
BRAAAINZZZ.
BRAINS!
YES. BRAINS. BRAINS ARE WHAT IT'S ALL ABOUT.
BRAINS ARE WHAT WE ZOMBIES WANT, AND BRAINS ARE WHAT'S NEEDED TO GET WHAT WE WANT, WHICH, AGAIN, IS BRAINS.
I'M GREG-GANTUAR.
AND I'M STILTS THE IMP.
WE'RE FROM THE ZOMBIE INSTITUTE FOR HIGHER LEARNING OF LOW DEEDS, AN ACCREDITED PART OF ZOMBIE UNIVERSITY.
BUT TODAY HERE AT BRAIN-Z, THE ZOMBIE BROADCASTING STUDIOS, WE'RE GOING TO BE TALKING TO MY OLD COLLEGE ROOMMATE...

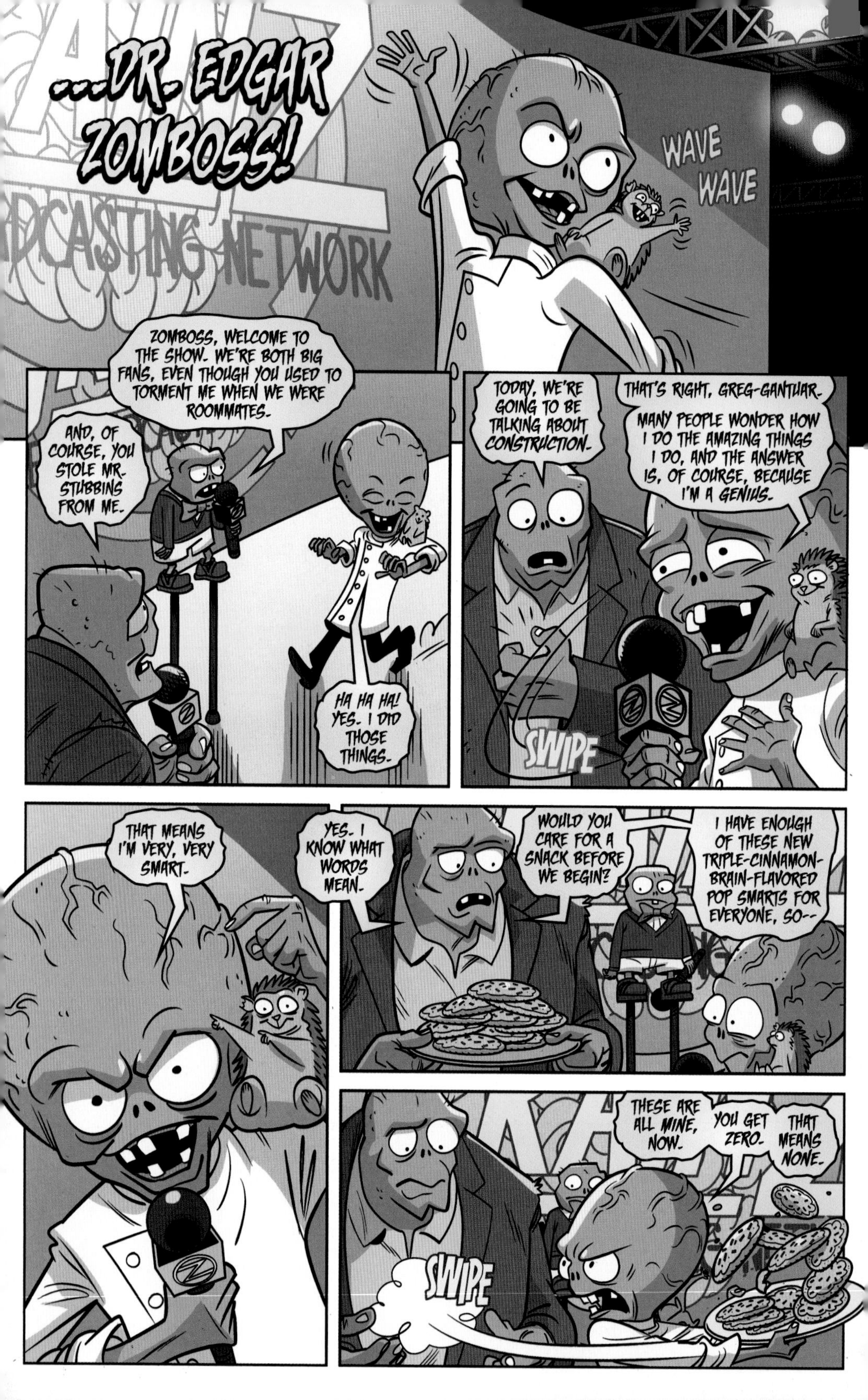
...DR. EDGAR ZOMBOSS!
WAVE WAVE
ADCASTING NETWORK
ZOMBOSS, WELCOME TO THE SHOW. WE'RE BOTH BIG FANS, EVEN THOUGH YOU USED TO TORMENT ME WHEN WE WERE ROOMMATES.
AND, OF COURSE, YOU STOLE MR. STUBBINS FROM ME.
HA HA HA! YES. I DID THOSE THINGS.
TODAY, WE'RE GOING TO BE TALKING ABOUT CONSTRUCTION.
THAT'S RIGHT, GREG-GANTUAR.
MANY PEOPLE WONDER HOW I DO THE AMAZING THINGS I DO, AND THE ANSWER IS, OF COURSE, BECAUSE I'M A GENIUS.
SWIPE
THAT MEANS I'M VERY, VERY SMART.
YES. I KNOW WHAT WORDS MEAN.
WOULD YOU CARE FOR A SNACK BEFORE WE BEGIN?
I HAVE ENOUGH OF THESE NEW TRIPLE-CINNAMON-BRAIN-FLAVORED POP SMARTS FOR EVERYONE, SO--
SWIPE
THESE ARE ALL MINE, NOW.
YOU GET ZERO.
THAT MEANS NONE.

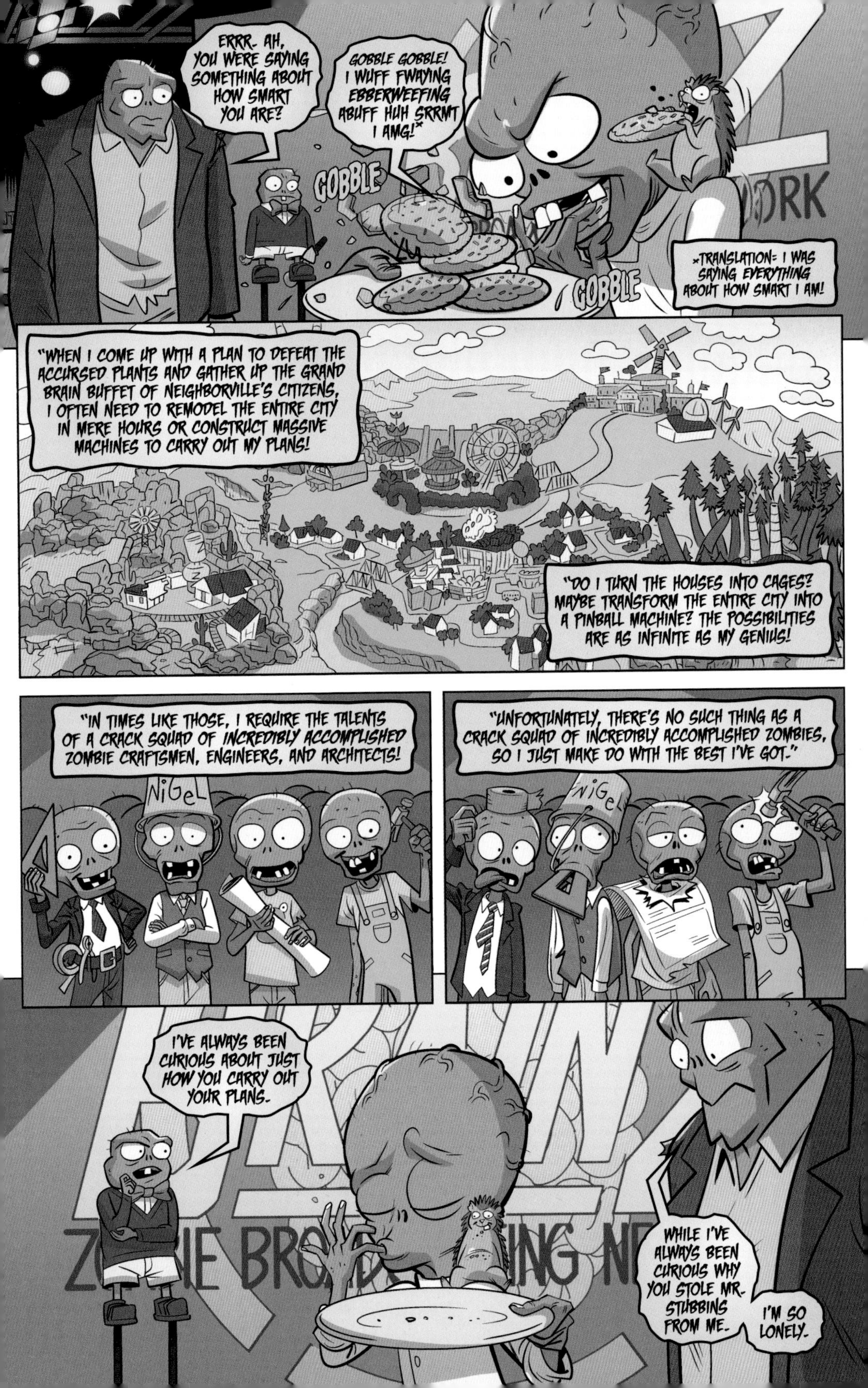
ERRR- AH, YOU WERE SAYING SOMETHING ABOUT HOW SMART YOU ARE?
GOBBLE GOBBLE! I WUFF FWAYING EBBERWEEFING ABUFF HUH SRRMT I AMG!*
GOBBLE
GOBBLE
*TRANSLATION: I WAS SAYING EVERYTHING ABOUT HOW SMART I AM!
"WHEN I COME UP WITH A PLAN TO DEFEAT THE ACCURSED PLANTS AND GATHER UP THE GRAND BRAIN BUFFET OF NEIGHBORVILLE'S CITIZENS, I OFTEN NEED TO REMODEL THE ENTIRE CITY IN MERE HOURS OR CONSTRUCT MASSIVE MACHINES TO CARRY OUT MY PLANS!
"DO I TURN THE HOUSES INTO CAGES? MAYBE TRANSFORM THE ENTIRE CITY INTO A PINBALL MACHINE? THE POSSIBILITIES ARE AS INFINITE AS MY GENIUS!
"IN TIMES LIKE THOSE, I REQUIRE THE TALENTS OF A CRACK SQUAD OF INCREDIBLY ACCOMPLISHED ZOMBIE CRAFTSMEN, ENGINEERS, AND ARCHITECTS!
NiGeL
"UNFORTUNATELY, THERE'S NO SUCH THING AS A CRACK SQUAD OF INCREDIBLY ACCOMPLISHED ZOMBIES, SO I JUST MAKE DO WITH THE BEST I'VE GOT."
NiGeL
I'VE ALWAYS BEEN CURIOUS ABOUT JUST HOW YOU CARRY OUT YOUR PLANS.
WHILE I'VE ALWAYS BEEN CURIOUS WHY YOU STOLE MR. STUBBING FROM ME.
I'M SO LONELY.

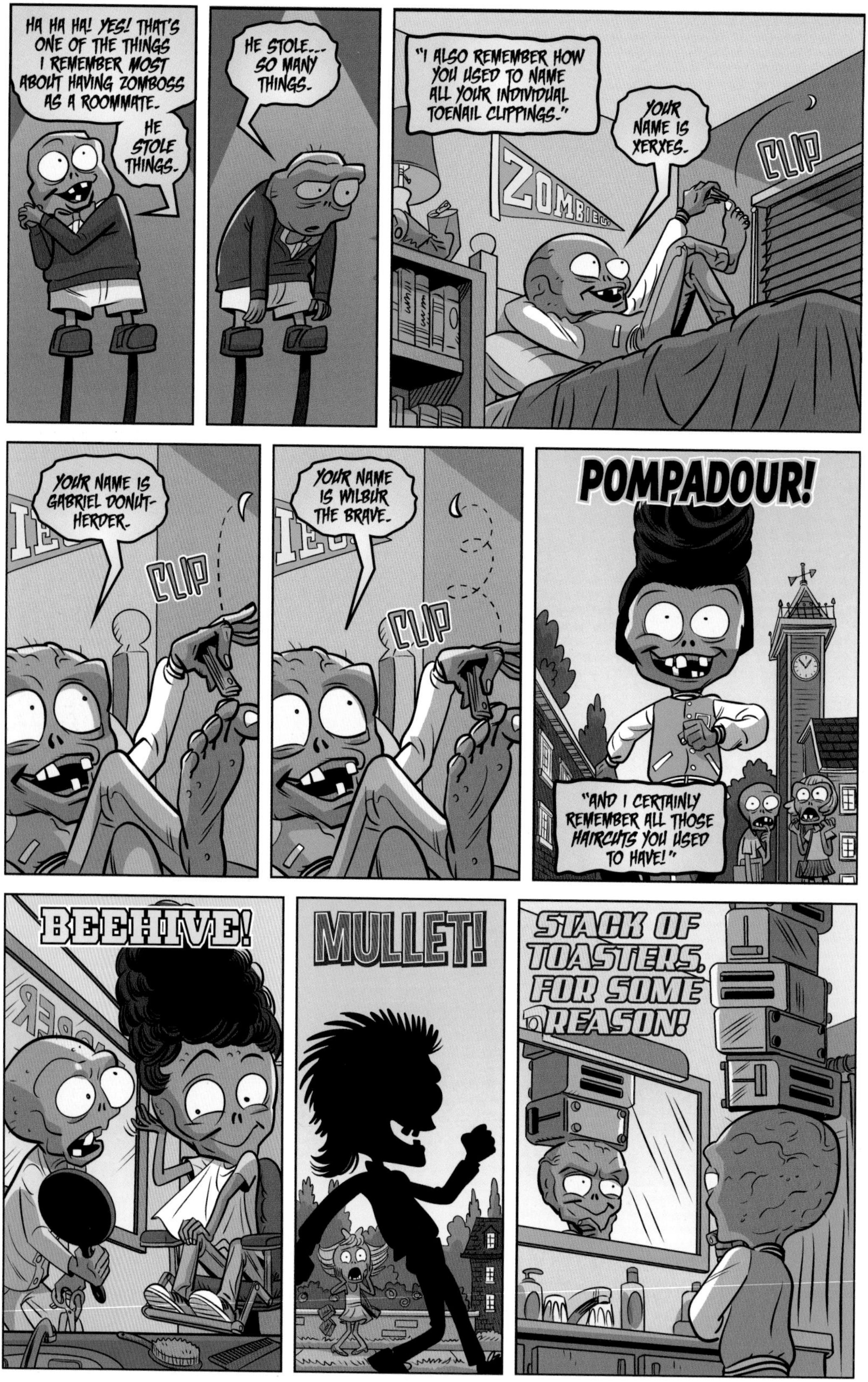

HA HA HA! YES! THAT'S ONE OF THE THINGS I REMEMBER MOST ABOUT HAVING ZOMBOSS AS A ROOMMATE.
HE STOLE THINGS.
HE STOLE... SO MANY THINGS.
"I ALSO REMEMBER HOW YOU USED TO NAME ALL YOUR INDIVIDUAL TOENAIL CLIPPINGS."
YOUR NAME IS XERXES.
ZOMBIEU
CLIP
YOUR NAME IS GABRIEL DONUT-HERDER.
CLIP
YOUR NAME IS WILBUR THE BRAVE.
CLIP
POMPADOUR!
"AND I CERTAINLY REMEMBER ALL THOSE HAIRCUTS YOU USED TO HAVE!"
BEEHIVE!
MULLET!
STACK OF TOASTERS, FOR SOME REASON!

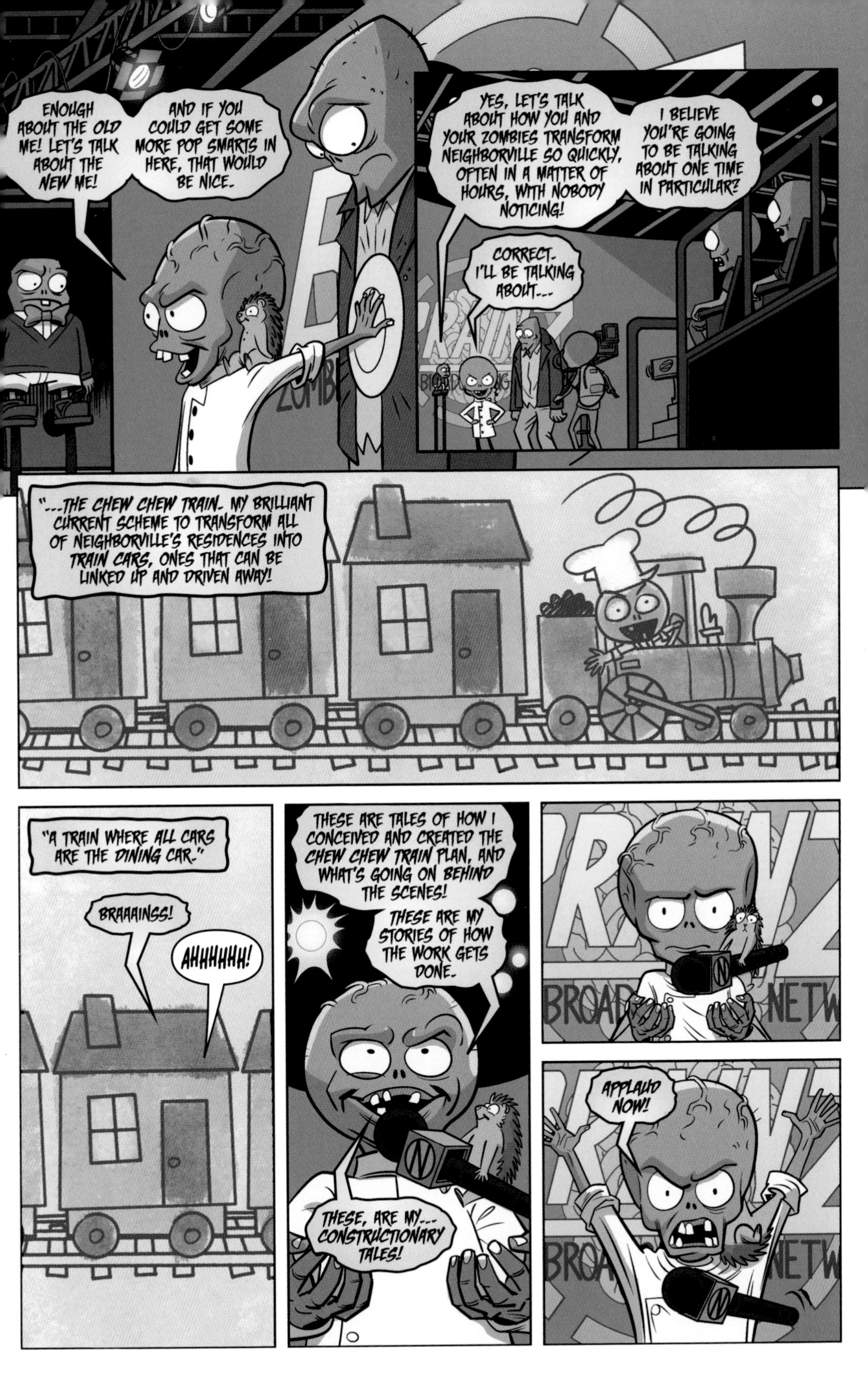
ENOUGH ABOUT THE OLD ME! LET'S TALK ABOUT THE NEW ME!
AND IF YOU COULD GET SOME MORE POP SMARTS IN HERE, THAT WOULD BE NICE.
YES, LET'S TALK ABOUT HOW YOU AND YOUR ZOMBIES TRANSFORM NEIGHBORVILLE SO QUICKLY, OFTEN IN A MATTER OF HOURS, WITH NOBODY NOTICING!
I BELIEVE YOU'RE GOING TO BE TALKING ABOUT ONE TIME IN PARTICULAR?
CORRECT. I'LL BE TALKING ABOUT...
"...THE CHEW CHEW TRAIN. MY BRILLIANT CURRENT SCHEME TO TRANSFORM ALL OF NEIGHBORVILLE'S RESIDENCES INTO TRAIN CARS, ONES THAT CAN BE LINKED UP AND DRIVEN AWAY!
"A TRAIN WHERE ALL CARS ARE THE DINING CAR."
BRAAAINSS!
AHHHHHH!
THESE ARE TALES OF HOW I CONCEIVED AND CREATED THE CHEW CHEW TRAIN PLAN, AND WHAT'S GOING ON BEHIND THE SCENES!
THESE ARE MY STORIES OF HOW THE WORK GETS DONE.
THESE, ARE MY... CONSTRUCTIONARY TALES!
APPLAUD NOW!

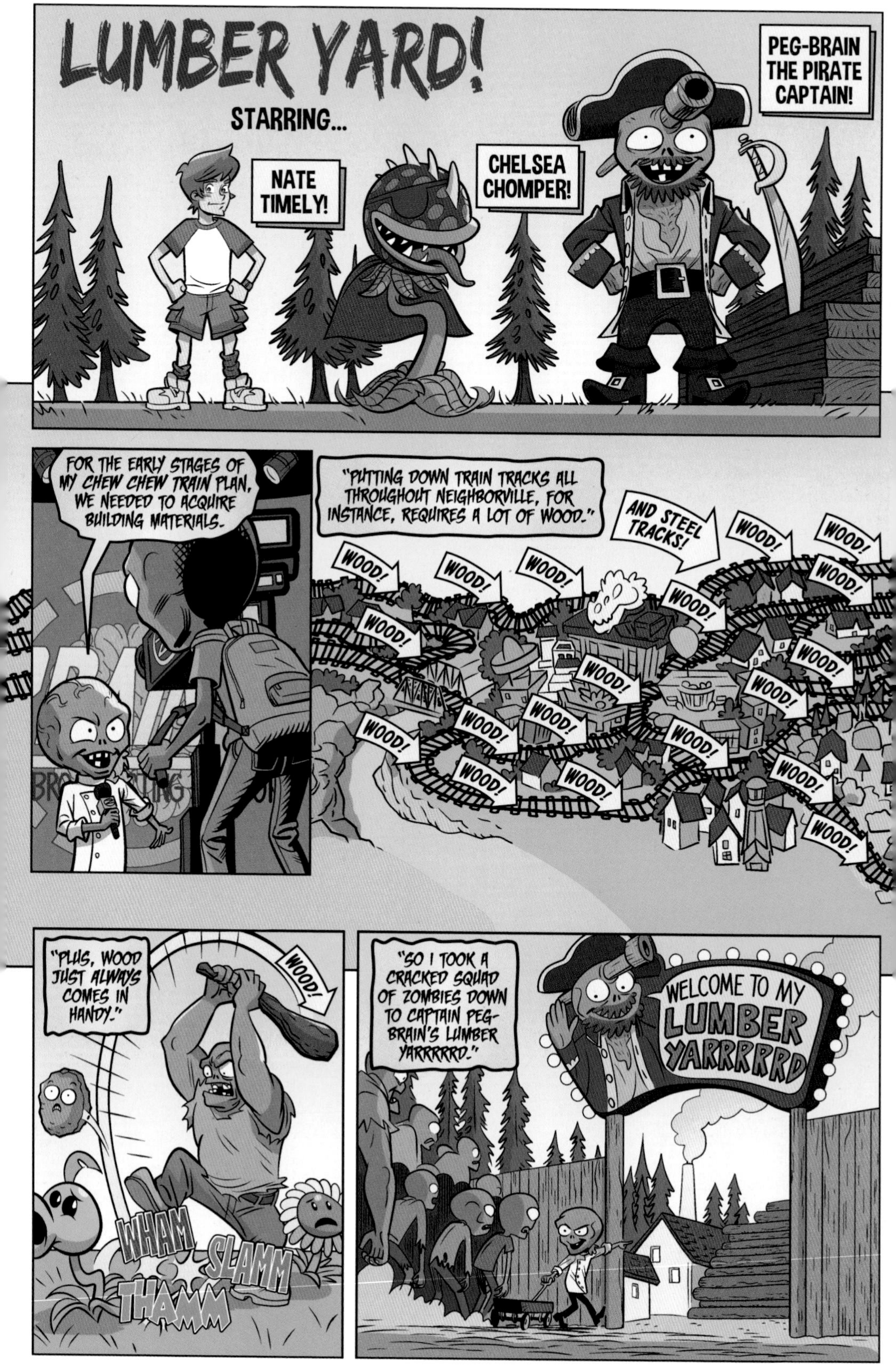
LUMBER YARD!
STARRING...
NATE TIMELY!
CHELSEA CHOMPER!
PEG-BRAIN THE PIRATE CAPTAIN!
FOR THE EARLY STAGES OF MY CHEW CHEW TRAIN PLAN, WE NEEDED TO ACQUIRE BUILDING MATERIALS.
"PUTTING DOWN TRAIN TRACKS ALL THROUGHOUT NEIGHBORVILLE, FOR INSTANCE, REQUIRES A LOT OF WOOD."
AND STEEL TRACKS!
WOOD!
"PLUS, WOOD JUST ALWAYS COMES IN HANDY."
WOOD!
WHAM
SLAMM
THAMM
"SO I TOOK A CRACKED SQUAD OF ZOMBIES DOWN TO CAPTAIN PEG-BRAIN'S LUMBER YARRRRRD."
WELCOME TO MY LUMBER YARRRRRD

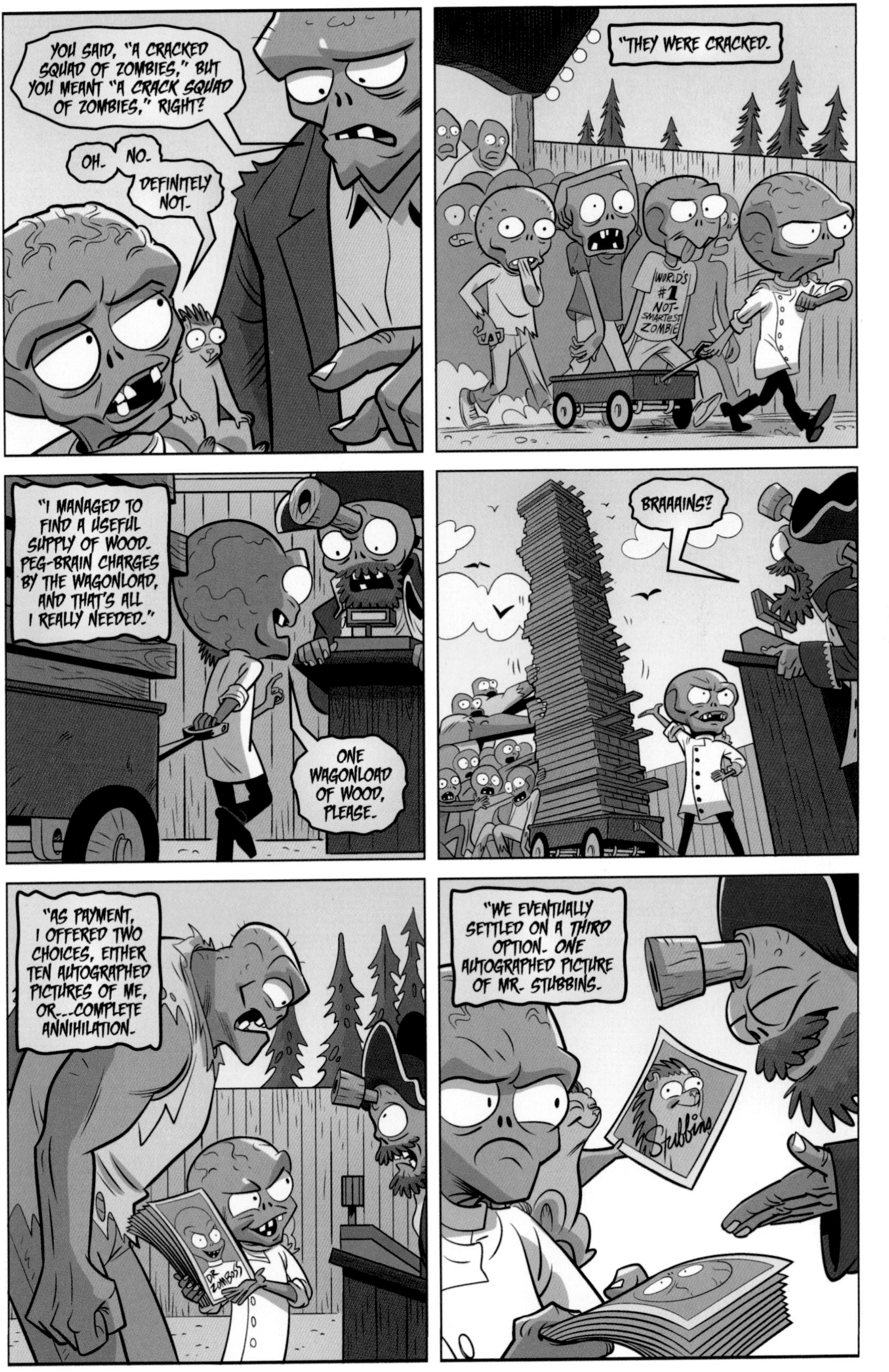
YOU SAID, "A CRACKED SQUAD OF ZOMBIES," BUT YOU MEANT "A CRACK SQUAD OF ZOMBIES," RIGHT?
OH.
NO.
DEFINITELY NOT.
"THEY WERE CRACKED.
WORLD'S #1 NOT-SMARTEST ZOMBIE
"I MANAGED TO FIND A USEFUL SUPPLY OF WOOD. PEG-BRAIN CHARGES BY THE WAGONLOAD, AND THAT'S ALL I REALLY NEEDED."
ONE WAGONLOAD OF WOOD, PLEASE.
BRAAAINS?
"AS PAYMENT, I OFFERED TWO CHOICES, EITHER TEN AUTOGRAPHED PICTURES OF ME, OR...COMPLETE ANNIHILATION.
DR. ZOMBOSS
"WE EVENTUALLY SETTLED ON A THIRD OPTION. ONE AUTOGRAPHED PICTURE OF MR. STUBBINS.
Stubbins

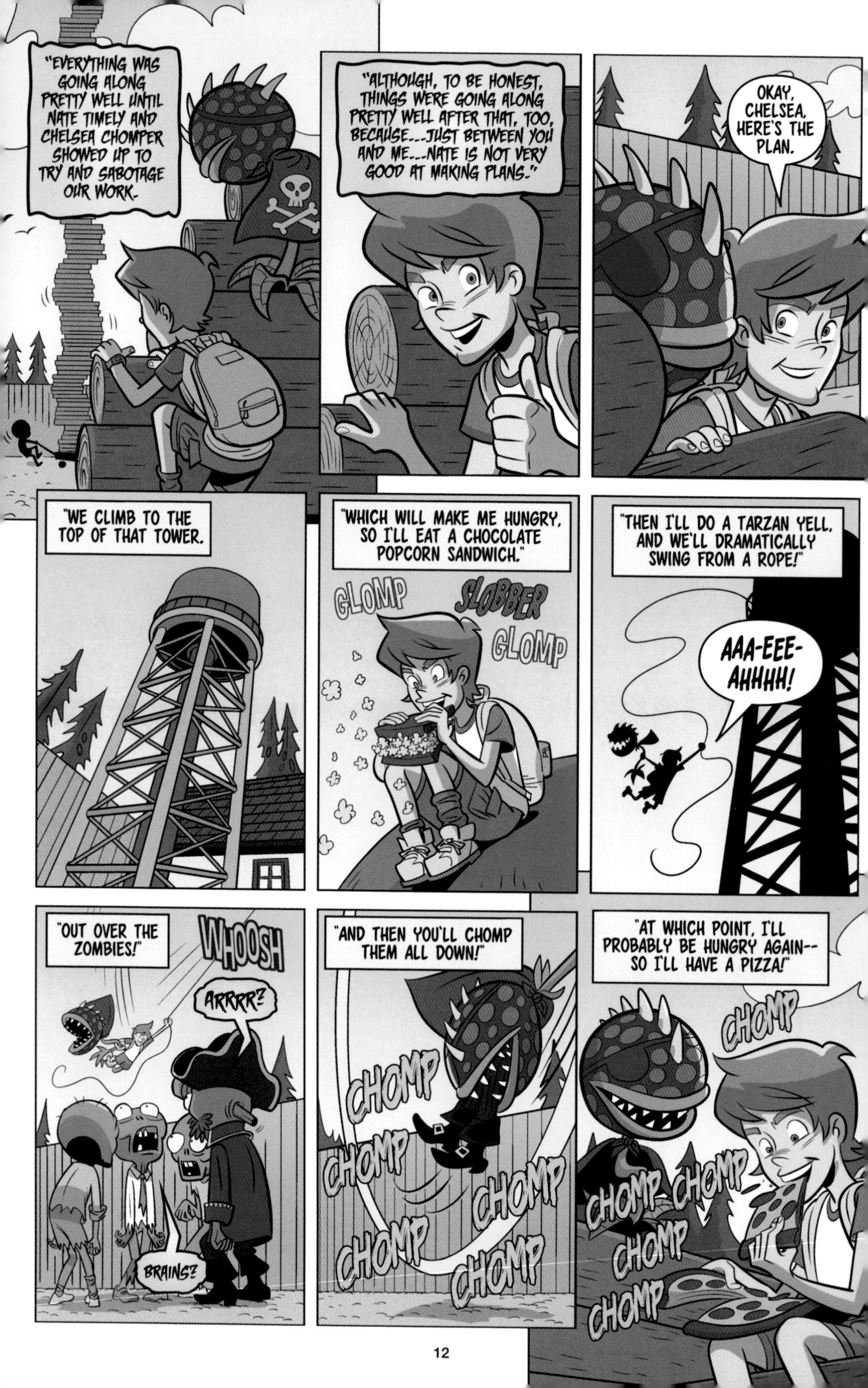
"EVERYTHING WAS GOING ALONG PRETTY WELL UNTIL NATE TIMELY AND CHELSEA CHOMPER SHOWED UP TO TRY AND SABOTAGE OUR WORK.
"ALTHOUGH, TO BE HONEST, THINGS WERE GOING ALONG PRETTY WELL AFTER THAT, TOO, BECAUSE...JUST BETWEEN YOU AND ME...NATE IS NOT VERY GOOD AT MAKING PLANS."
OKAY, CHELSEA, HERE'S THE PLAN.
"WE CLIMB TO THE TOP OF THAT TOWER.
"WHICH WILL MAKE ME HUNGRY, SO I'LL EAT A CHOCOLATE POPCORN SANDWICH."
GLOMP
SLOBBER
GLOMP
"THEN I'LL DO A TARZAN YELL, AND WE'LL DRAMATICALLY SWING FROM A ROPE!"
AAA-EEE-AHHHH!
"OUT OVER THE ZOMBIES!"
WHOOSH
ARRRR?
BRAINS?
"AND THEN YOU'LL CHOMP THEM ALL DOWN!"
CHOMP
CHOMP
CHOMP
CHOMP
CHOMP
"AT WHICH POINT, I'LL PROBABLY BE HUNGRY AGAIN--SO I'LL HAVE A PIZZA!"
CHOMP
CHOMP CHOMP
CHOMP
CHOMP

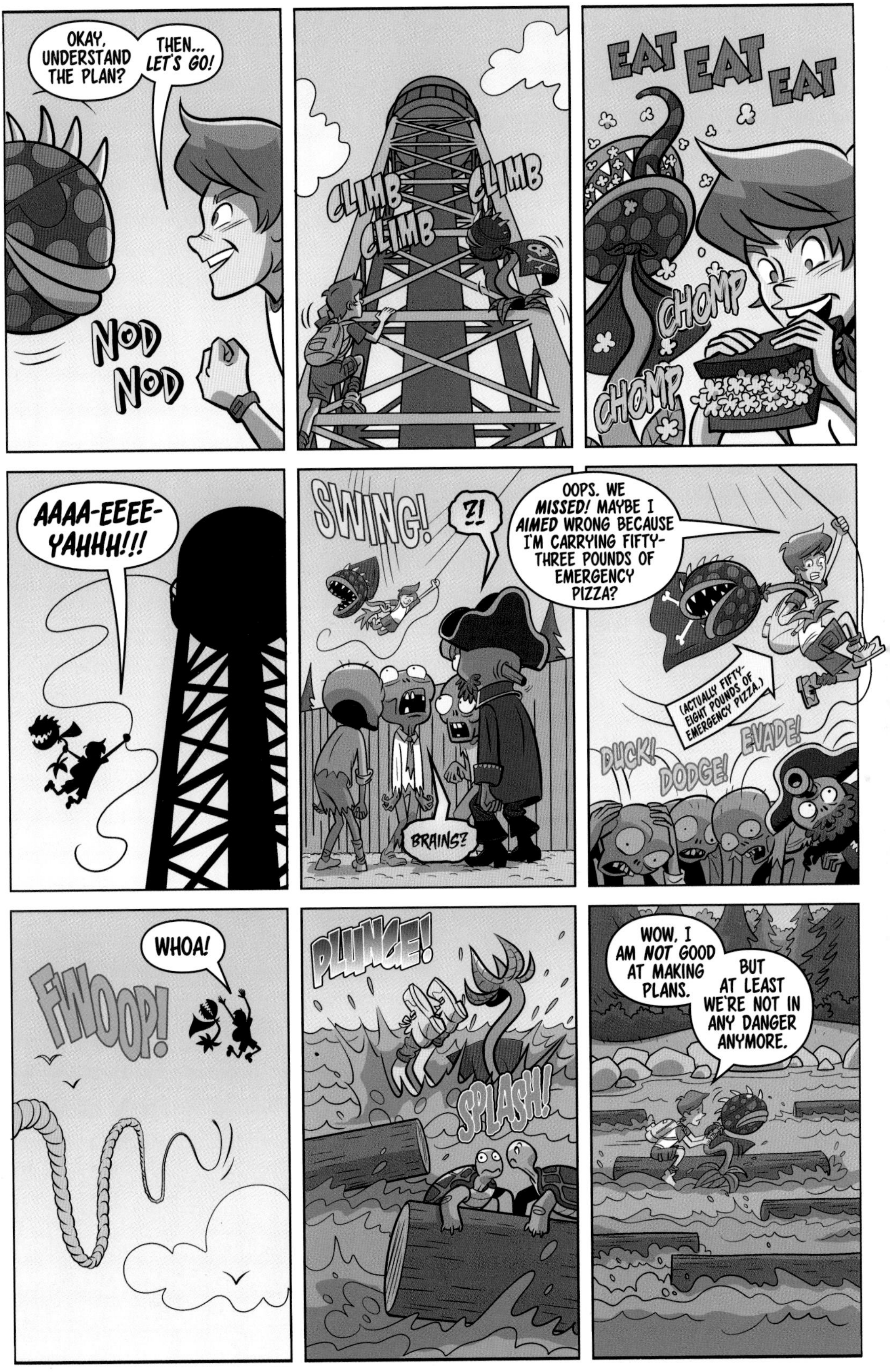

OKAY, UNDERSTAND THE PLAN?
THEN... LET'S GO!
NOD NOD
CLIMB CLIMB CLIMB
EAT EAT EAT
CHOMP CHOMP
AAAA-EEEE-YAHHH!!!
SWING!
?!
BRAINS?
OOPS. WE MISSED! MAYBE I AIMED WRONG BECAUSE I'M CARRYING FIFTY-THREE POUNDS OF EMERGENCY PIZZA?
(ACTUALLY FIFTY-EIGHT POUNDS OF EMERGENCY PIZZA.)
DUCK! DODGE! EVADE!
FWOOP!
WHOA!
PLUNGE!
SPLASH!
WOW, I AM NOT GOOD AT MAKING PLANS.
BUT AT LEAST WE'RE NOT IN ANY DANGER ANYMORE.

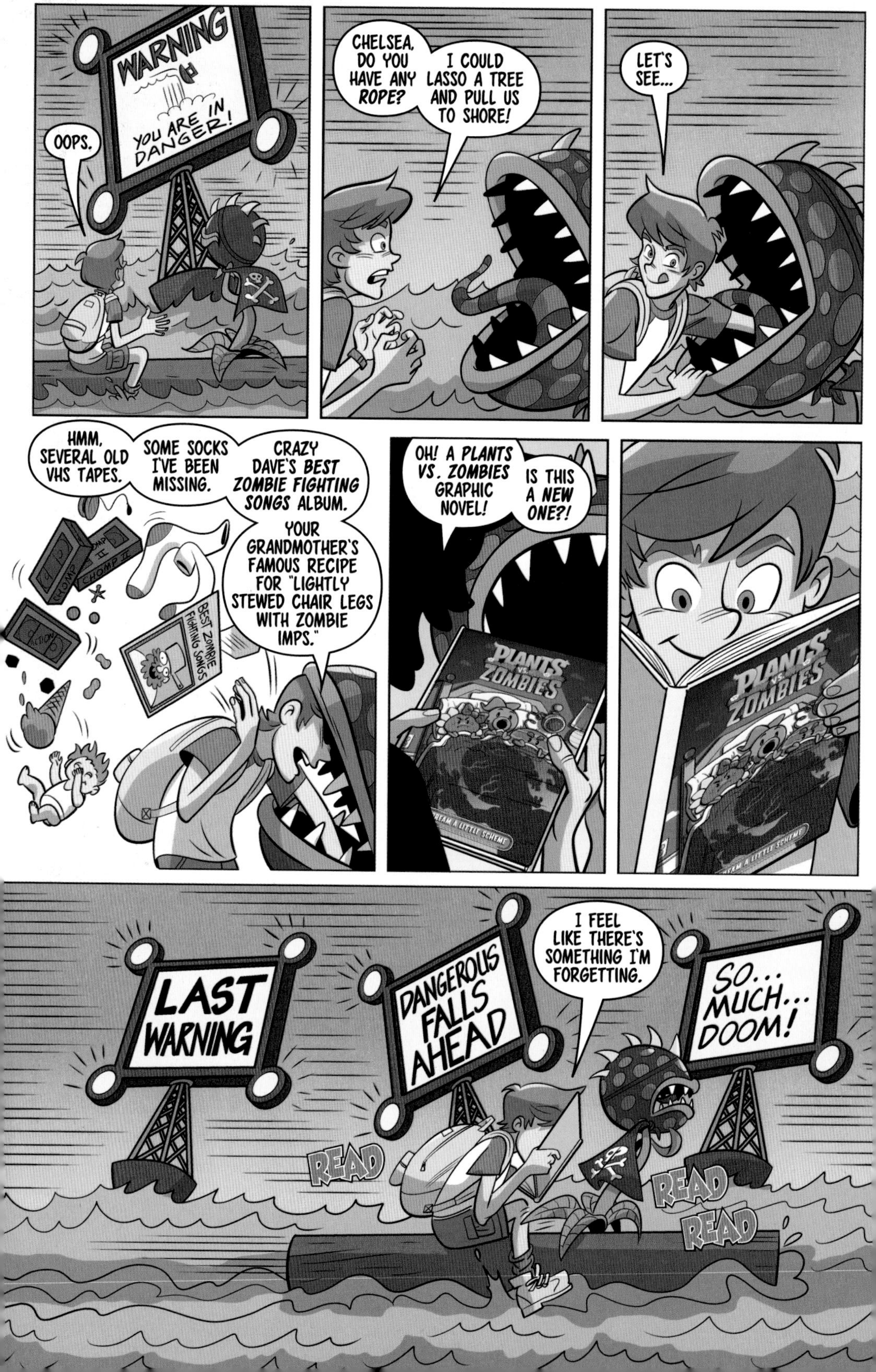

WARNING
YOU ARE IN DANGER!
OOPS.
CHELSEA, DO YOU HAVE ANY ROPE?
I COULD LASSO A TREE AND PULL US TO SHORE!
LET'S SEE...
HMM, SEVERAL OLD VHS TAPES.
SOME SOCKS I'VE BEEN MISSING.
CRAZY DAVE'S BEST ZOMBIE FIGHTING SONGS ALBUM.
YOUR GRANDMOTHER'S FAMOUS RECIPE FOR "LIGHTLY STEWED CHAIR LEGS WITH ZOMBIE IMPS."
CHOMP II
BEST ZOMBIE FIGHTING SONGS
OH! A PLANTS VS. ZOMBIES GRAPHIC NOVEL!
IS THIS A NEW ONE?!
PLANTS VS. ZOMBIES
LAST WARNING
DANGEROUS FALLS AHEAD
I FEEL LIKE THERE'S SOMETHING I'M FORGETTING.
SO... MUCH... DOOM!
READ
READ
READ

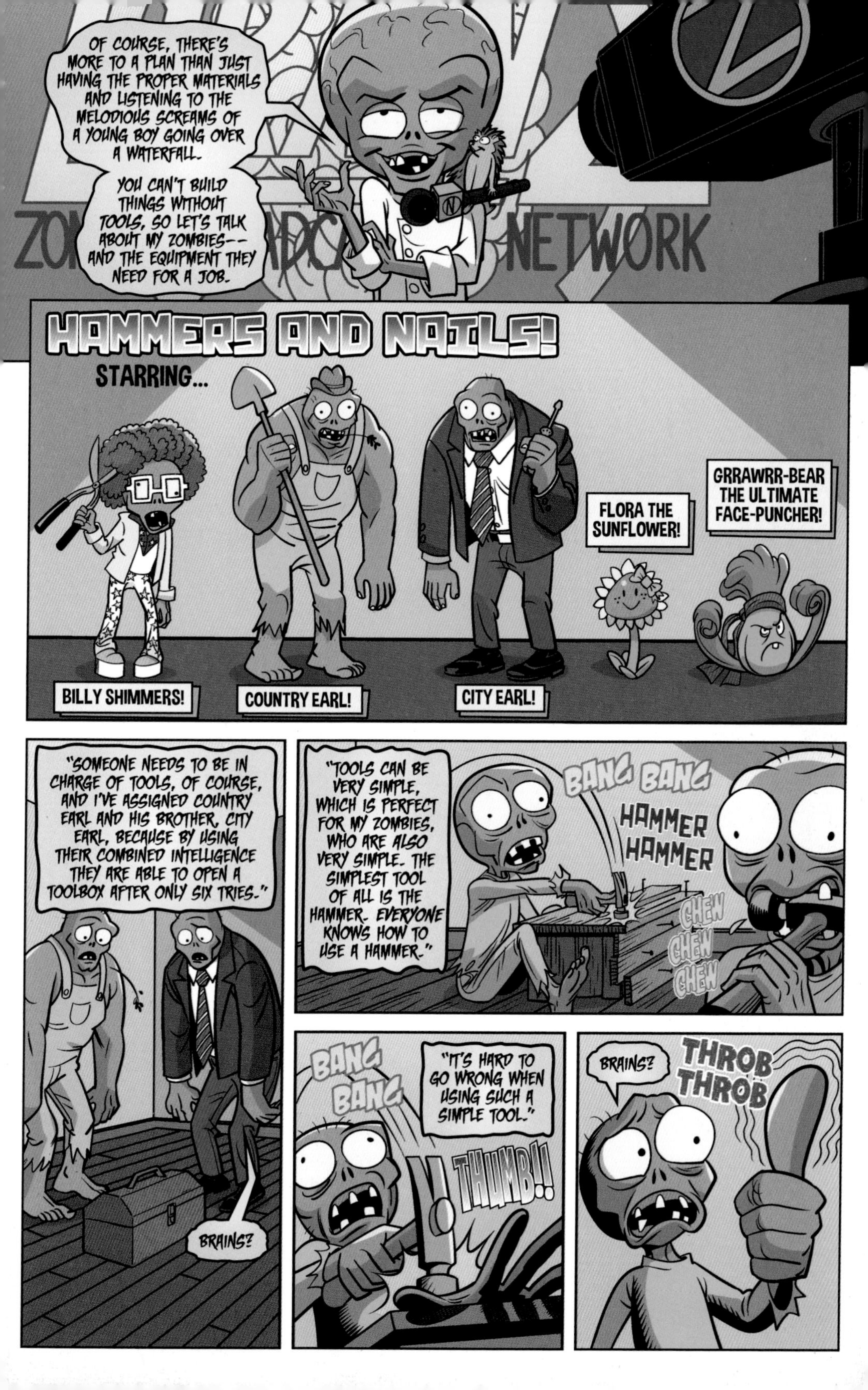
OF COURSE, THERE'S MORE TO A PLAN THAN JUST HAVING THE PROPER MATERIALS AND LISTENING TO THE MELODIOUS SCREAMS OF A YOUNG BOY GOING OVER A WATERFALL.
YOU CAN'T BUILD THINGS WITHOUT TOOLS, SO LET'S TALK ABOUT MY ZOMBIES-- AND THE EQUIPMENT THEY NEED FOR A JOB.
NETWORK
HAMMERS AND NAILS!
STARRING...
BILLY SHIMMERS!
COUNTRY EARL!
CITY EARL!
FLORA THE SUNFLOWER!
GRRAWRR-BEAR THE ULTIMATE FACE-PUNCHER!
"SOMEONE NEEDS TO BE IN CHARGE OF TOOLS, OF COURSE, AND I'VE ASSIGNED COUNTRY EARL AND HIS BROTHER, CITY EARL, BECAUSE BY USING THEIR COMBINED INTELLIGENCE THEY ARE ABLE TO OPEN A TOOLBOX AFTER ONLY SIX TRIES."
BRAINS?
"TOOLS CAN BE VERY SIMPLE, WHICH IS PERFECT FOR MY ZOMBIES, WHO ARE ALSO VERY SIMPLE. THE SIMPLEST TOOL OF ALL IS THE HAMMER. EVERYONE KNOWS HOW TO USE A HAMMER."
BANG BANG
HAMMER HAMMER
CHEW CHEW CHEW
BANG BANG
"IT'S HARD TO GO WRONG WHEN USING SUCH A SIMPLE TOOL."
THUMB!!
BRAINS?
THROB THROB

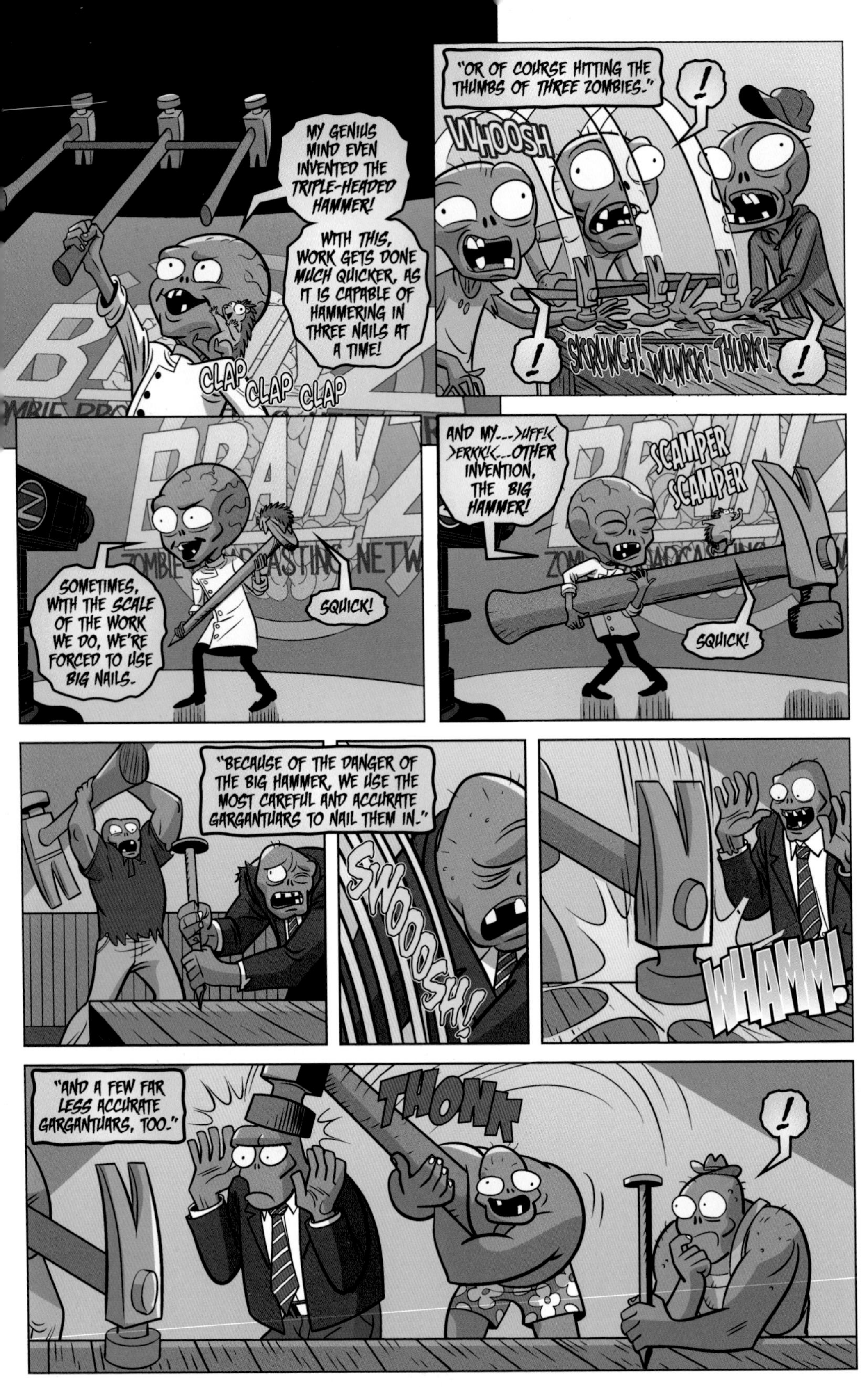
MY GENIUS MIND EVEN INVENTED THE TRIPLE-HEADED HAMMER!
WITH THIS, WORK GETS DONE MUCH QUICKER, AS IT IS CAPABLE OF HAMMERING IN THREE NAILS AT A TIME!
CLAP CLAP CLAP
"OR OF COURSE HITTING THE THUMBS OF THREE ZOMBIES."
WHOOSH
!
!
SKRUNCH! WUNKK! THURK!
!
SOMETIMES, WITH THE SCALE OF THE WORK WE DO, WE'RE FORCED TO USE BIG NAILS.
SQUICK!
AND MY...>UFF!< >ERKK!<...OTHER INVENTION, THE BIG HAMMER!
SCAMPER SCAMPER
SQUICK!
"BECAUSE OF THE DANGER OF THE BIG HAMMER, WE USE THE MOST CAREFUL AND ACCURATE GARGANTUARS TO NAIL THEM IN."
SWOOOOSH!
WHAMM!
"AND A FEW FAR LESS ACCURATE GARGANTUARS, TOO."
THONK
!

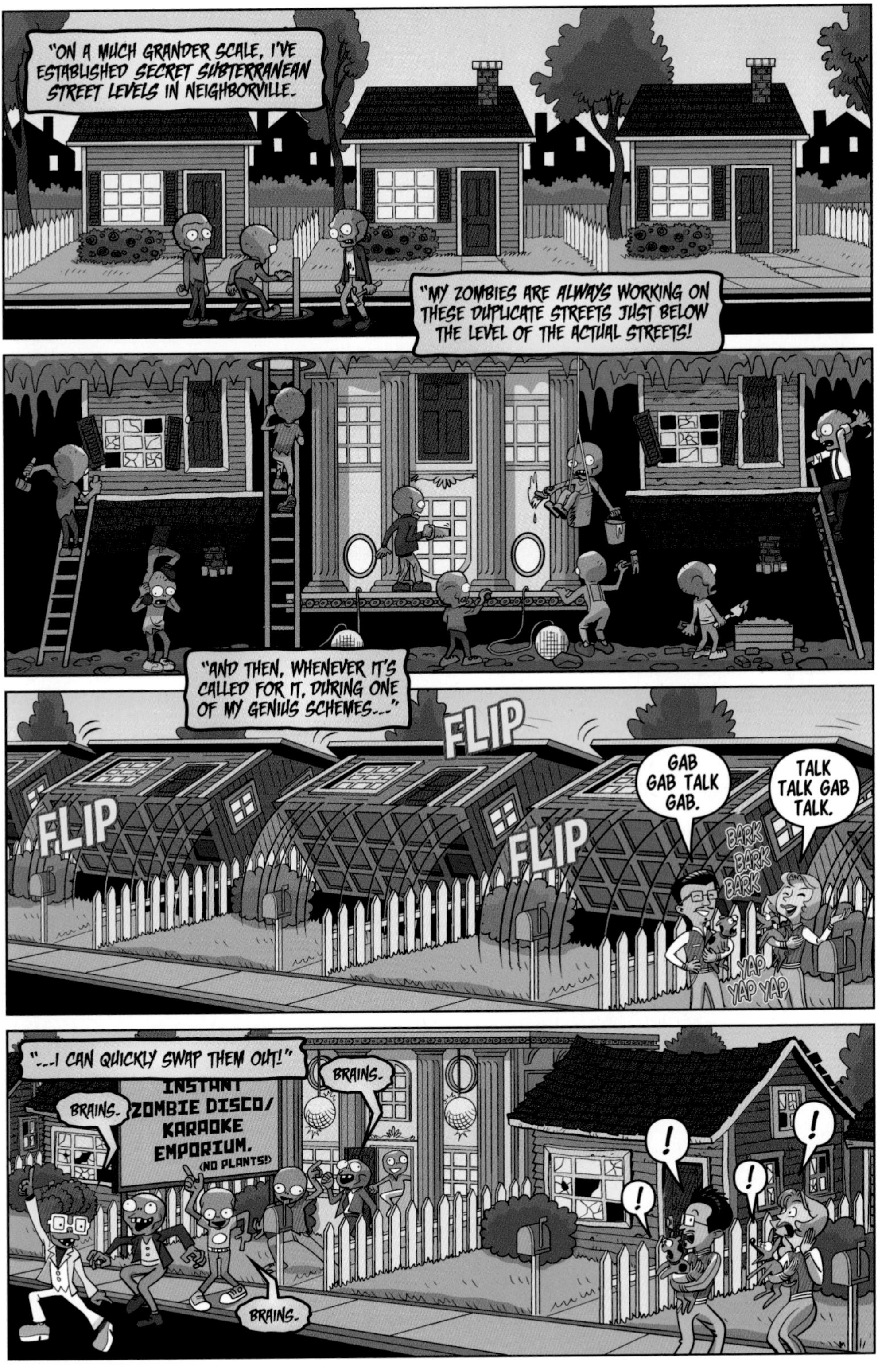

"ON A MUCH GRANDER SCALE, I'VE ESTABLISHED SECRET SUBTERRANEAN STREET LEVELS IN NEIGHBORVILLE.
"MY ZOMBIES ARE ALWAYS WORKING ON THESE DUPLICATE STREETS JUST BELOW THE LEVEL OF THE ACTUAL STREETS!
"AND THEN, WHENEVER IT'S CALLED FOR IT, DURING ONE OF MY GENIUS SCHEMES..."
FLIP
FLIP
FLIP
GAB GAB TALK GAB.
TALK TALK GAB TALK.
BARK BARK BARK
YAP YAP YAP
"...I CAN QUICKLY SWAP THEM OUT!"
INSTANT ZOMBIE DISCO/ KARAOKE EMPORIUM. (NO PLANTS!)
BRAINS.
BRAINS.
BRAINS.
!
!
!
!

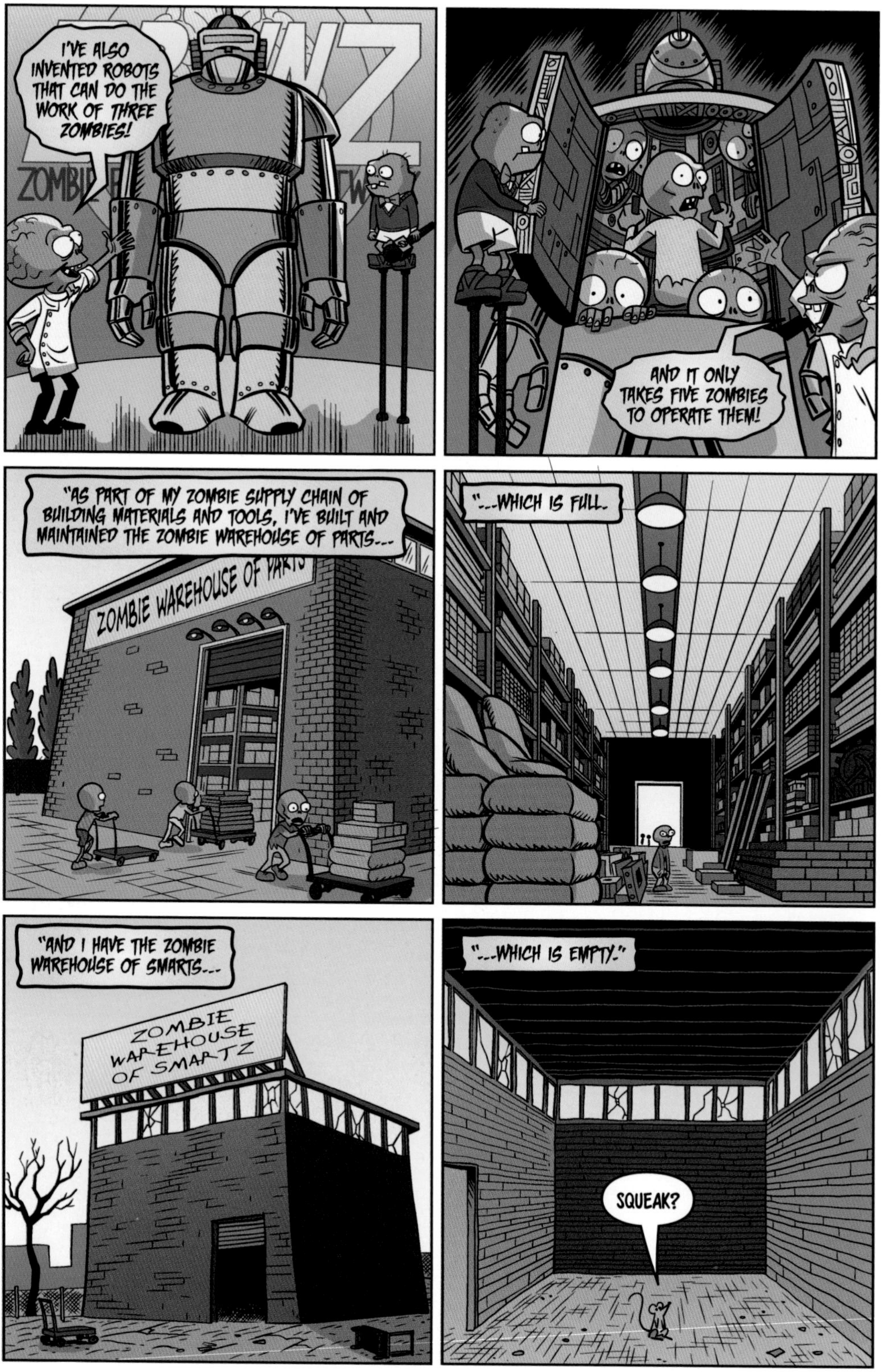
I'VE ALSO INVENTED ROBOTS THAT CAN DO THE WORK OF THREE ZOMBIES!
AND IT ONLY TAKES FIVE ZOMBIES TO OPERATE THEM!
"AS PART OF MY ZOMBIE SUPPLY CHAIN OF BUILDING MATERIALS AND TOOLS, I'VE BUILT AND MAINTAINED THE ZOMBIE WAREHOUSE OF PARTS...
ZOMBIE WAREHOUSE OF PARTS
"...WHICH IS FULL.
"AND I HAVE THE ZOMBIE WAREHOUSE OF SMARTS...
ZOMBIE WAREHOUSE OF SMARTZ
"...WHICH IS EMPTY."
SQUEAK?

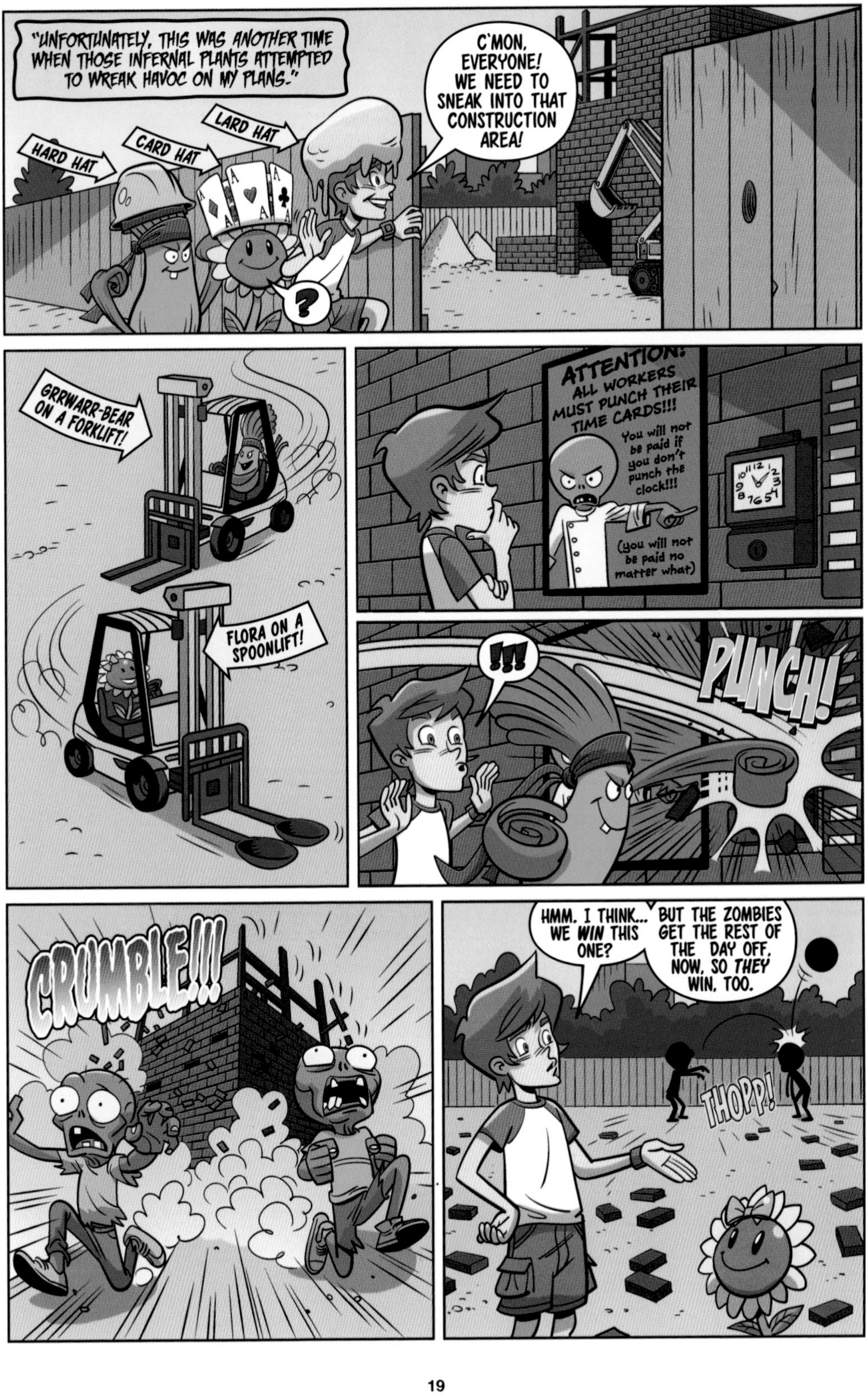

"UNFORTUNATELY, THIS WAS ANOTHER TIME WHEN THOSE INFERNAL PLANTS ATTEMPTED TO WREAK HAVOC ON MY PLANS."
HARD HAT
CARD HAT
LARD HAT
C'MON, EVERYONE! WE NEED TO SNEAK INTO THAT CONSTRUCTION AREA!
?
GRRWARR-BEAR ON A FORKLIFT!
FLORA ON A SPOONLIFT!
ATTENTION: ALL WORKERS MUST PUNCH THEIR TIME CARDS!!!
You will not be paid if you don't punch the clock!!!
(you will not be paid no matter what)
!!!
PUNCH!
CRUMBLE!!!
HMM. I THINK... WE WIN THIS ONE?
BUT THE ZOMBIES GET THE REST OF THE DAY OFF, NOW, SO THEY WIN, TOO.
THOPP!

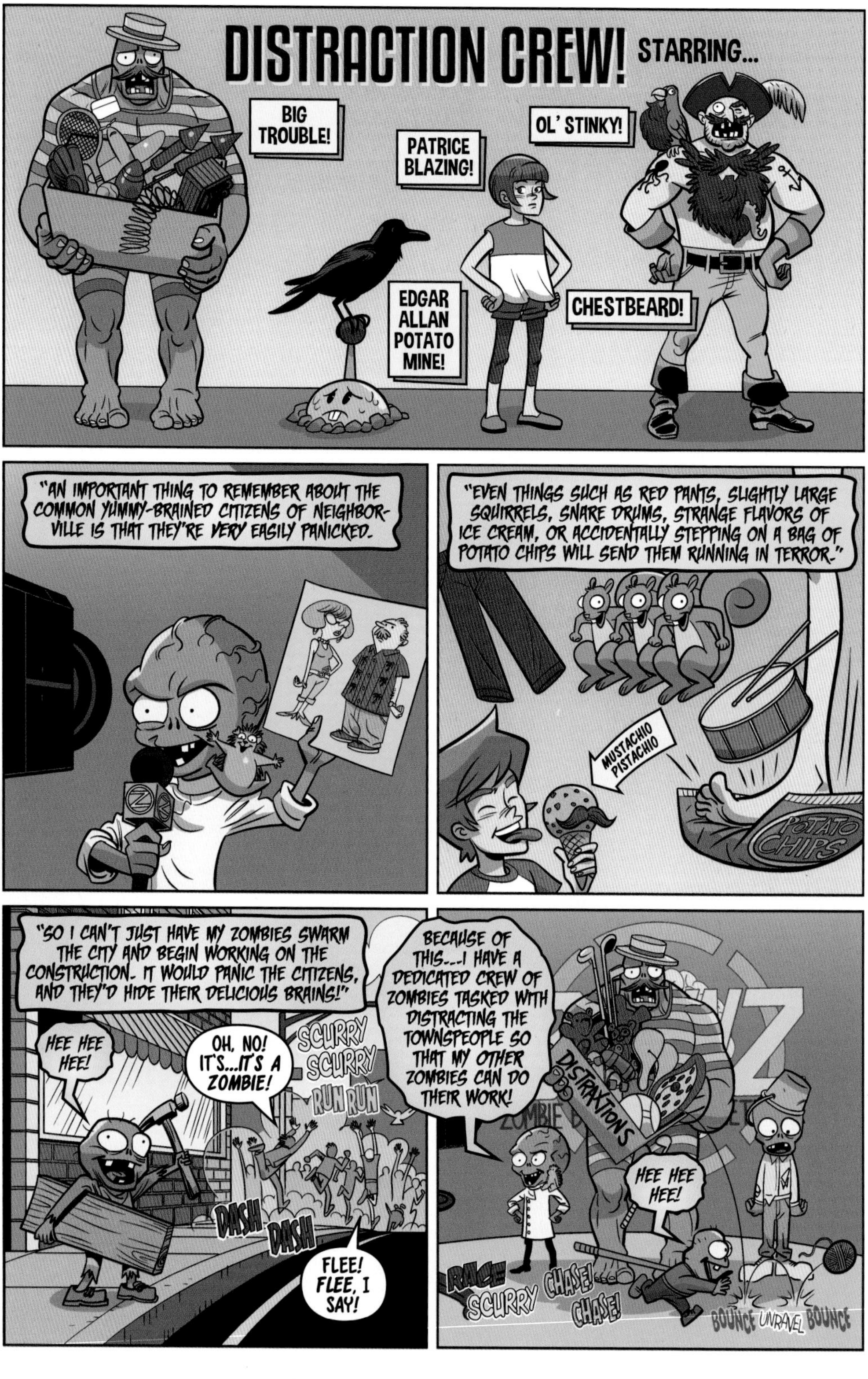

DISTRACTION CREW! STARRING...
BIG TROUBLE!
PATRICE BLAZING!
OL' STINKY!
EDGAR ALLAN POTATO MINE!
CHESTBEARD!
"AN IMPORTANT THING TO REMEMBER ABOUT THE COMMON YUMMY-BRAINED CITIZENS OF NEIGHBORVILLE IS THAT THEY'RE VERY EASILY PANICKED.
"EVEN THINGS SUCH AS RED PANTS, SLIGHTLY LARGE SQUIRRELS, SNARE DRUMS, STRANGE FLAVORS OF ICE CREAM, OR ACCIDENTALLY STEPPING ON A BAG OF POTATO CHIPS WILL SEND THEM RUNNING IN TERROR."
MUSTACHIO PISTACHIO
POTATO CHIPS
"SO I CAN'T JUST HAVE MY ZOMBIES SWARM THE CITY AND BEGIN WORKING ON THE CONSTRUCTION. IT WOULD PANIC THE CITIZENS, AND THEY'D HIDE THEIR DELICIOUS BRAINS!"
HEE HEE HEE!
OH, NO! IT'S...IT'S A ZOMBIE!
SCURRY SCURRY
RUN RUN
DASH DASH
FLEE! FLEE, I SAY!
BECAUSE OF THIS...I HAVE A DEDICATED CREW OF ZOMBIES TASKED WITH DISTRACTING THE TOWNSPEOPLE SO THAT MY OTHER ZOMBIES CAN DO THEIR WORK!
DISTRAXTIONS
HEE HEE HEE!
RACE
SCURRY
CHASE! CHASE!
BOUNCE UNRAVEL BOUNCE

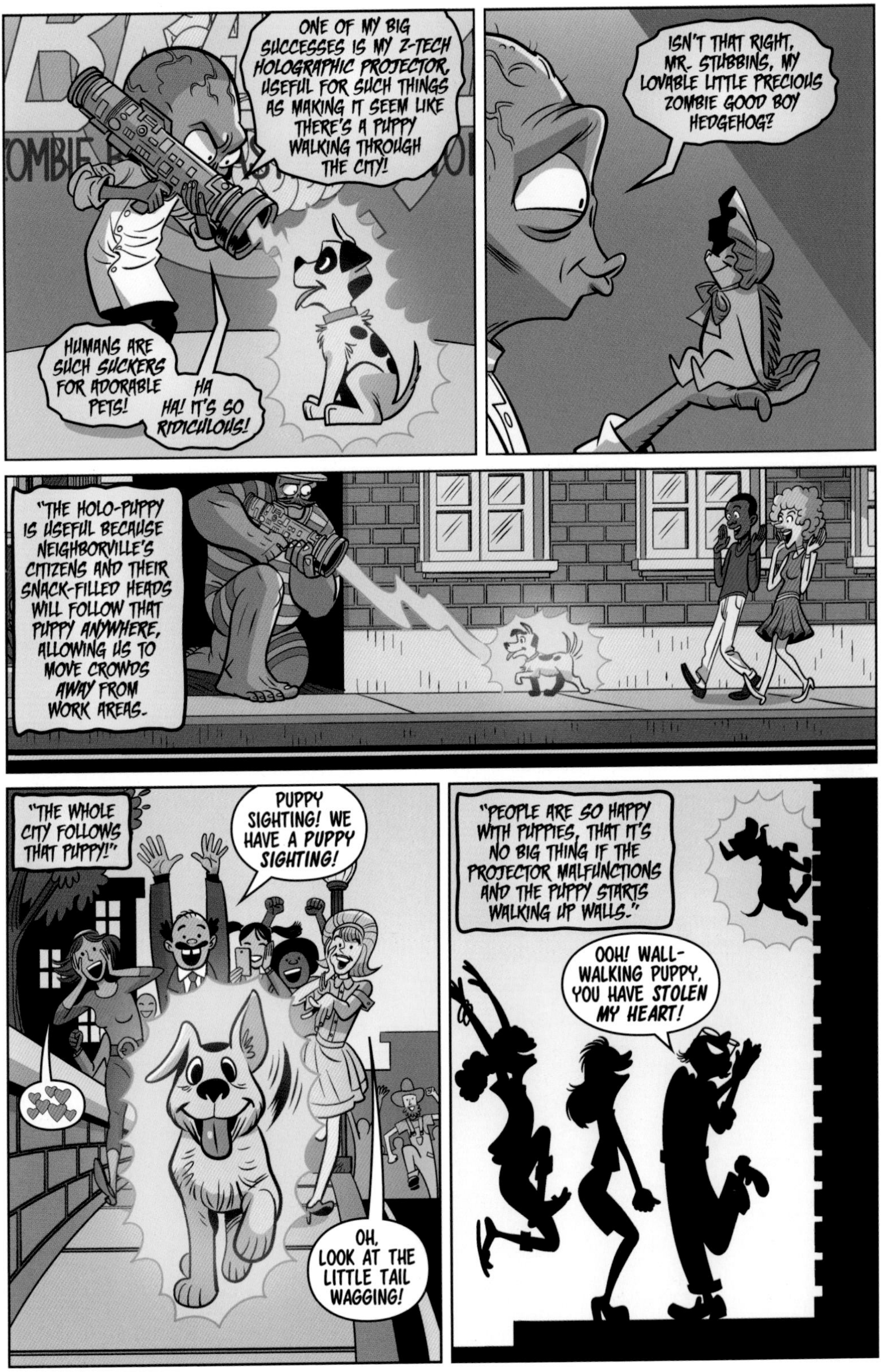
ONE OF MY BIG SUCCESSES IS MY Z-TECH HOLOGRAPHIC PROJECTOR, USEFUL FOR SUCH THINGS AS MAKING IT SEEM LIKE THERE'S A PUPPY WALKING THROUGH THE CITY!
HUMANS ARE SUCH SUCKERS FOR ADORABLE PETS!
HA HA! IT'S SO RIDICULOUS!
ISN'T THAT RIGHT, MR. STUBBINS, MY LOVABLE LITTLE PRECIOUS ZOMBIE GOOD BOY HEDGEHOG?
"THE HOLO-PUPPY IS USEFUL BECAUSE NEIGHBORVILLE'S CITIZENS AND THEIR SNACK-FILLED HEADS WILL FOLLOW THAT PUPPY ANYWHERE, ALLOWING US TO MOVE CROWDS AWAY FROM WORK AREAS.
"THE WHOLE CITY FOLLOWS THAT PUPPY!"
PUPPY SIGHTING! WE HAVE A PUPPY SIGHTING!
OH, LOOK AT THE LITTLE TAIL WAGGING!
"PEOPLE ARE SO HAPPY WITH PUPPIES, THAT IT'S NO BIG THING IF THE PROJECTOR MALFUNCTIONS AND THE PUPPY STARTS WALKING UP WALLS."
OOH! WALL-WALKING PUPPY, YOU HAVE STOLEN MY HEART!

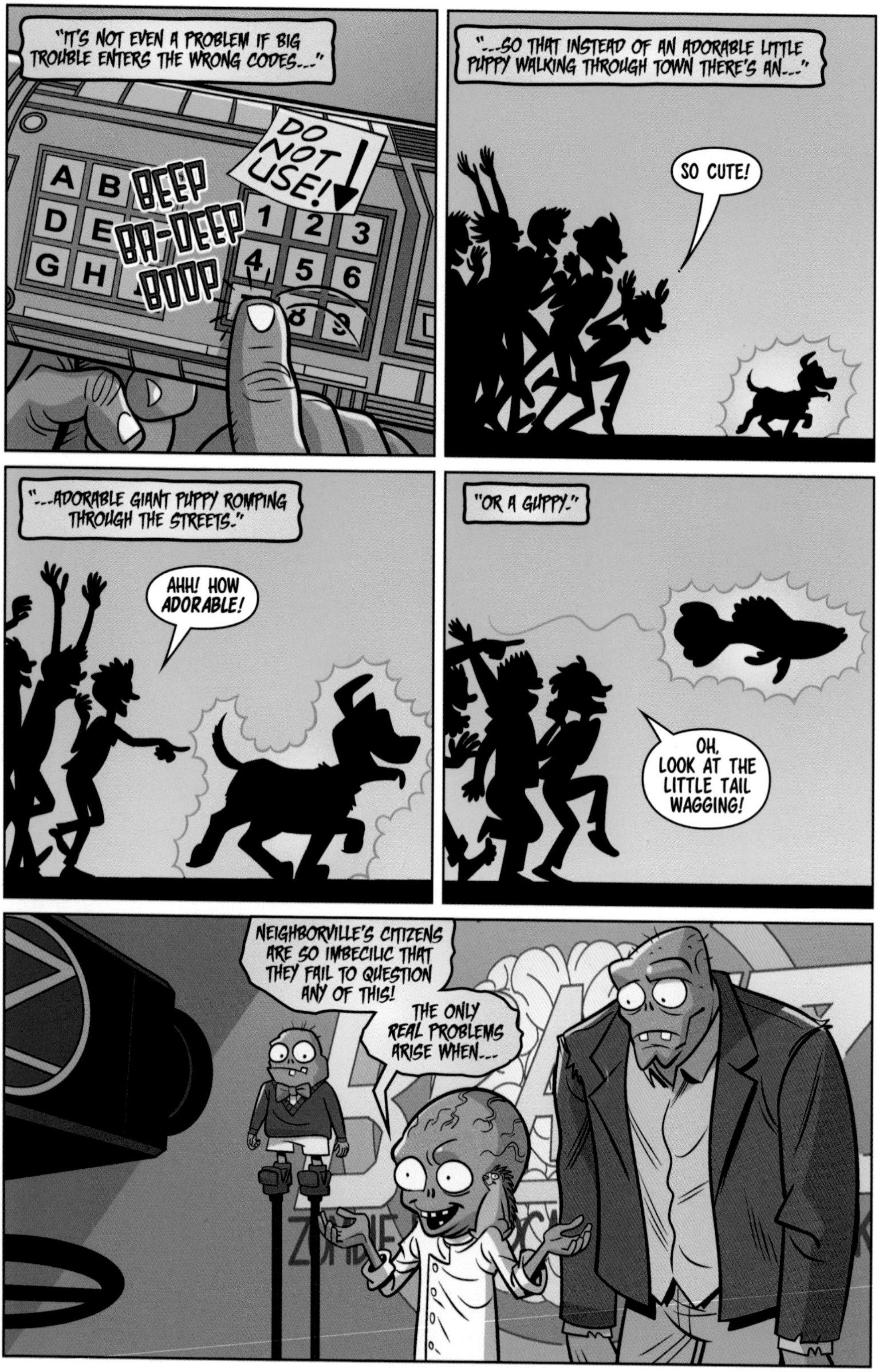
"IT'S NOT EVEN A PROBLEM IF BIG TROUBLE ENTERS THE WRONG CODES..."
DO NOT USE!
BEEP BA-DEEP BOOP
"...SO THAT INSTEAD OF AN ADORABLE LITTLE PUPPY WALKING THROUGH TOWN THERE'S AN..."
SO CUTE!
"...ADORABLE GIANT PUPPY ROMPING THROUGH THE STREETS."
AHH! HOW ADORABLE!
"OR A GUPPY."
OH, LOOK AT THE LITTLE TAIL WAGGING!
NEIGHBORVILLE'S CITIZENS ARE SO IMBECILIC THAT THEY FAIL TO QUESTION ANY OF THIS!
THE ONLY REAL PROBLEMS ARISE WHEN...

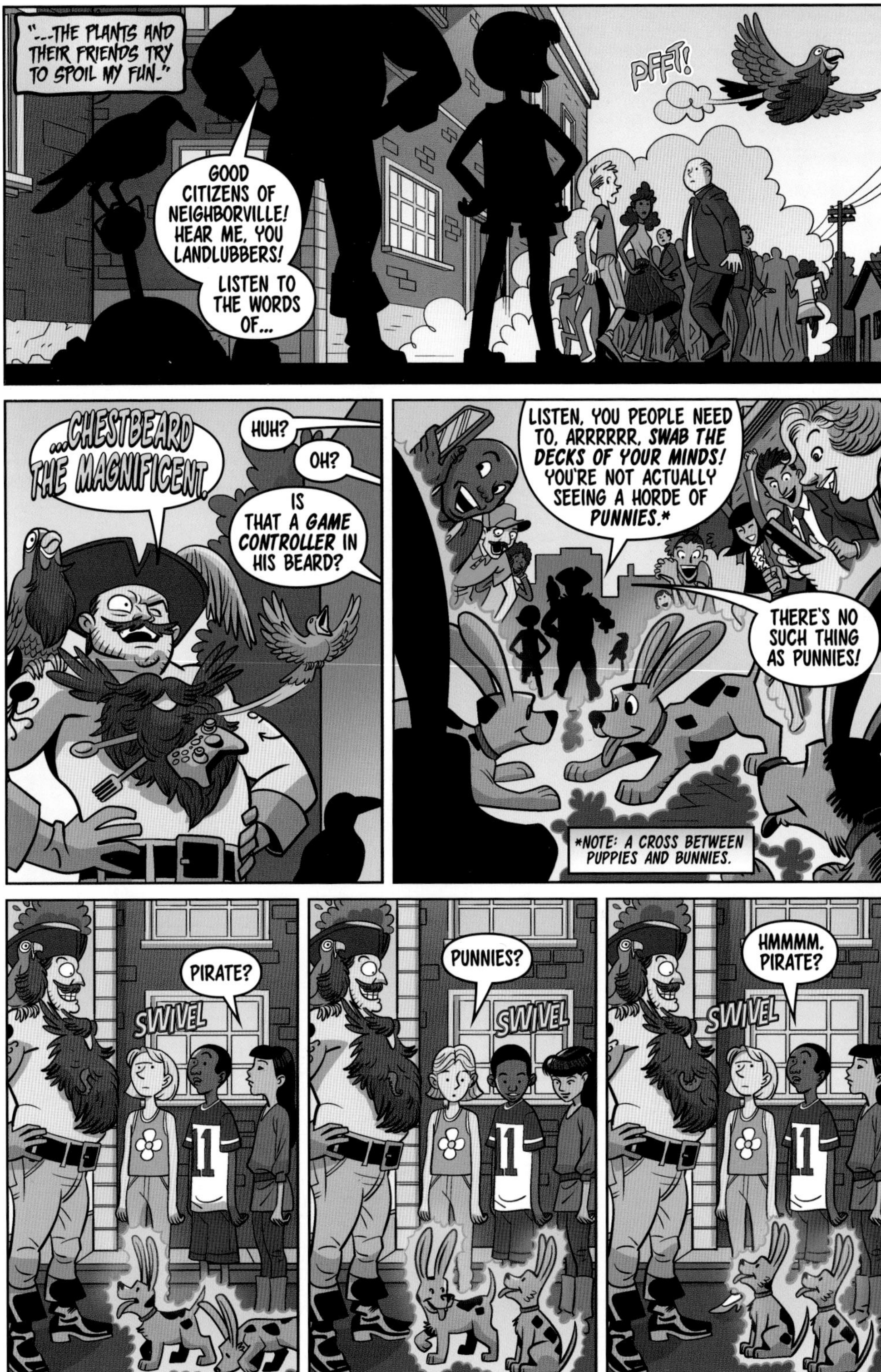
"...THE PLANTS AND THEIR FRIENDS TRY TO SPOIL MY FUN."
GOOD CITIZENS OF NEIGHBORVILLE! HEAR ME, YOU LANDLUBBERS!
LISTEN TO THE WORDS OF...
PFFT!
...CHESTBEARD THE MAGNIFICENT.
HUH?
OH?
IS THAT A GAME CONTROLLER IN HIS BEARD?
LISTEN, YOU PEOPLE NEED TO, ARRRRRR, SWAB THE DECKS OF YOUR MINDS! YOU'RE NOT ACTUALLY SEEING A HORDE OF PUNNIES.*
THERE'S NO SUCH THING AS PUNNIES!
*NOTE: A CROSS BETWEEN PUPPIES AND BUNNIES.
PIRATE?
SWIVEL
PUNNIES?
SWIVEL
HMMMM. PIRATE?
SWIVEL

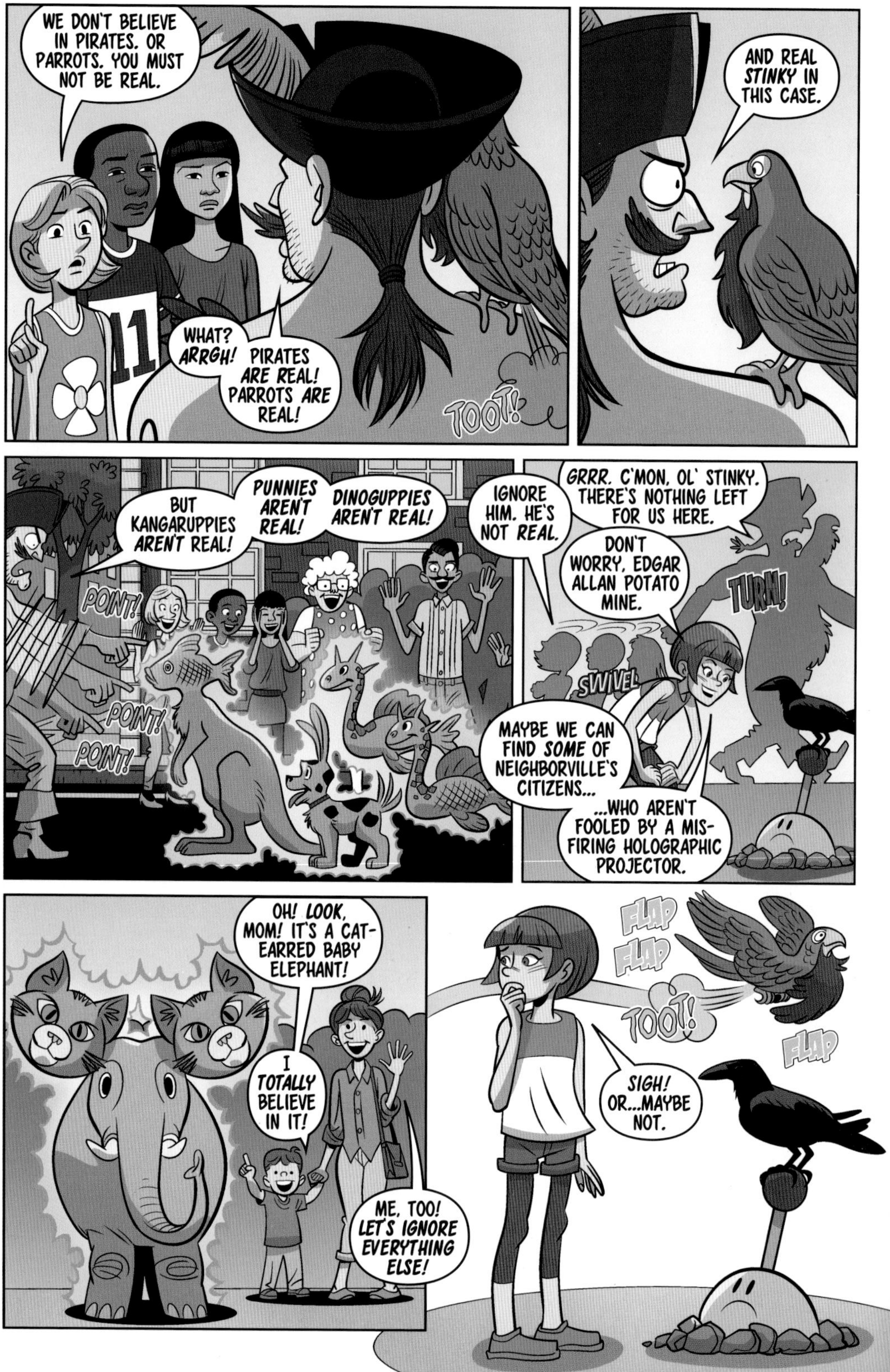

WE DON'T BELIEVE IN PIRATES. OR PARROTS. YOU MUST NOT BE REAL.
WHAT? ARRGH! PIRATES ARE REAL! PARROTS ARE REAL!
TOOT!
AND REAL STINKY IN THIS CASE.
BUT KANGARUPPIES AREN'T REAL!
PUNNIES AREN'T REAL!
DINOGUPPIES AREN'T REAL!
POINT!
POINT!
POINT!
IGNORE HIM. HE'S NOT REAL.
GRRR. C'MON, OL' STINKY. THERE'S NOTHING LEFT FOR US HERE.
TURN!
DON'T WORRY, EDGAR ALLAN POTATO MINE.
SWIVEL
MAYBE WE CAN FIND SOME OF NEIGHBORVILLE'S CITIZENS...
...WHO AREN'T FOOLED BY A MIS-FIRING HOLOGRAPHIC PROJECTOR.
OH! LOOK, MOM! IT'S A CAT-EARRED BABY ELEPHANT!
I TOTALLY BELIEVE IN IT!
ME, TOO! LET'S IGNORE EVERYTHING ELSE!
FLAP
FLAP
TOOT!
FLAP
SIGH! OR...MAYBE NOT.

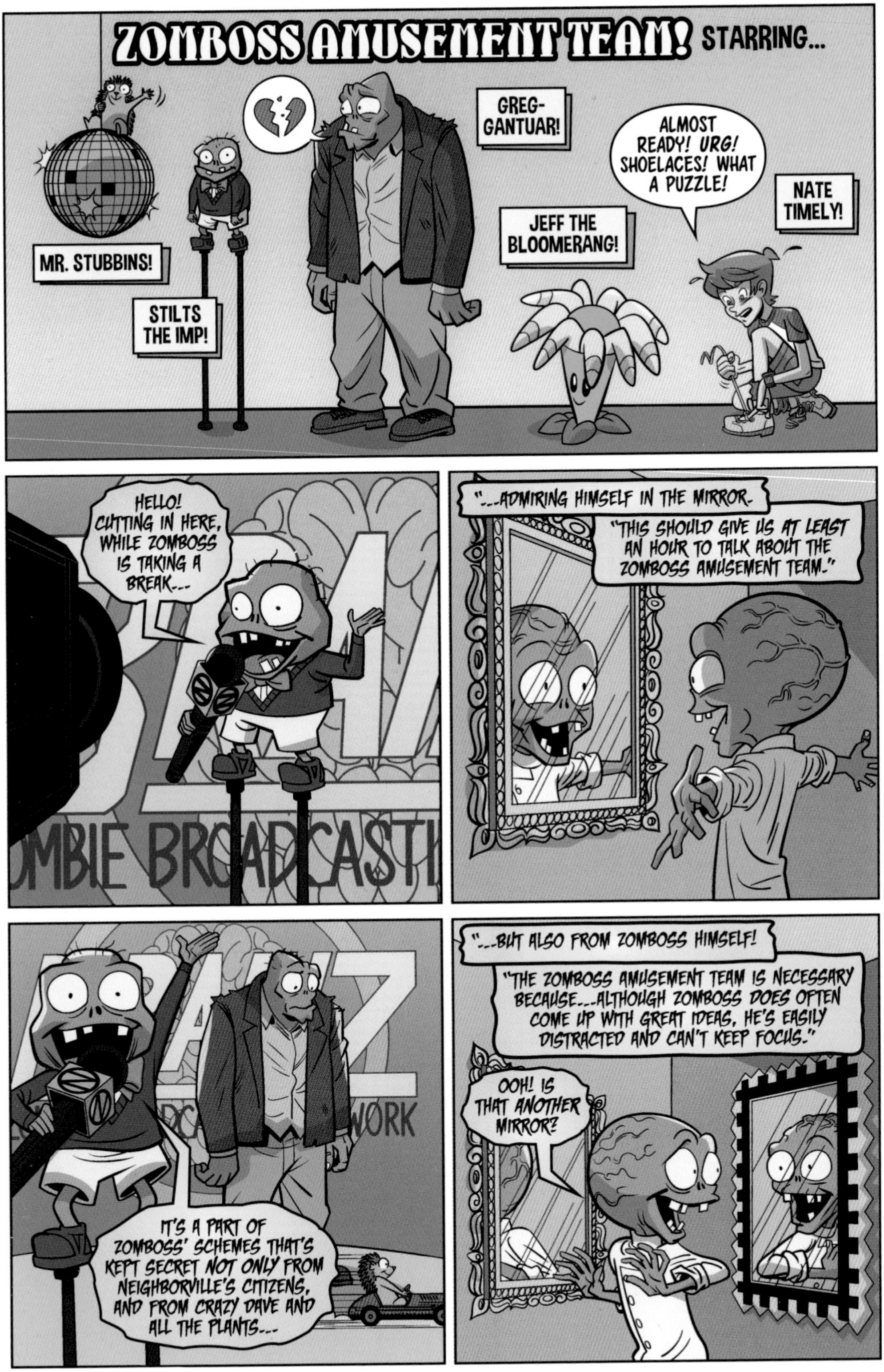
ZOMBOSS AMUSEMENT TEAM! STARRING...
MR. STUBBINS!
STILTS THE IMP!
GREG-GANTUAR!
JEFF THE BLOOMERANG!
ALMOST READY! URG! SHOELACES! WHAT A PUZZLE!
NATE TIMELY!
HELLO! CUTTING IN HERE, WHILE ZOMBOSS IS TAKING A BREAK...
ZOMBIE BROADCASTI
"...ADMIRING HIMSELF IN THE MIRROR.
"THIS SHOULD GIVE US AT LEAST AN HOUR TO TALK ABOUT THE ZOMBOSS AMUSEMENT TEAM."
IT'S A PART OF ZOMBOSS' SCHEMES THAT'S KEPT SECRET NOT ONLY FROM NEIGHBORVILLE'S CITIZENS, AND FROM CRAZY DAVE AND ALL THE PLANTS...
"...BUT ALSO FROM ZOMBOSS HIMSELF!
"THE ZOMBOSS AMUSEMENT TEAM IS NECESSARY BECAUSE...ALTHOUGH ZOMBOSS DOES OFTEN COME UP WITH GREAT IDEAS, HE'S EASILY DISTRACTED AND CAN'T KEEP FOCUS."
OOH! IS THAT ANOTHER MIRROR?

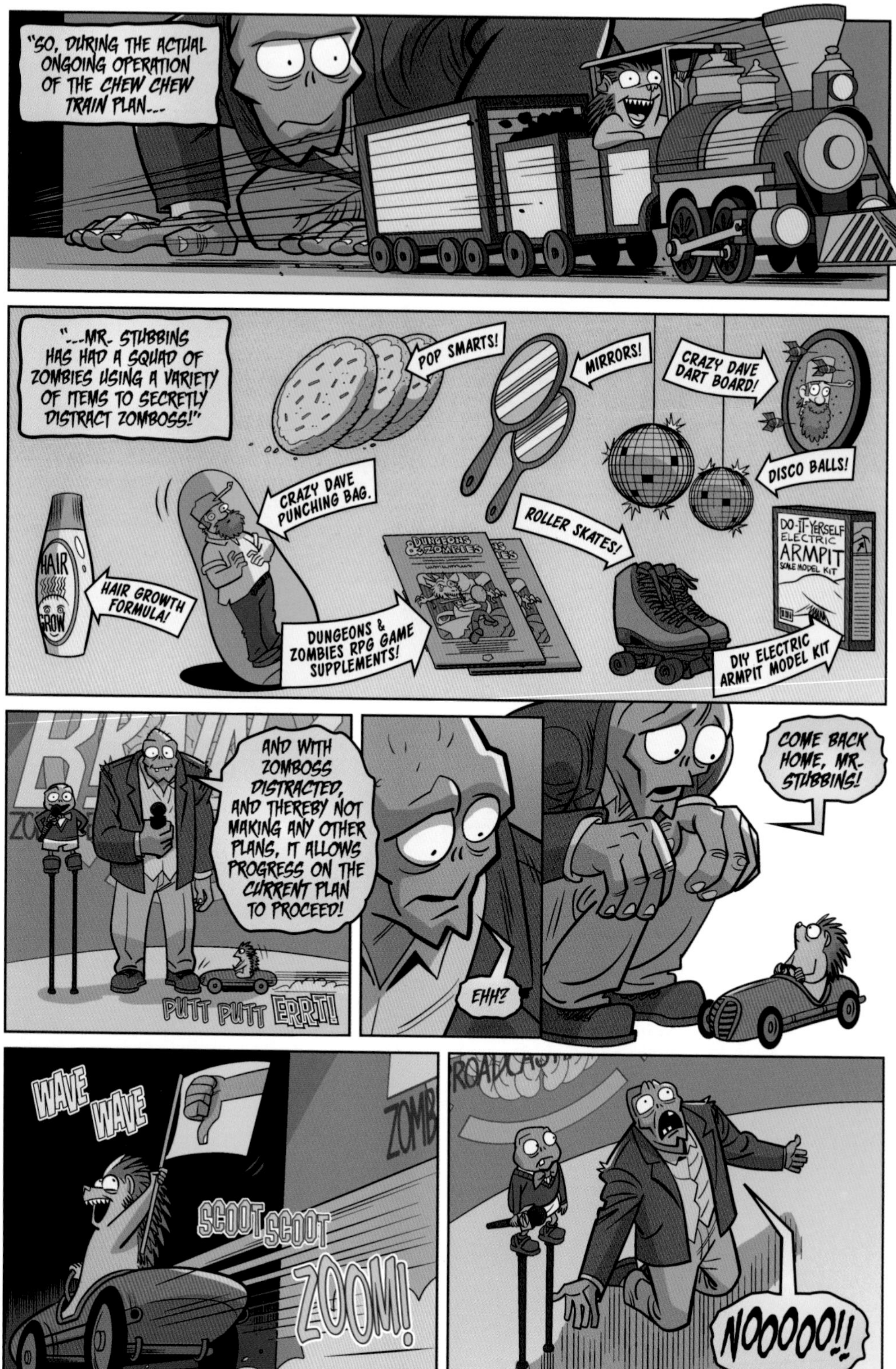
"SO, DURING THE ACTUAL ONGOING OPERATION OF THE CHEW CHEW TRAIN PLAN...
"...MR. STUBBINS HAS HAD A SQUAD OF ZOMBIES USING A VARIETY OF ITEMS TO SECRETLY DISTRACT ZOMBOSS!"
POP SMARTS!
MIRRORS!
CRAZY DAVE DART BOARD!
DISCO BALLS!
CRAZY DAVE PUNCHING BAG.
ROLLER SKATES!
HAIR GROW
HAIR GROWTH FORMULA!
DUNGEONS & ZOMBIES
DUNGEONS & ZOMBIES RPG GAME SUPPLEMENTS!
DO-IT-YERSELF ELECTRIC ARMPIT SCALE MODEL KIT
DIY ELECTRIC ARMPIT MODEL KIT
AND WITH ZOMBOSS DISTRACTED, AND THEREBY NOT MAKING ANY OTHER PLANS, IT ALLOWS PROGRESS ON THE CURRENT PLAN TO PROCEED!
PUTT PUTT ERRT!
EHH?
COME BACK HOME, MR. STUBBINS!
WAVE WAVE
SCOOT SCOOT
ZOOM!
NOOOOO!!

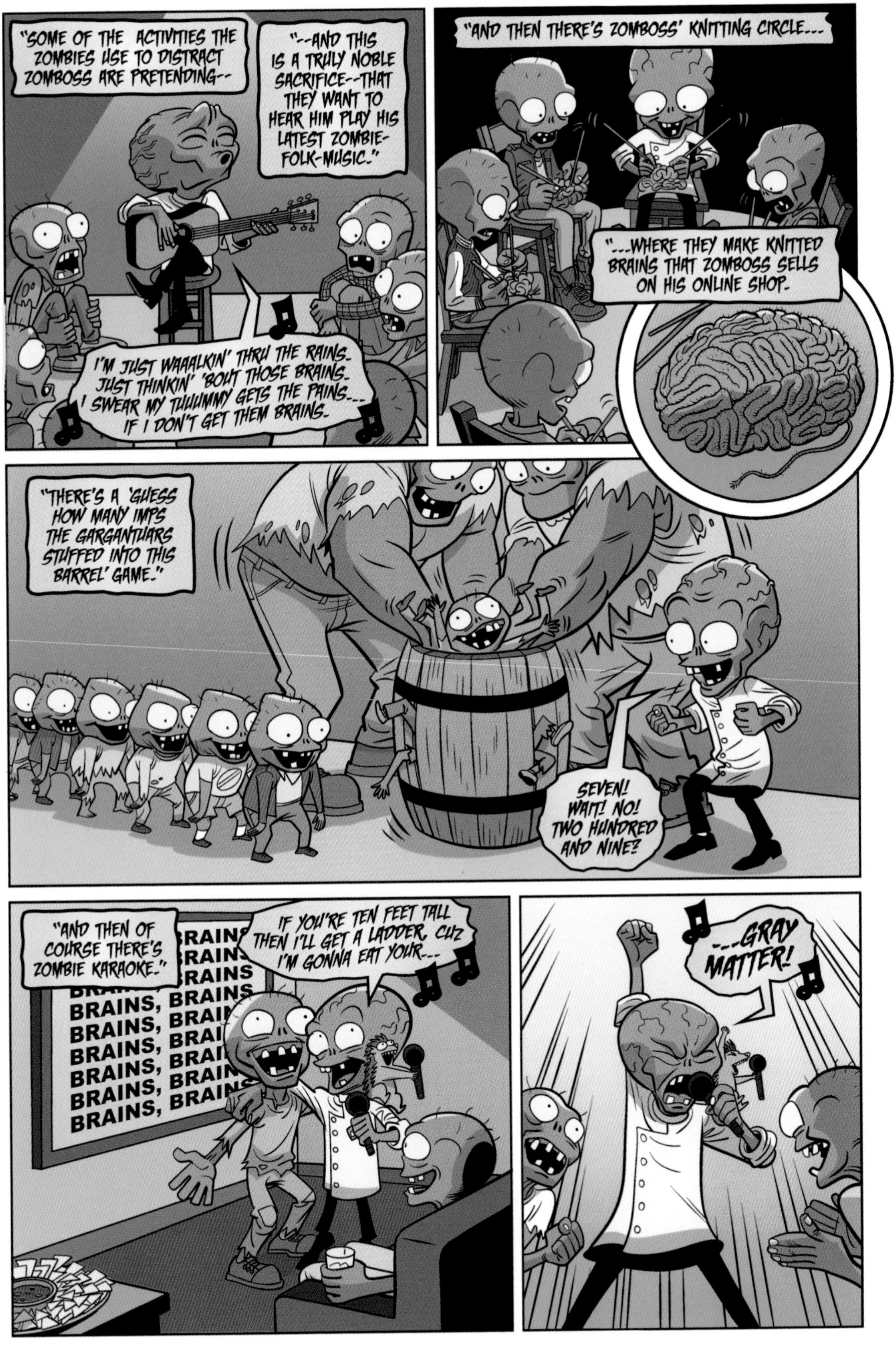
"SOME OF THE ACTIVITIES THE ZOMBIES USE TO DISTRACT ZOMBOSS ARE PRETENDING--
"--AND THIS IS A TRULY NOBLE SACRIFICE--THAT THEY WANT TO HEAR HIM PLAY HIS LATEST ZOMBIE-FOLK-MUSIC."
I'M JUST WAAALKIN' THRU THE RAINS. JUST THINKIN' 'BOUT THOSE BRAINS. I SWEAR MY TUUUMMY GETS THE PAINS... IF I DON'T GET THEM BRAINS.
"AND THEN THERE'S ZOMBOSS' KNITTING CIRCLE...
"...WHERE THEY MAKE KNITTED BRAINS THAT ZOMBOSS SELLS ON HIS ONLINE SHOP.
"THERE'S A 'GUESS HOW MANY IMPS THE GARGANTUARS STUFFED INTO THIS BARREL' GAME."
SEVEN! WAIT! NO! TWO HUNDRED AND NINE?
"AND THEN OF COURSE THERE'S ZOMBIE KARAOKE."
IF YOU'RE TEN FEET TALL THEN I'LL GET A LADDER, CUZ I'M GONNA EAT YOUR...
BRAINS, BRAINS
...GRAY MATTER!

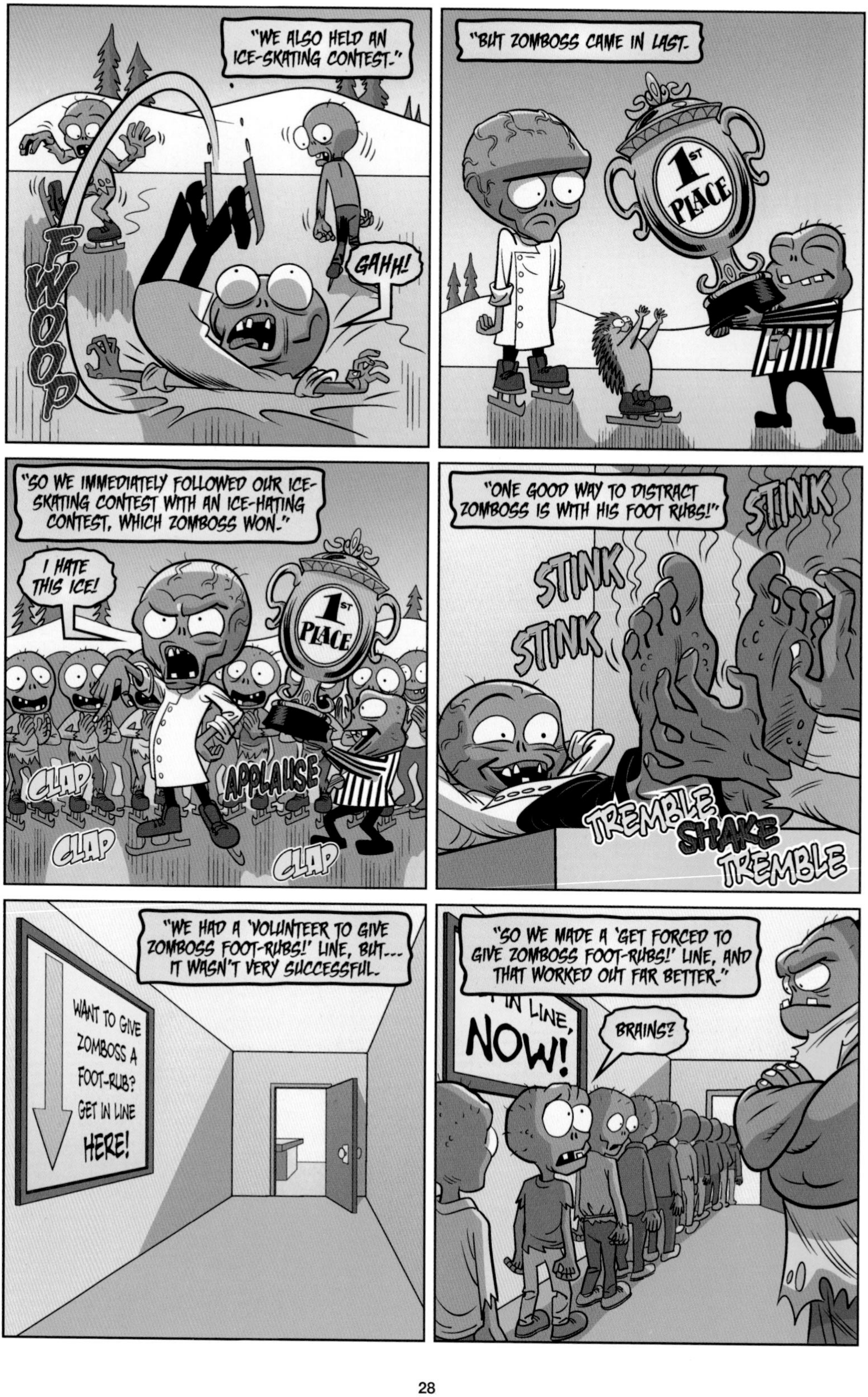

"WE ALSO HELD AN ICE-SKATING CONTEST."
FWOOP
GAHH!
"BUT ZOMBOSS CAME IN LAST.
1ST PLACE
"SO WE IMMEDIATELY FOLLOWED OUR ICE-SKATING CONTEST WITH AN ICE-HATING CONTEST, WHICH ZOMBOSS WON."
I HATE THIS ICE!
1ST PLACE
CLAP
APPLAUSE
CLAP
CLAP
"ONE GOOD WAY TO DISTRACT ZOMBOSS IS WITH HIS FOOT RUBS!"
STINK
STINK
STINK
TREMBLE
SHAKE
TREMBLE
"WE HAD A 'VOLUNTEER TO GIVE ZOMBOSS FOOT-RUBS!' LINE, BUT... IT WASN'T VERY SUCCESSFUL.
WANT TO GIVE ZOMBOSS A FOOT-RUB? GET IN LINE HERE!
"SO WE MADE A 'GET FORCED TO GIVE ZOMBOSS FOOT-RUBS!' LINE, AND THAT WORKED OUT FAR BETTER."
IN LINE, NOW!
BRAINS?

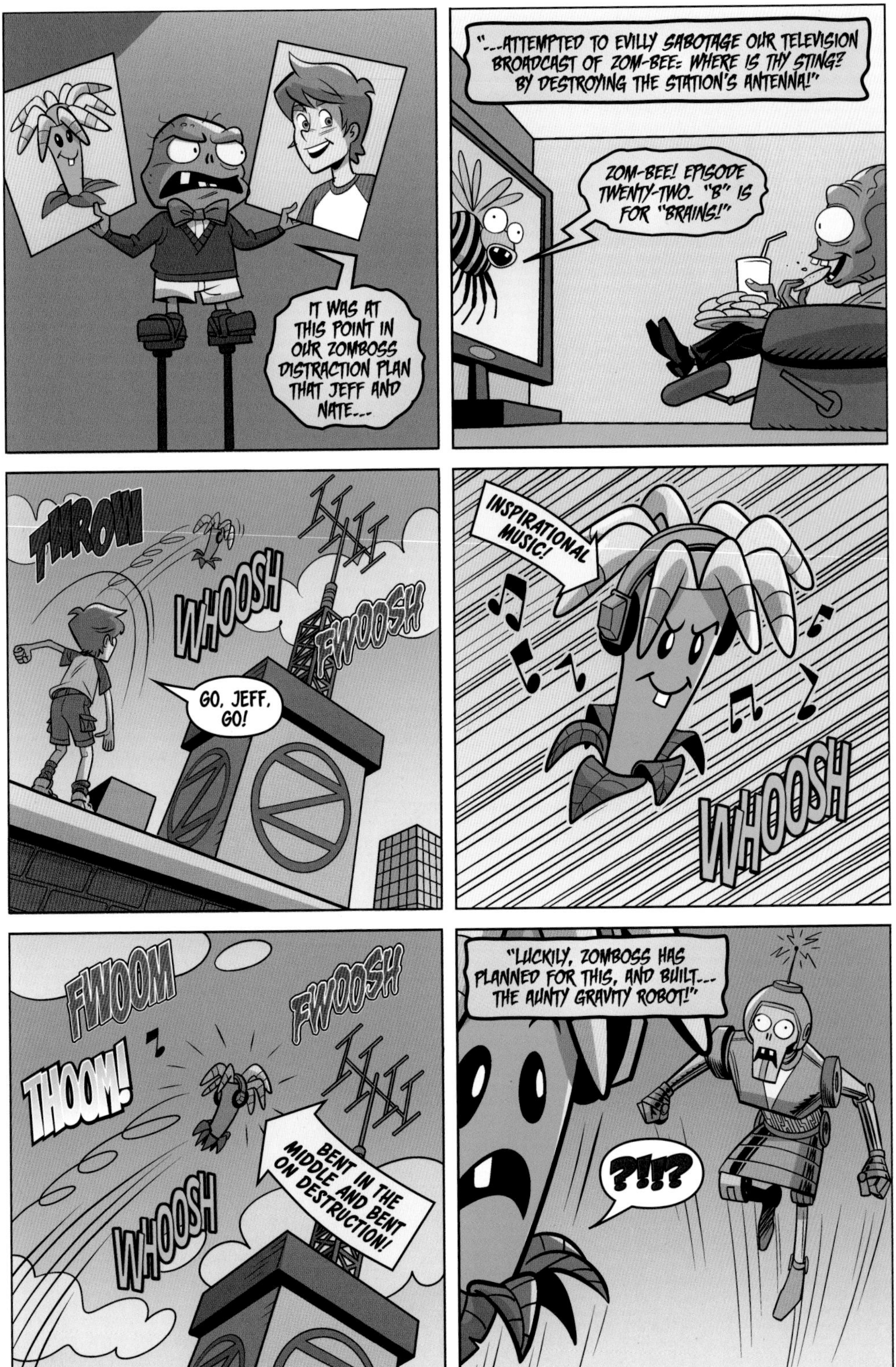
IT WAS AT THIS POINT IN OUR ZOMBOSS DISTRACTION PLAN THAT JEFF AND NATE...
"...ATTEMPTED TO EVILLY SABOTAGE OUR TELEVISION BROADCAST OF ZOM-BEE: WHERE IS THY STING? BY DESTROYING THE STATION'S ANTENNA!"
ZOM-BEE! EPISODE TWENTY-TWO. "B" IS FOR "BRAINS!"
THROW
WHOOSH
FWOOSH
GO, JEFF, GO!
INSPIRATIONAL MUSIC!
WHOOSH
FWOOM
FWOOSH
THOOM!
BENT IN THE MIDDLE AND BENT ON DESTRUCTION!
WHOOSH
"LUCKILY, ZOMBOSS HAS PLANNED FOR THIS, AND BUILT... THE AUNTY GRAVITY ROBOT!"
?!!?

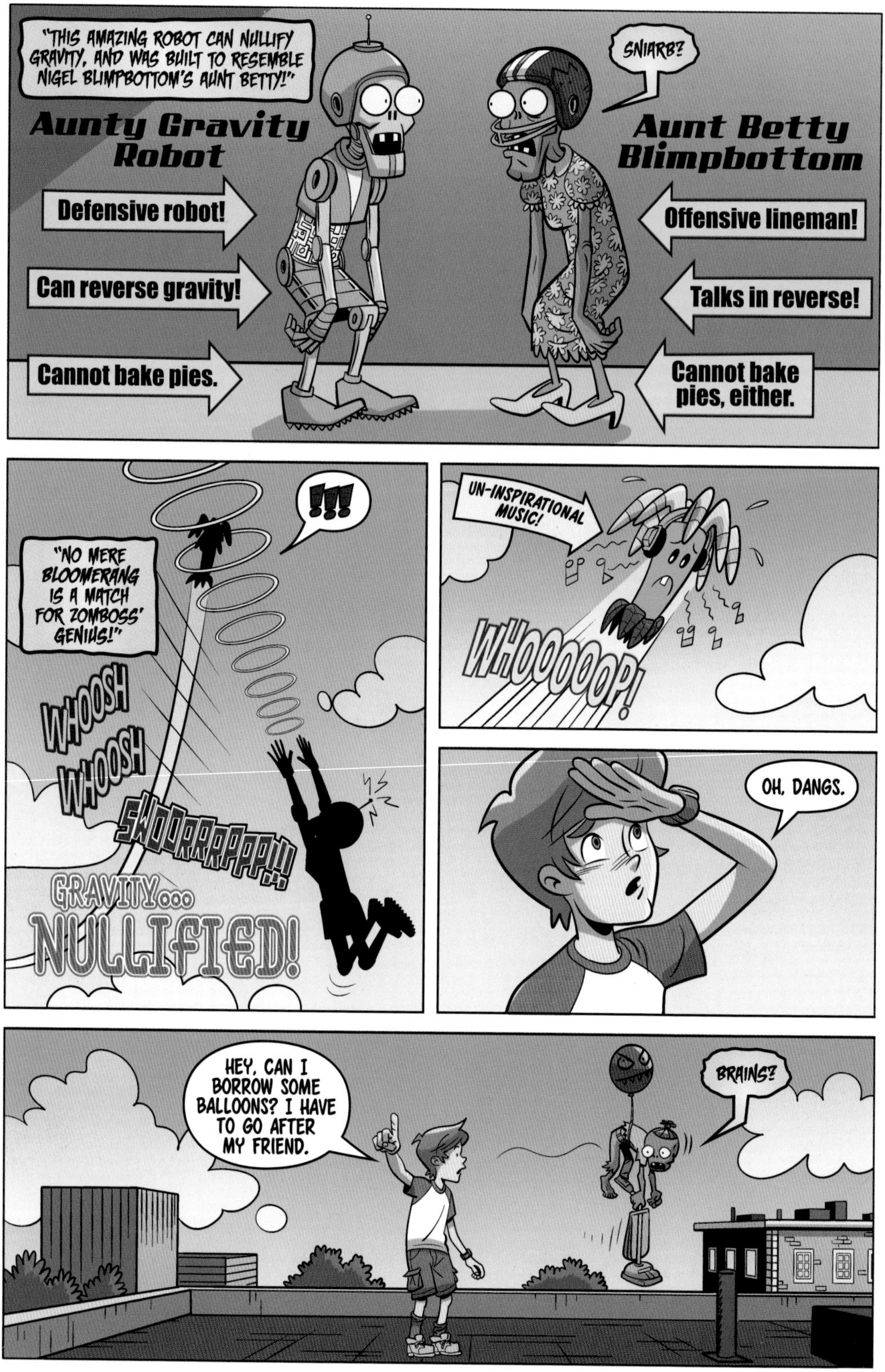
"THIS AMAZING ROBOT CAN NULLIFY GRAVITY, AND WAS BUILT TO RESEMBLE NIGEL BLIMPBOTTOM'S AUNT BETTY!"
SNIARB?
Aunty Gravity Robot
Aunt Betty Blimpbottom
Defensive robot!
Offensive lineman!
Can reverse gravity!
Talks in reverse!
Cannot bake pies.
Cannot bake pies, either.
"NO MERE BLOOMERANG IS A MATCH FOR ZOMBOSS' GENIUS!"
!!!
WHOOSH
WHOOSH
SWOORRRPPP!!!
GRAVITY...
NULLIFIED!
UN-INSPIRATIONAL MUSIC!
WHOOOOOP!
OH, DANGS.
HEY, CAN I BORROW SOME BALLOONS? I HAVE TO GO AFTER MY FRIEND.
BRAINS?

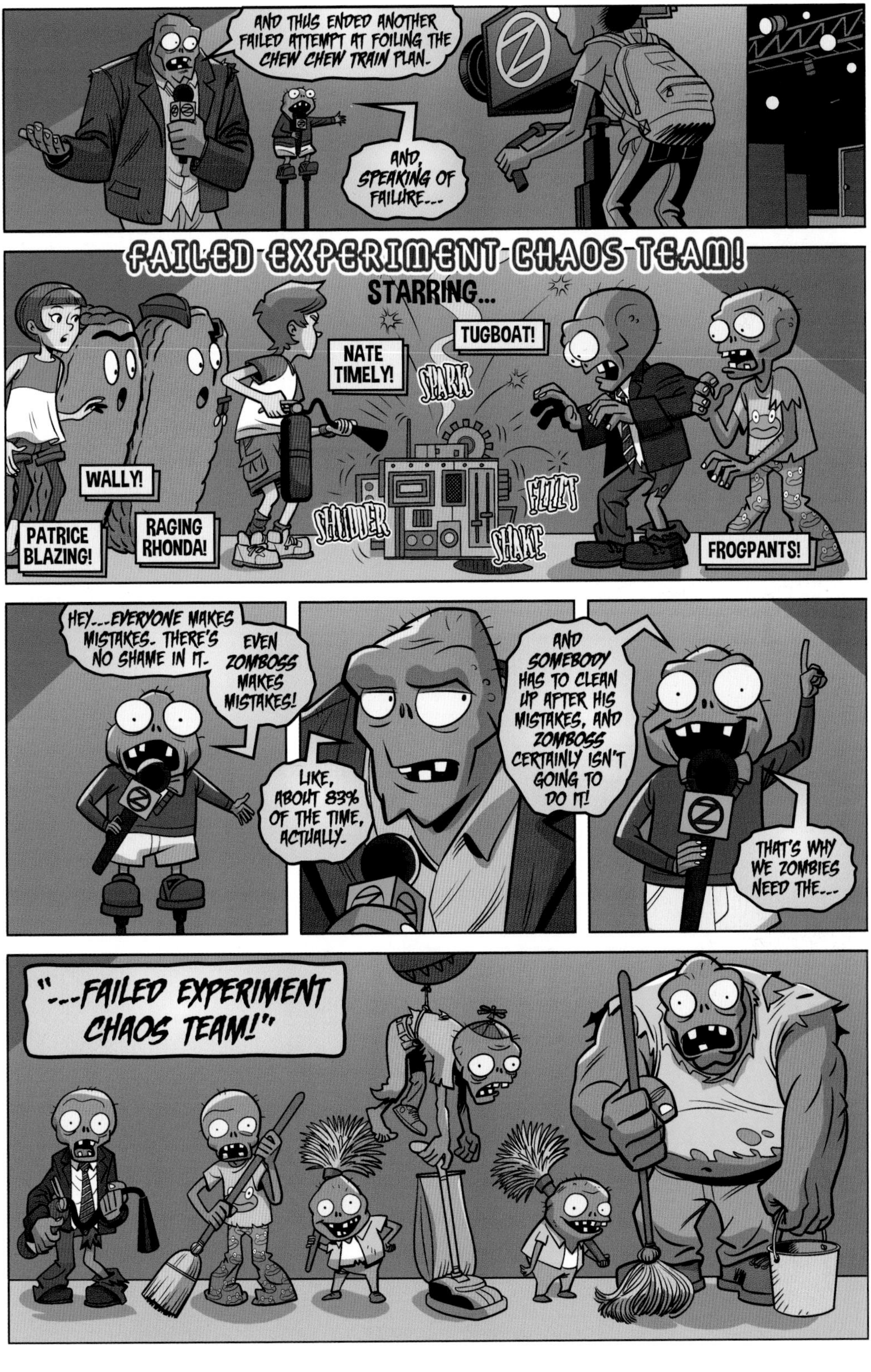
AND THUS ENDED ANOTHER FAILED ATTEMPT AT FOILING THE CHEW CHEW TRAIN PLAN.
AND, SPEAKING OF FAILURE...
FAILED EXPERIMENT CHAOS TEAM!
STARRING...
NATE TIMELY!
TUGBOAT!
WALLY!
PATRICE BLAZING!
RAGING RHONDA!
FROGPANTS!
SPARK
SHUDDER
FZZZT
SHAKE
HEY...EVERYONE MAKES MISTAKES. THERE'S NO SHAME IN IT.
EVEN ZOMBOSS MAKES MISTAKES!
LIKE, ABOUT 83% OF THE TIME, ACTUALLY.
AND SOMEBODY HAS TO CLEAN UP AFTER HIS MISTAKES, AND ZOMBOSS CERTAINLY ISN'T GOING TO DO IT!
THAT'S WHY WE ZOMBIES NEED THE...
"...FAILED EXPERIMENT CHAOS TEAM!"

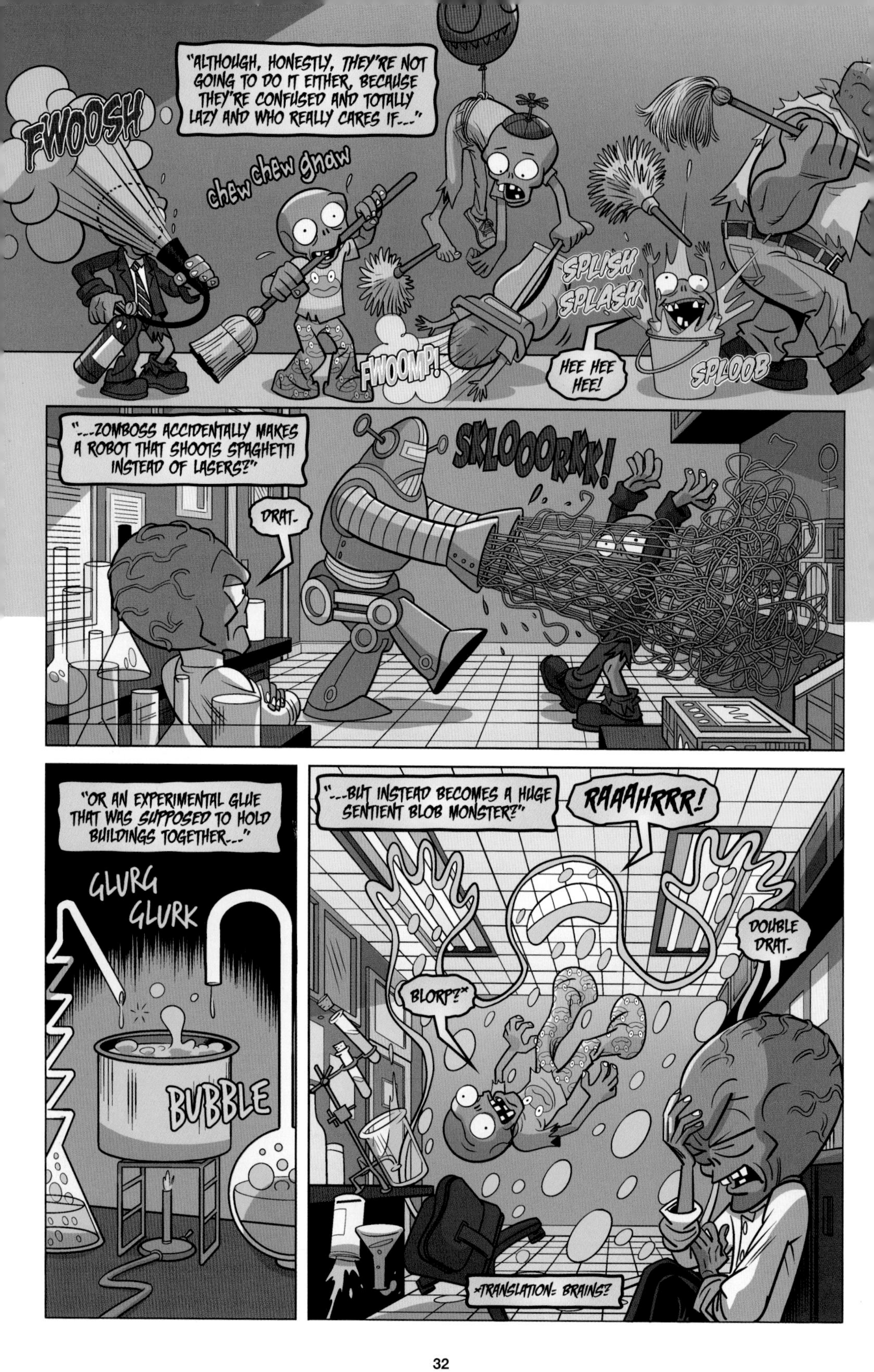
"ALTHOUGH, HONESTLY, THEY'RE NOT GOING TO DO IT EITHER, BECAUSE THEY'RE CONFUSED AND TOTALLY LAZY AND WHO REALLY CARES IF--"
FWOOSH
chew chew gnaw
SPLISH SPLASH
FWOOMP!
HEE HEE HEE!
SPLOOB
"--ZOMBOSS ACCIDENTALLY MAKES A ROBOT THAT SHOOTS SPAGHETTI INSTEAD OF LASERS?"
SKLOOORKK!
DRAT.
"OR AN EXPERIMENTAL GLUE THAT WAS SUPPOSED TO HOLD BUILDINGS TOGETHER--"
GLURG GLURK
BUBBLE
"--BUT INSTEAD BECOMES A HUGE SENTIENT BLOB MONSTER?"
RAAAHRRR!
DOUBLE DRAT.
BLORP?*
*TRANSLATION: BRAINS?

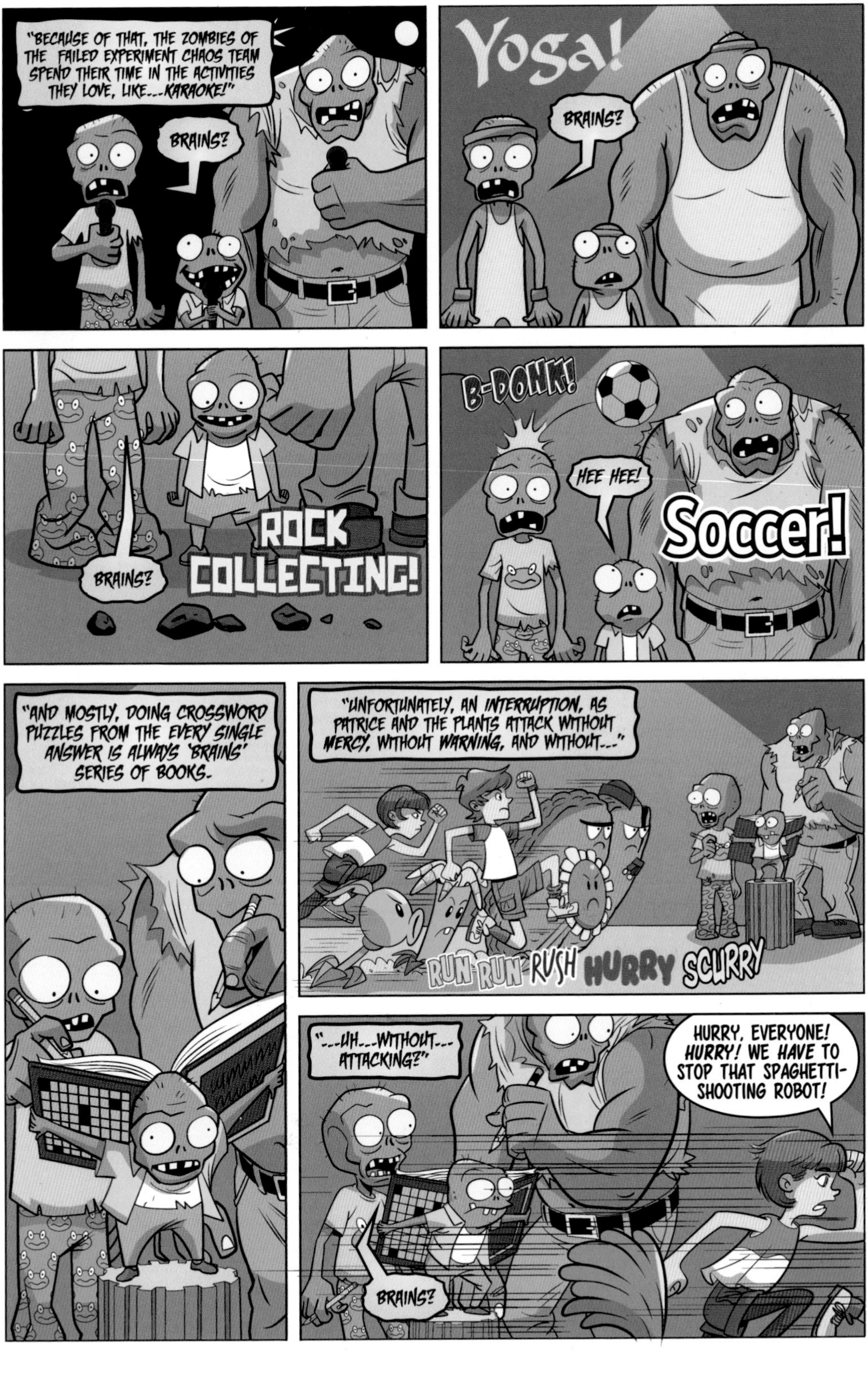
"BECAUSE OF THAT, THE ZOMBIES OF THE FAILED EXPERIMENT CHAOS TEAM SPEND THEIR TIME IN THE ACTIVITIES THEY LOVE, LIKE...KARAOKE!"
BRAINS?
Yoga!
BRAINS?
BRAINS?
ROCK COLLECTING!
B-DONK!
HEE HEE!
Soccer!
"AND MOSTLY, DOING CROSSWORD PUZZLES FROM THE EVERY SINGLE ANSWER IS ALWAYS 'BRAINS' SERIES OF BOOKS.
"UNFORTUNATELY, AN INTERRUPTION, AS PATRICE AND THE PLANTS ATTACK WITHOUT MERCY, WITHOUT WARNING, AND WITHOUT..."
RUN RUN RUSH HURRY SCURRY
"...UH...WITHOUT... ATTACKING?"
HURRY, EVERYONE! HURRY! WE HAVE TO STOP THAT SPAGHETTI-SHOOTING ROBOT!
BRAINS?

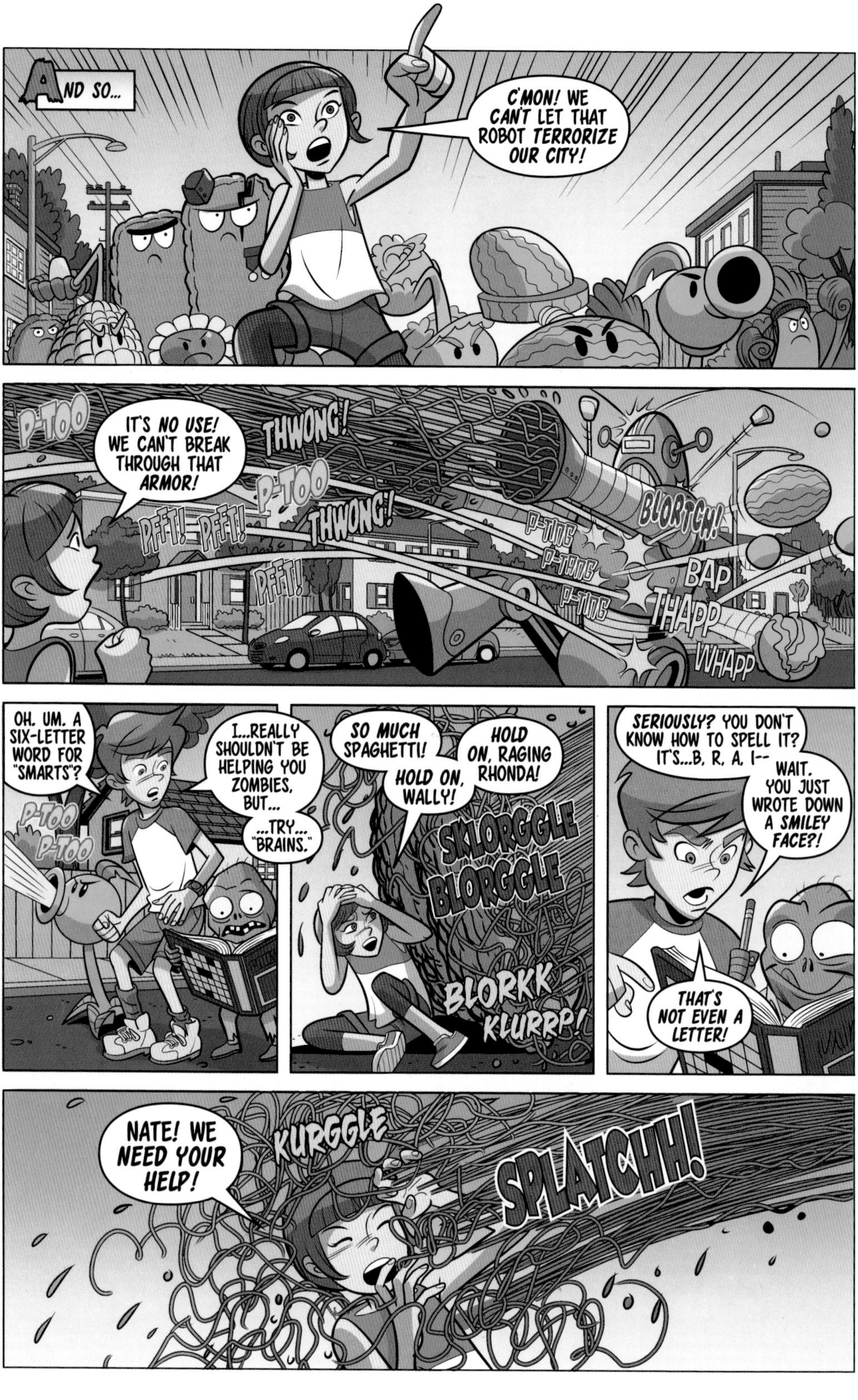
AND SO...
C'MON! WE CAN'T LET THAT ROBOT TERRORIZE OUR CITY!
P-TOO
IT'S NO USE! WE CAN'T BREAK THROUGH THAT ARMOR!
THWONG!
P-TOO
PFFT! PFFT!
THWONG!
PFFT!
BLORTCH!
P-TING
P-TANG
P-TING
BAP
THAPP
WHAPP
OH. UM. A SIX-LETTER WORD FOR "SMARTS"?
P-TOO
P-TOO
I...REALLY SHOULDN'T BE HELPING YOU ZOMBIES, BUT...
...TRY... "BRAINS."
SO MUCH SPAGHETTI!
HOLD ON, RAGING RHONDA!
HOLD ON, WALLY!
SKLORGGLE
BLORGGLE
BLORKK
KLURRP!
SERIOUSLY? YOU DON'T KNOW HOW TO SPELL IT? IT'S...B, R, A, I--
WAIT. YOU JUST WROTE DOWN A SMILEY FACE?!
THAT'S NOT EVEN A LETTER!
NATE! WE NEED YOUR HELP!
KURGGLE
SPLATCHH!

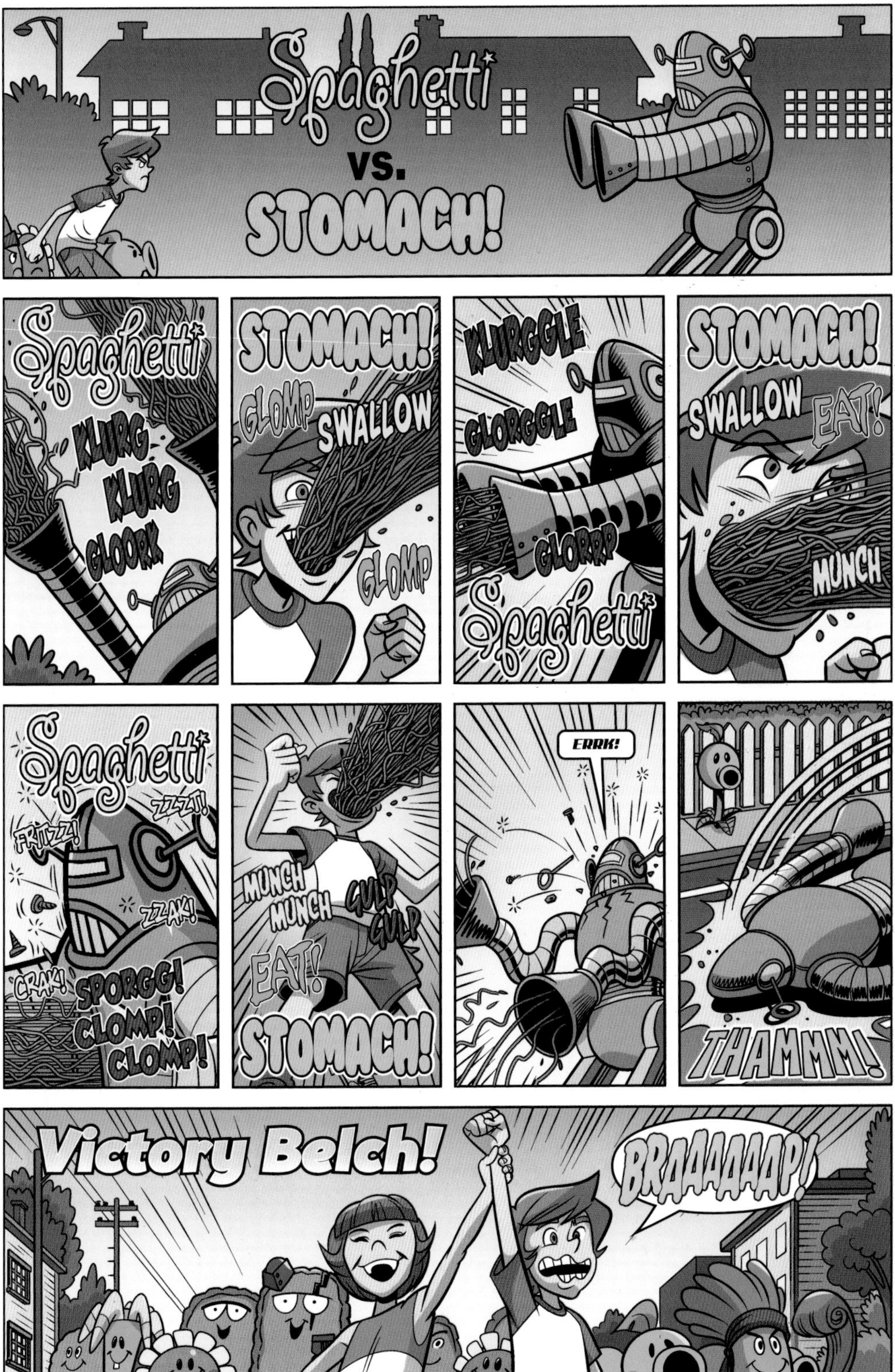

Spaghetti vs. STOMACH!
Spaghetti
KLURG KLURG
GLOORK
STOMACH!
GLOMP
SWALLOW
GLOMP
KLURGGLE
GLORGGLE
GLORRP
Spaghetti
STOMACH!
SWALLOW
EAT!
MUNCH
Spaghetti
ZZZZT!
FRITZZZ!
ZZAK!
CRAK!
SPORGG!
CLOMP!
CLOMP!
MUNCH
MUNCH
GULP
GULP
EAT!
STOMACH!
ERRK!
THAMMM!
Victory Belch!
BRAAAAAAP!

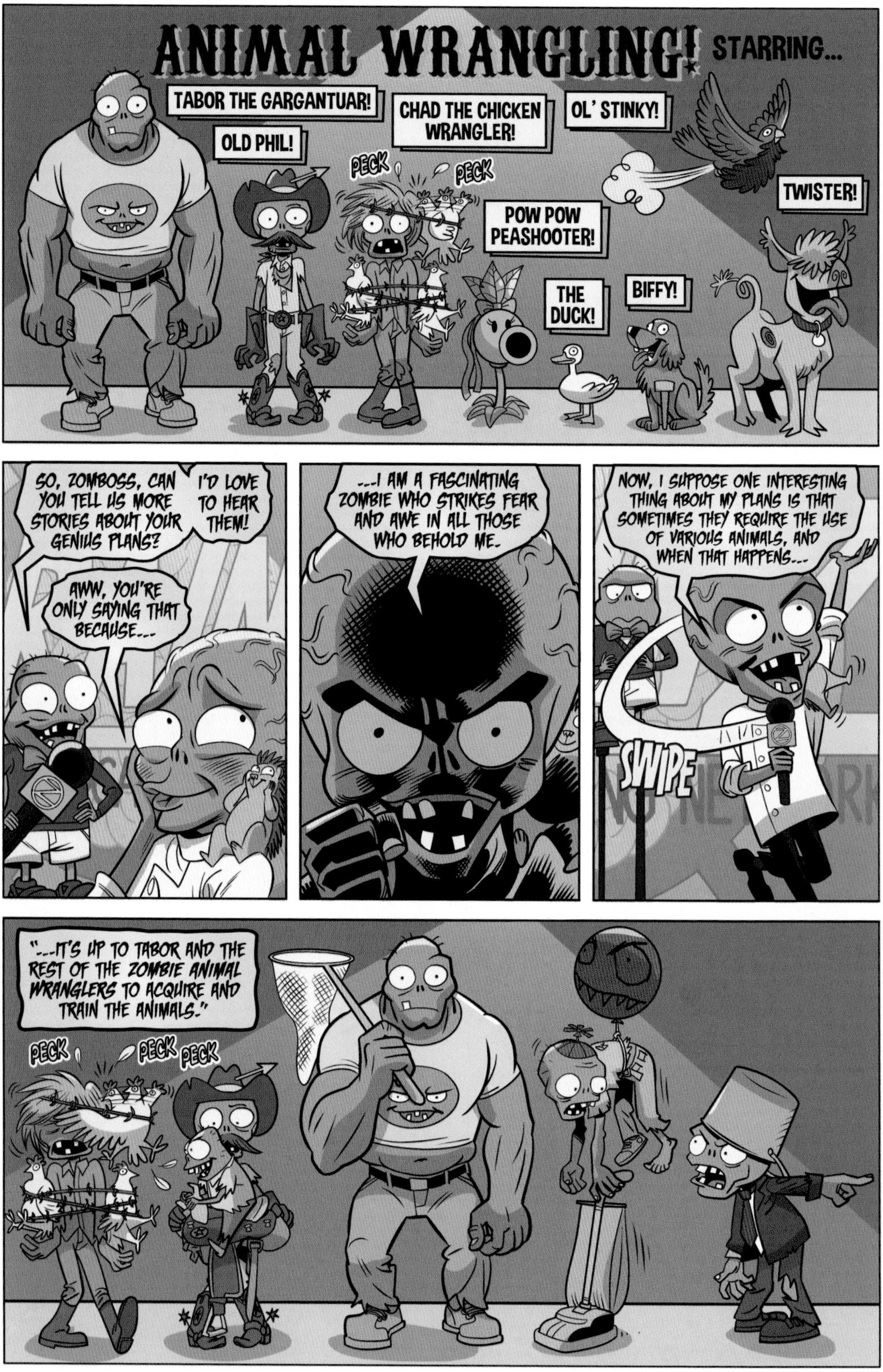
ANIMAL WRANGLING! STARRING...
TABOR THE GARGANTUAR!
OLD PHIL!
CHAD THE CHICKEN WRANGLER!
OL' STINKY!
PECK PECK
POW POW PEASHOOTER!
TWISTER!
THE DUCK!
BIFFY!
SO, ZOMBOSS, CAN YOU TELL US MORE STORIES ABOUT YOUR GENIUS PLANS?
I'D LOVE TO HEAR THEM!
AWW, YOU'RE ONLY SAYING THAT BECAUSE...
...I AM A FASCINATING ZOMBIE WHO STRIKES FEAR AND AWE IN ALL THOSE WHO BEHOLD ME.
NOW, I SUPPOSE ONE INTERESTING THING ABOUT MY PLANS IS THAT SOMETIMES THEY REQUIRE THE USE OF VARIOUS ANIMALS, AND WHEN THAT HAPPENS...
SWIPE
"...IT'S UP TO TABOR AND THE REST OF THE ZOMBIE ANIMAL WRANGLERS TO ACQUIRE AND TRAIN THE ANIMALS."
PECK PECK PECK

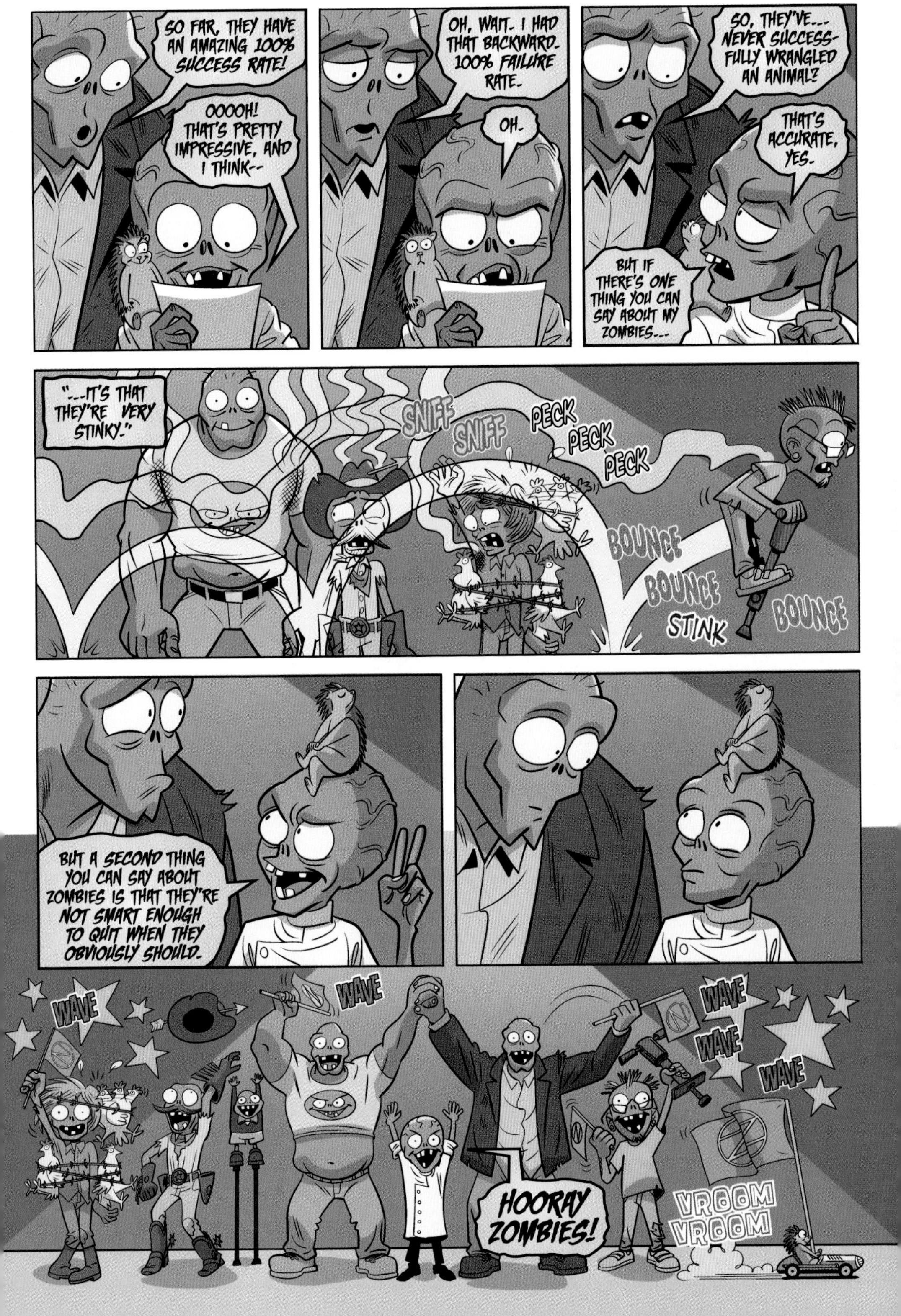
SO FAR, THEY HAVE AN AMAZING 100% SUCCESS RATE!
OOOOH! THAT'S PRETTY IMPRESSIVE, AND I THINK--
OH, WAIT. I HAD THAT BACKWARD. 100% FAILURE RATE.
OH.
SO, THEY'VE... NEVER SUCCESSFULLY WRANGLED AN ANIMAL?
THAT'S ACCURATE, YES.
BUT IF THERE'S ONE THING YOU CAN SAY ABOUT MY ZOMBIES...
"...IT'S THAT THEY'RE VERY STINKY."
SNIFF
SNIFF
PECK
PECK
PECK
BOUNCE
BOUNCE
BOUNCE
STINK
BUT A SECOND THING YOU CAN SAY ABOUT ZOMBIES IS THAT THEY'RE NOT SMART ENOUGH TO QUIT WHEN THEY OBVIOUSLY SHOULD.
WAVE
WAVE
WAVE
WAVE
WAVE
HOORAY ZOMBIES!
VROOM
VROOM

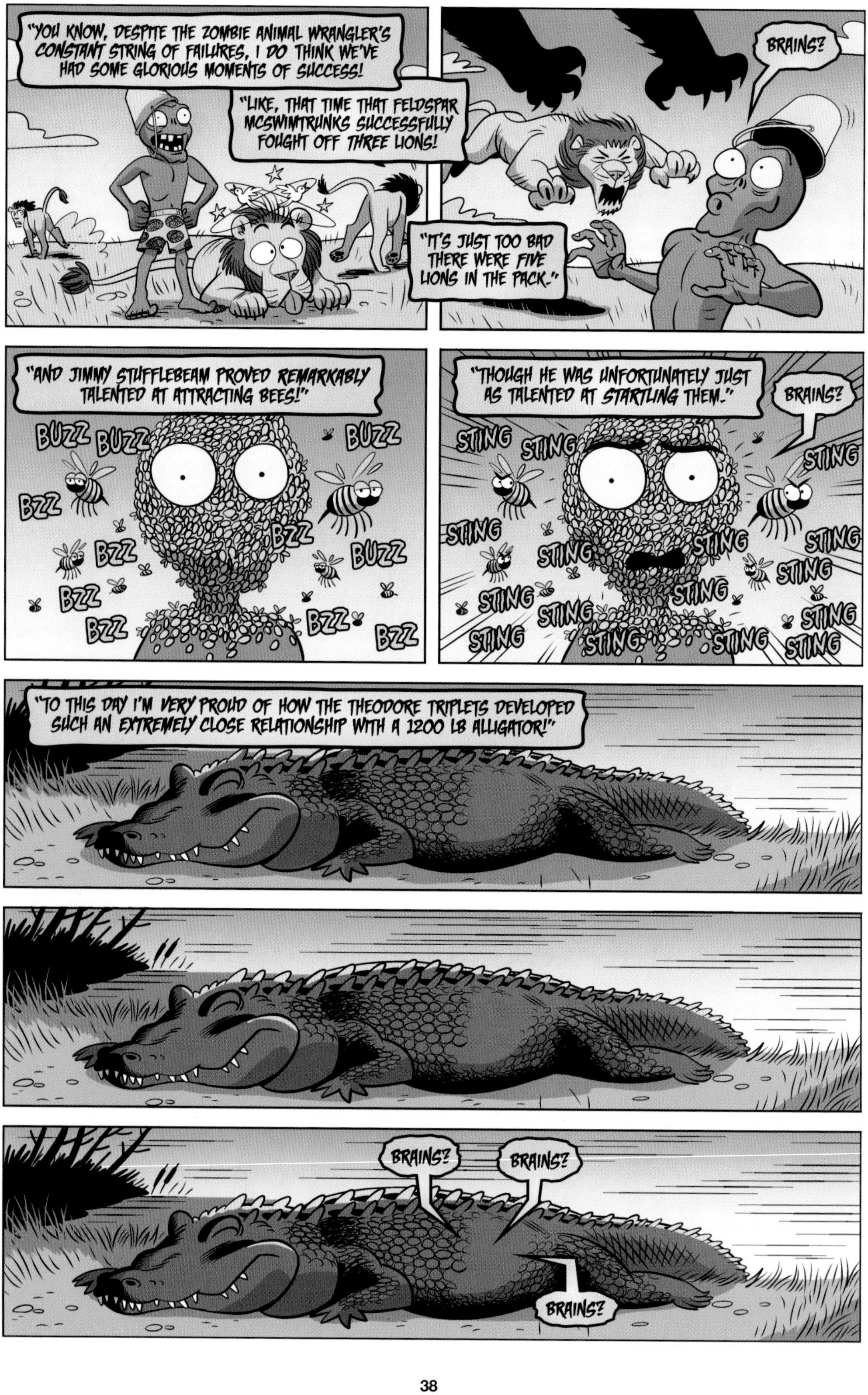
"YOU KNOW, DESPITE THE ZOMBIE ANIMAL WRANGLER'S CONSTANT STRING OF FAILURES, I DO THINK WE'VE HAD SOME GLORIOUS MOMENTS OF SUCCESS!
"LIKE, THAT TIME THAT FELDSPAR MCSWIMTRUNKS SUCCESSFULLY FOUGHT OFF THREE LIONS!
BRAINS?
"IT'S JUST TOO BAD THERE WERE FIVE LIONS IN THE PACK."
"AND JIMMY STUFFLEBEAM PROVED REMARKABLY TALENTED AT ATTRACTING BEES!"
BUZZ BUZZ BZZ BUZZ BZZ BZZ BUZZ BZZ BZZ BZZ BZZ
"THOUGH HE WAS UNFORTUNATELY JUST AS TALENTED AT STARTLING THEM."
BRAINS?
STING STING STING STING STING STING STING STING STING STING STING STING STING STING STING
"TO THIS DAY I'M VERY PROUD OF HOW THE THEODORE TRIPLETS DEVELOPED SUCH AN EXTREMELY CLOSE RELATIONSHIP WITH A 1200 LB ALLIGATOR!"
BRAINS?
BRAINS?
BRAINS?

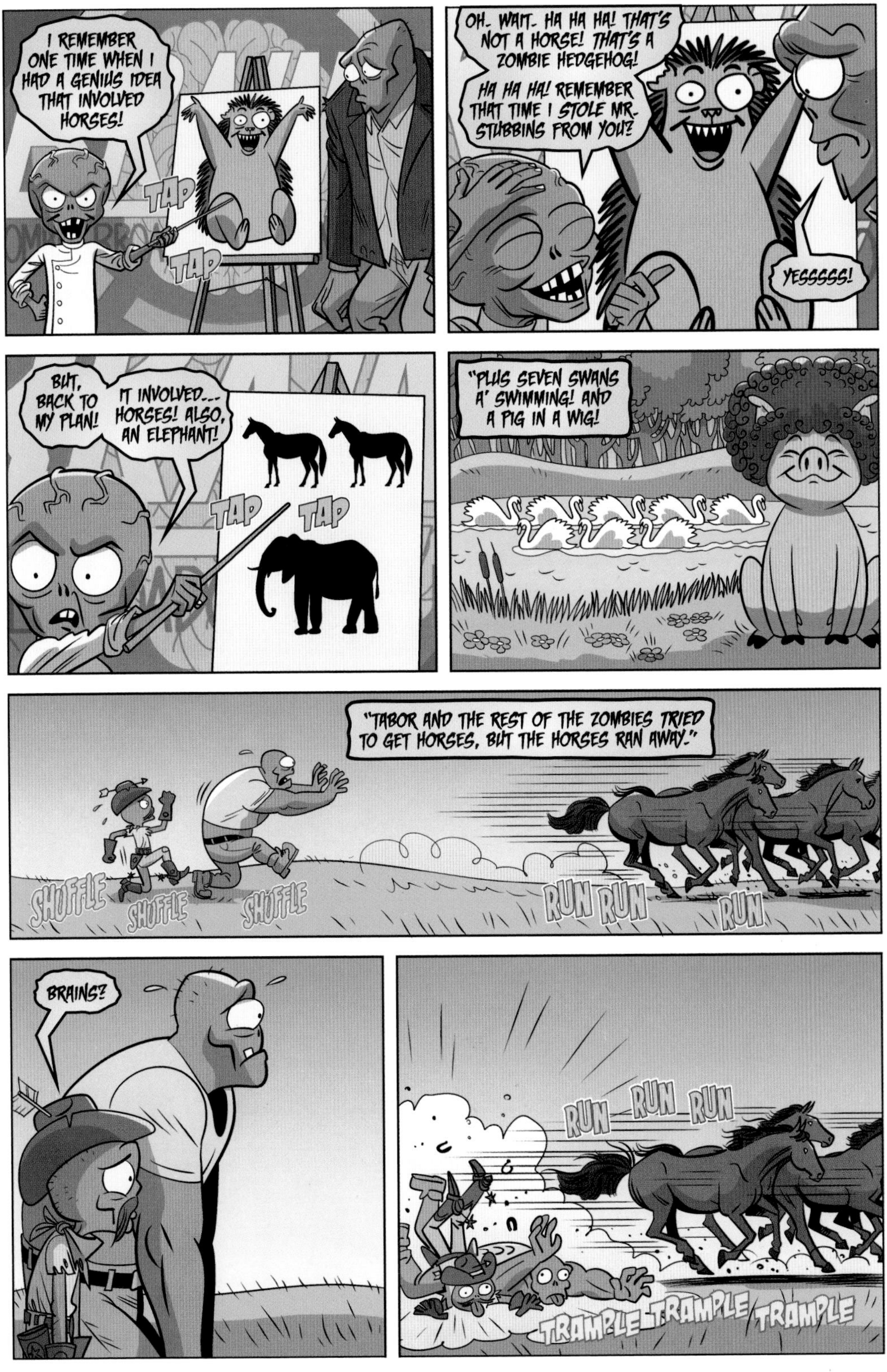
I REMEMBER ONE TIME WHEN I HAD A GENIUS IDEA THAT INVOLVED HORSES!
TAP
TAP
OH. WAIT. HA HA HA! THAT'S NOT A HORSE! THAT'S A ZOMBIE HEDGEHOG!
HA HA HA! REMEMBER THAT TIME I STOLE MR. STUBBINS FROM YOU?
YESSSSS!
BUT, BACK TO MY PLAN!
IT INVOLVED... HORSES! ALSO, AN ELEPHANT!
TAP
TAP
"PLUS SEVEN SWANS A' SWIMMING! AND A PIG IN A WIG!
"TABOR AND THE REST OF THE ZOMBIES TRIED TO GET HORSES, BUT THE HORSES RAN AWAY."
SHUFFLE
SHUFFLE
SHUFFLE
RUN RUN
RUN
BRAINS?
RUN RUN RUN
TRAMPLE TRAMPLE TRAMPLE

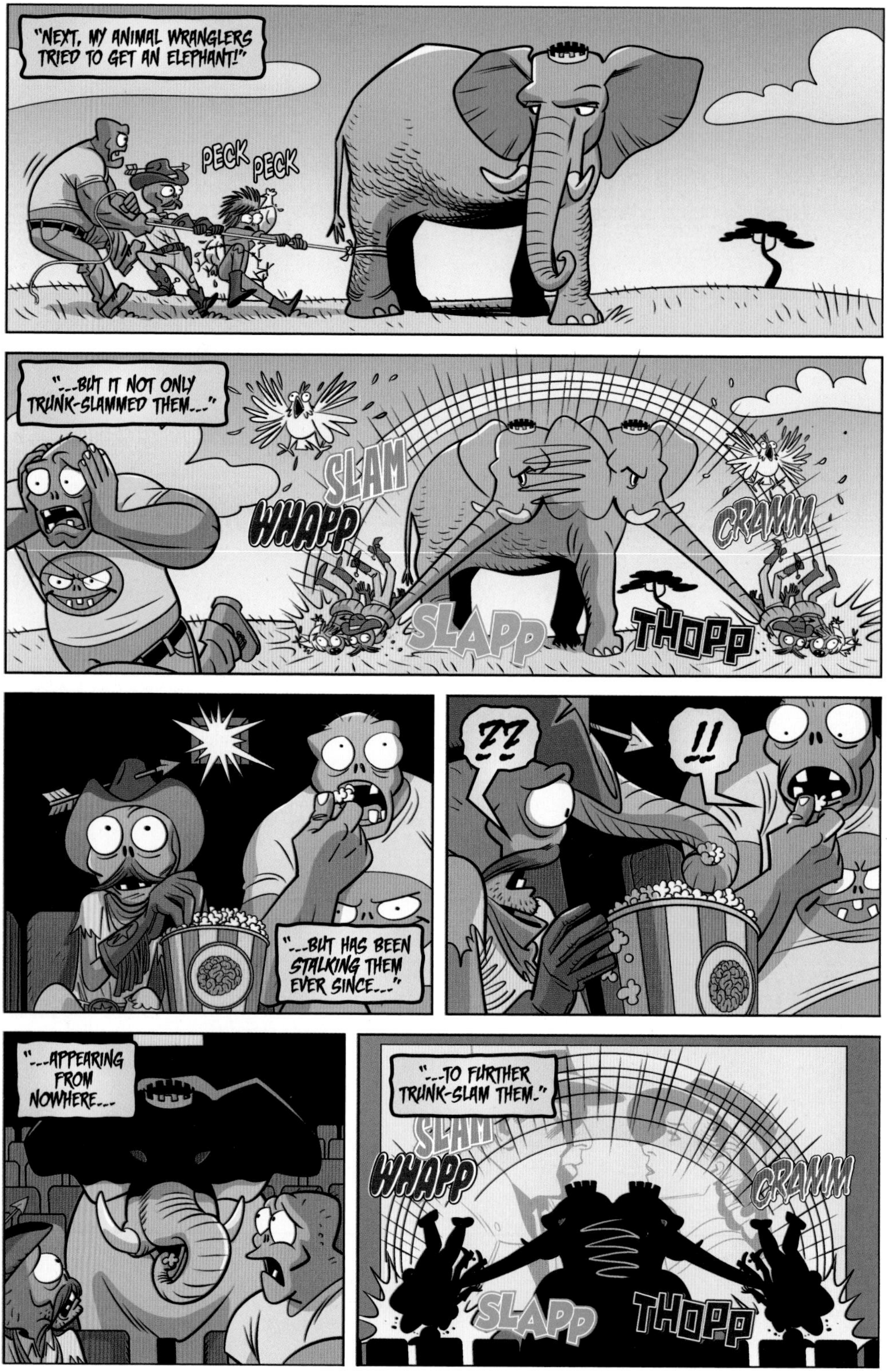
"NEXT, MY ANIMAL WRANGLERS TRIED TO GET AN ELEPHANT!"
PECK PECK
"...BUT IT NOT ONLY TRUNK-SLAMMED THEM..."
SLAM
WHAPP
CRAMM
SLAPP
THOPP
"...BUT HAS BEEN STALKING THEM EVER SINCE..."
??
!!
"...APPEARING FROM NOWHERE..."
"...TO FURTHER TRUNK-SLAM THEM."
SLAM
WHAPP
CRAMM
SLAPP
THOPP

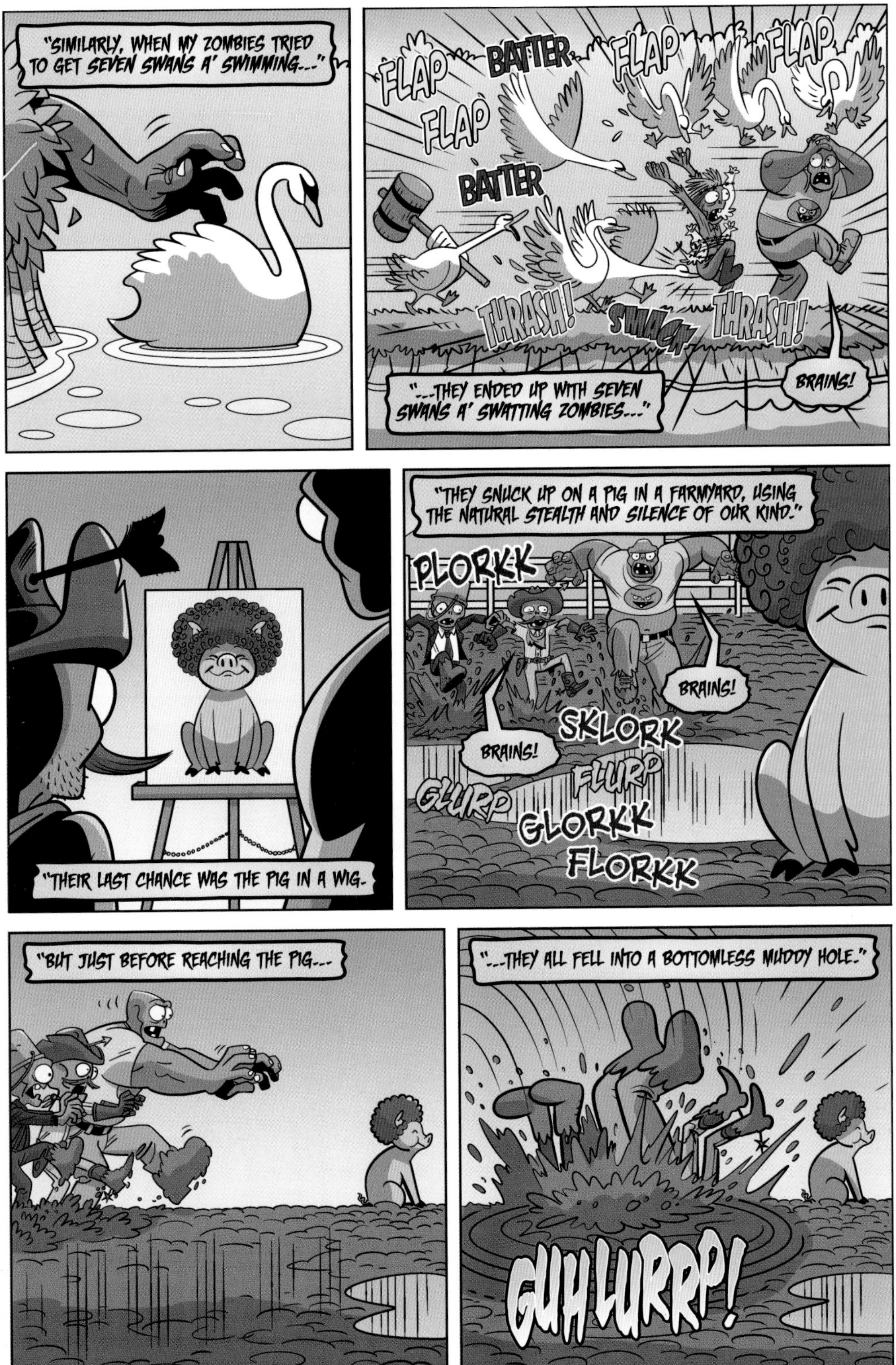
"SIMILARLY, WHEN MY ZOMBIES TRIED TO GET SEVEN SWANS A' SWIMMING..."
FLAP
BATTER
FLAP
FLAP
FLAP
BATTER
THRASH!
SWACK
THRASH!
"...THEY ENDED UP WITH SEVEN SWANS A' SWATTING ZOMBIES..."
BRAINS!
"THEIR LAST CHANCE WAS THE PIG IN A WIG.
"THEY SNUCK UP ON A PIG IN A FARMYARD, USING THE NATURAL STEALTH AND SILENCE OF OUR KIND."
PLORKK
BRAINS!
SKLORK
BRAINS!
FLURP
GLURP
GLORKK
FLORKK
"BUT JUST BEFORE REACHING THE PIG...
"...THEY ALL FELL INTO A BOTTOMLESS MUDDY HOLE."
GUH LURRP!

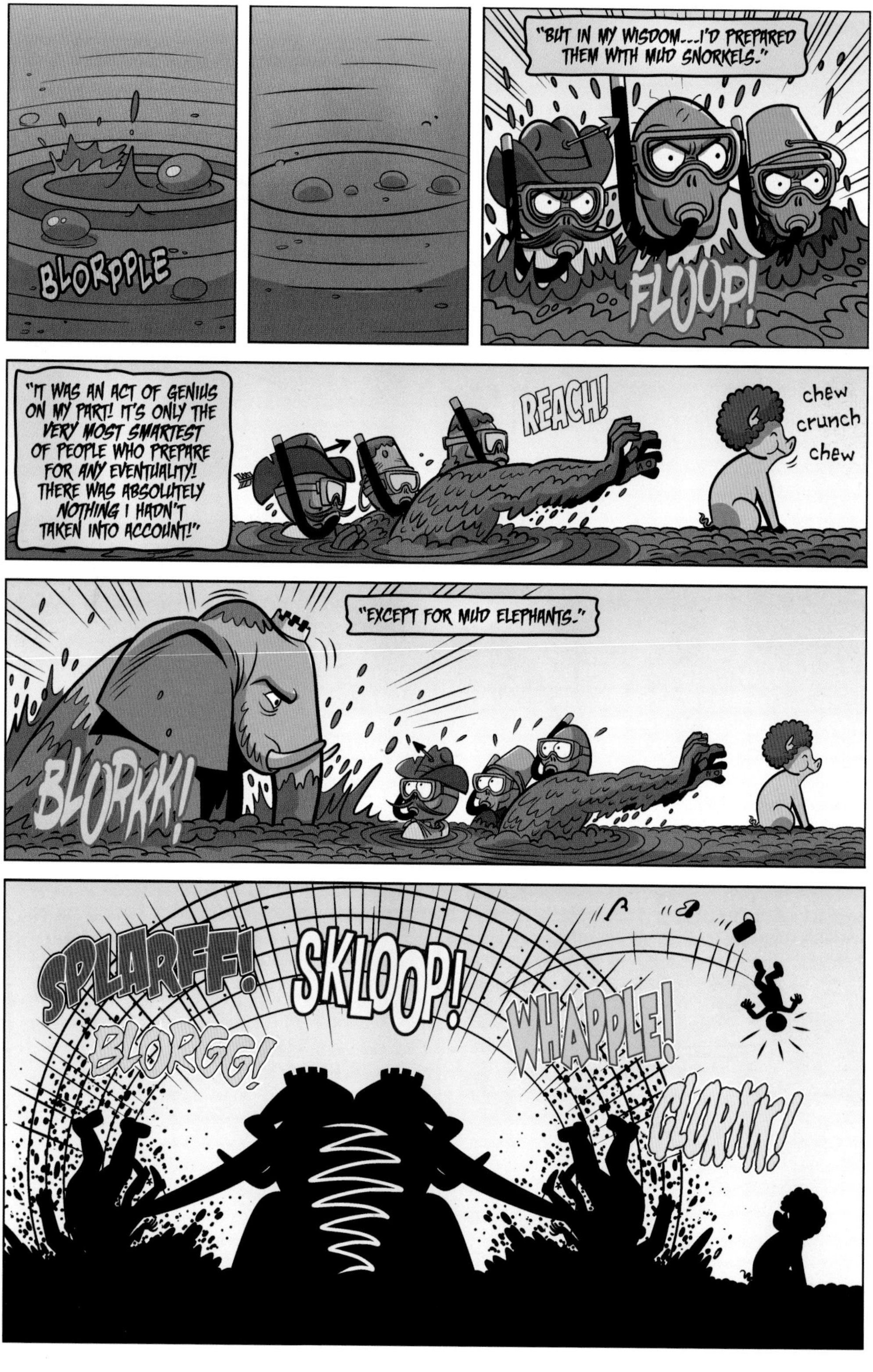
BLORPPLE
"BUT IN MY WISDOM...I'D PREPARED THEM WITH MUD SNORKELS."
FLOOP!
"IT WAS AN ACT OF GENIUS ON MY PART! IT'S ONLY THE VERY MOST SMARTEST OF PEOPLE WHO PREPARE FOR ANY EVENTUALITY! THERE WAS ABSOLUTELY NOTHING I HADN'T TAKEN INTO ACCOUNT!"
REACH!
chew
crunch
chew
"EXCEPT FOR MUD ELEPHANTS."
BLORKK!
SPLARFF!
SKLOOP!
BLORGG!
WHAPPLE!
CLORKK!

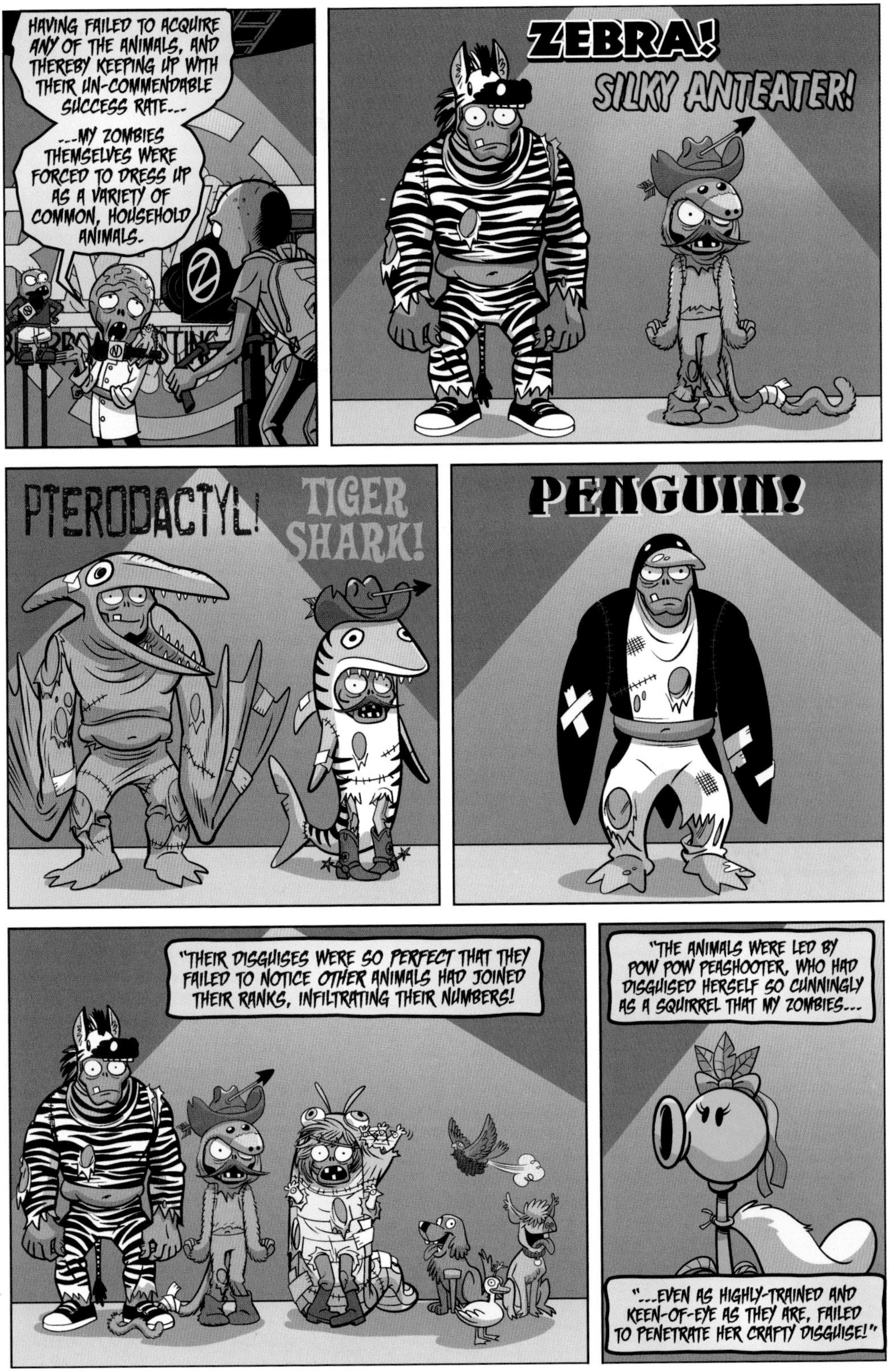
HAVING FAILED TO ACQUIRE ANY OF THE ANIMALS, AND THEREBY KEEPING UP WITH THEIR UN-COMMENDABLE SUCCESS RATE...
...MY ZOMBIES THEMSELVES WERE FORCED TO DRESS UP AS A VARIETY OF COMMON, HOUSEHOLD ANIMALS.
ZEBRA!
SILKY ANTEATER!
PTERODACTYL!
TIGER SHARK!
PENGUIN!
"THEIR DISGUISES WERE SO PERFECT THAT THEY FAILED TO NOTICE OTHER ANIMALS HAD JOINED THEIR RANKS, INFILTRATING THEIR NUMBERS!
"THE ANIMALS WERE LED BY POW POW PEASHOOTER, WHO HAD DISGUISED HERSELF SO CUNNINGLY AS A SQUIRREL THAT MY ZOMBIES...
"...EVEN AS HIGHLY-TRAINED AND KEEN-OF-EYE AS THEY ARE, FAILED TO PENETRATE HER CRAFTY DISGUISE!"

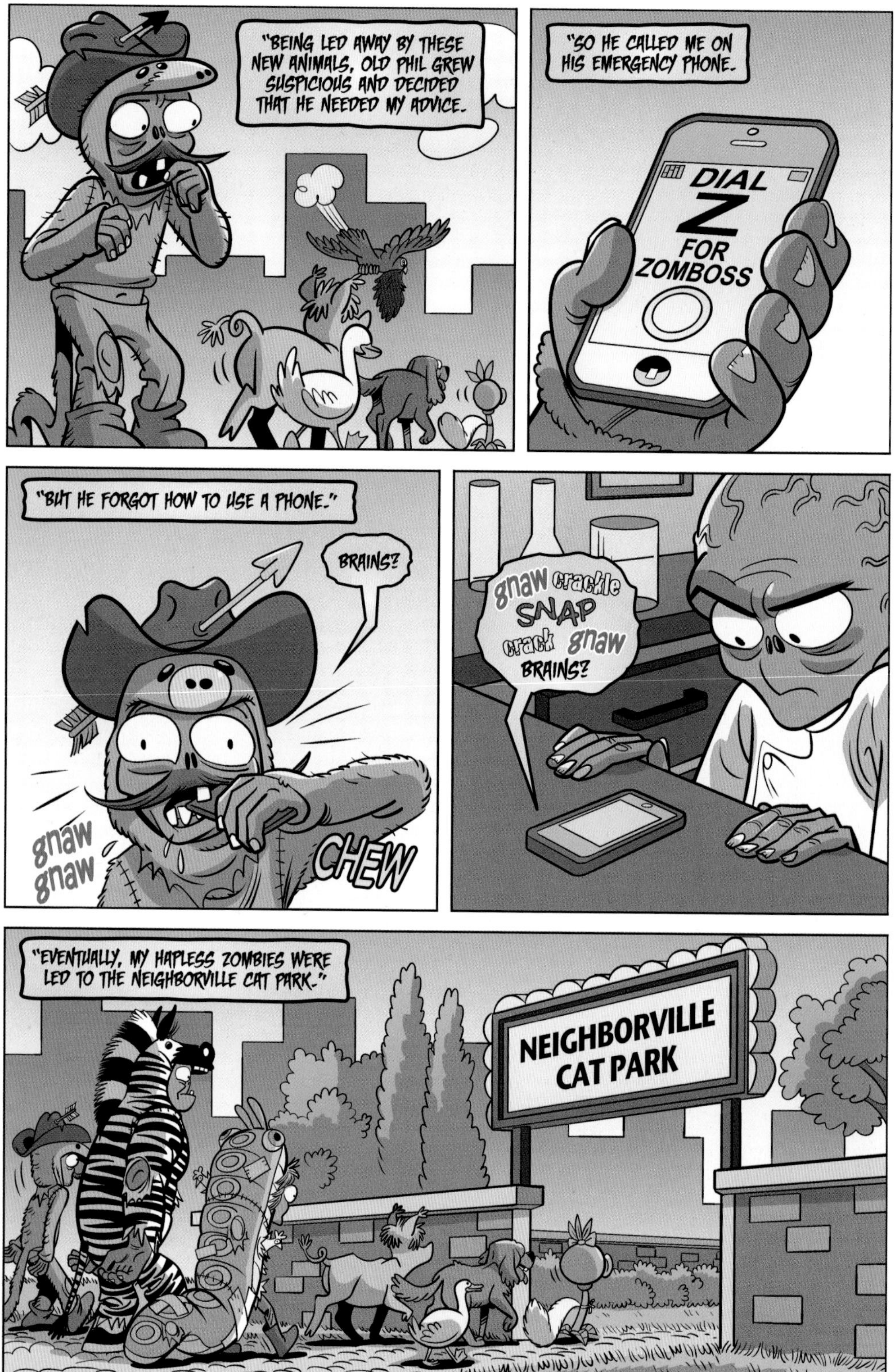

"BEING LED AWAY BY THESE NEW ANIMALS, OLD PHIL GREW SUSPICIOUS AND DECIDED THAT HE NEEDED MY ADVICE.
"SO HE CALLED ME ON HIS EMERGENCY PHONE.
DIAL Z FOR ZOMBOSS
"BUT HE FORGOT HOW TO USE A PHONE."
BRAINS?
gnaw gnaw
CHEW
gnaw crackle SNAP crack gnaw BRAINS?
"EVENTUALLY, MY HAPLESS ZOMBIES WERE LED TO THE NEIGHBORVILLE CAT PARK."
NEIGHBORVILLE CAT PARK

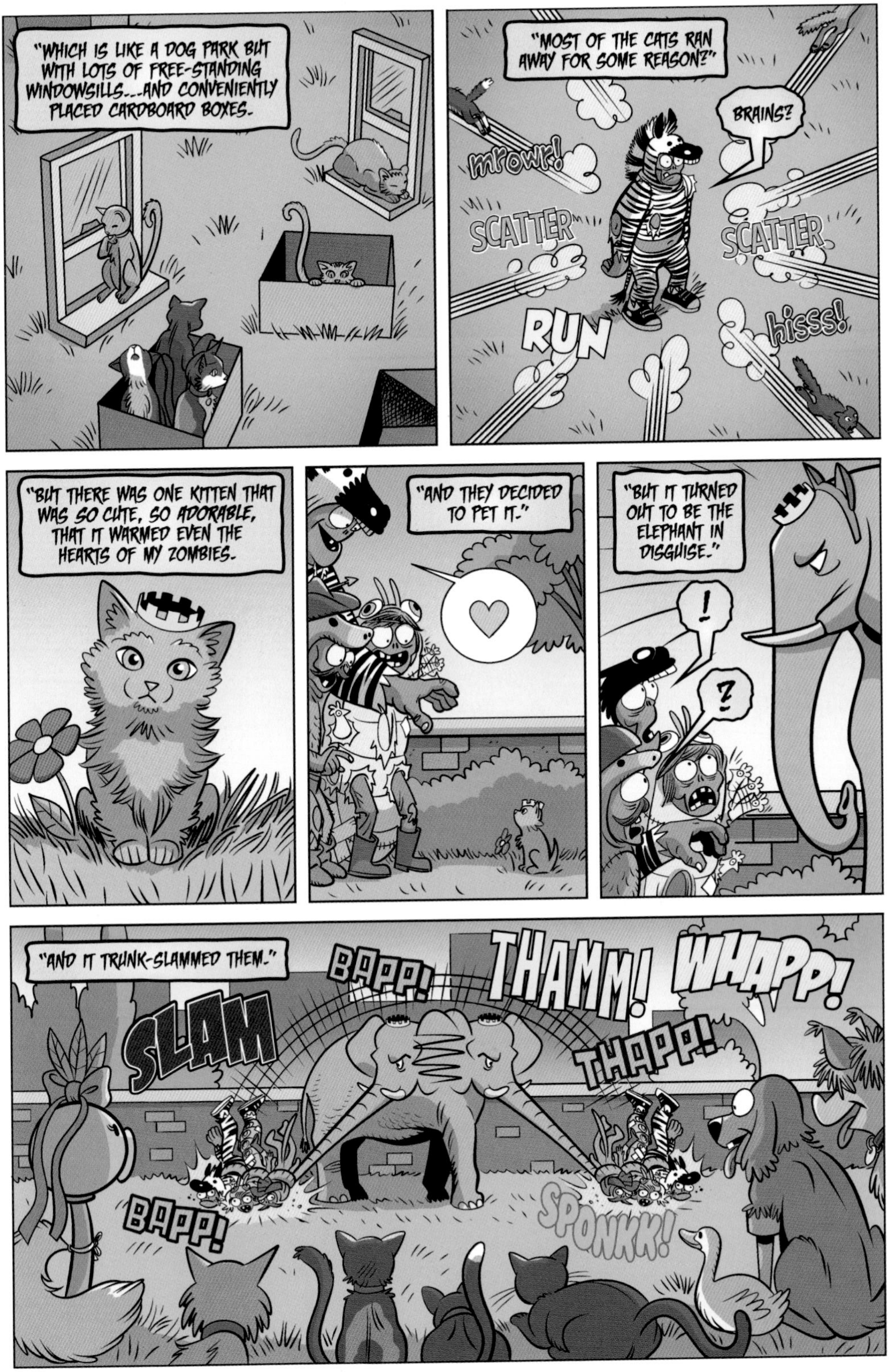
"WHICH IS LIKE A DOG PARK BUT WITH LOTS OF FREE-STANDING WINDOWSILLS...AND CONVENIENTLY PLACED CARDBOARD BOXES.
"MOST OF THE CATS RAN AWAY FOR SOME REASON?"
mrowr!
BRAINS?
SCATTER
SCATTER
RUN
hisss!
"BUT THERE WAS ONE KITTEN THAT WAS SO CUTE, SO ADORABLE, THAT IT WARMED EVEN THE HEARTS OF MY ZOMBIES.
"AND THEY DECIDED TO PET IT."
"BUT IT TURNED OUT TO BE THE ELEPHANT IN DISGUISE."
!
?
"AND IT TRUNK-SLAMMED THEM."
BAPP!
THAMM!
WHAPP!
SLAM
THAPP!
BAPP!
SPONKK!

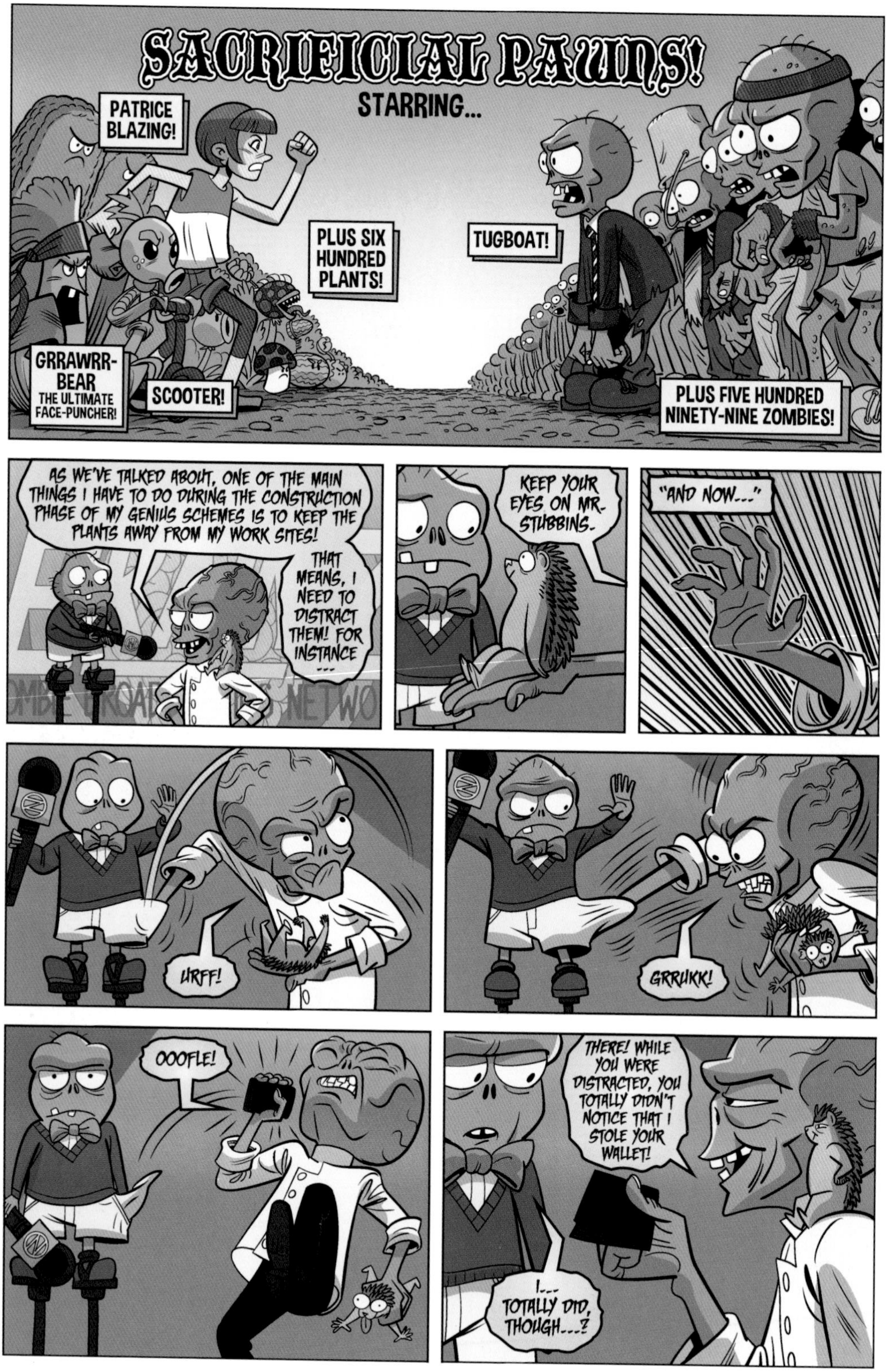
SACRIFICIAL PAWNS!
STARRING...
PATRICE BLAZING!
PLUS SIX HUNDRED PLANTS!
TUGBOAT!
GRRAWRR-BEAR THE ULTIMATE FACE-PUNCHER!
SCOOTER!
PLUS FIVE HUNDRED NINETY-NINE ZOMBIES!
AS WE'VE TALKED ABOUT, ONE OF THE MAIN THINGS I HAVE TO DO DURING THE CONSTRUCTION PHASE OF MY GENIUS SCHEMES IS TO KEEP THE PLANTS AWAY FROM MY WORK SITES!
THAT MEANS, I NEED TO DISTRACT THEM! FOR INSTANCE...
KEEP YOUR EYES ON MR. STUBBINS.
"AND NOW..."
URFF!
GRRUKK!
OOOFLE!
THERE! WHILE YOU WERE DISTRACTED, YOU TOTALLY DIDN'T NOTICE THAT I STOLE YOUR WALLET!
I... TOTALLY DID, THOUGH...?

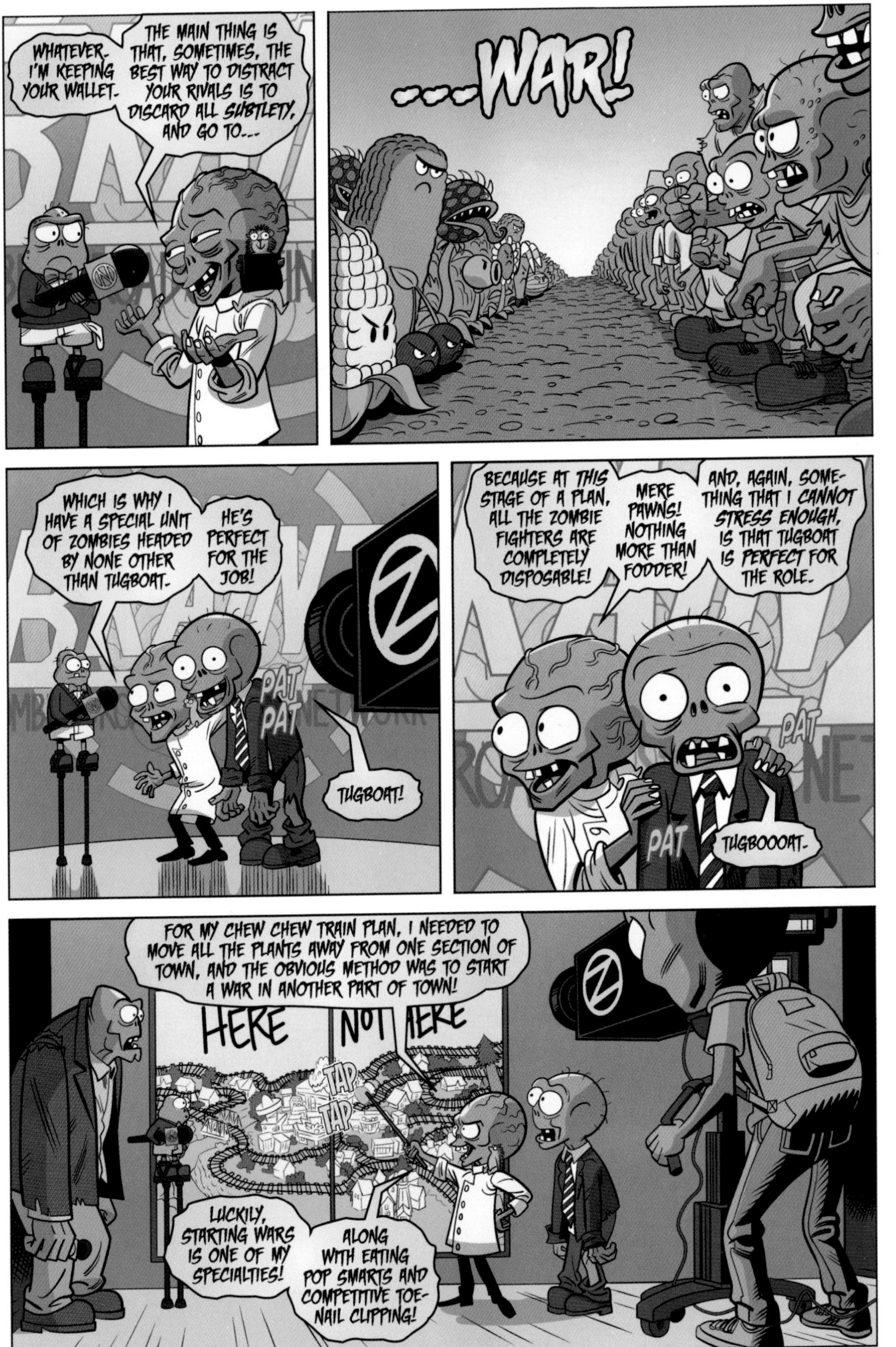
THE MAIN THING IS THAT, SOMETIMES, THE BEST WAY TO DISTRACT YOUR RIVALS IS TO DISCARD ALL SUBTLETY, AND GO TO...
WHATEVER. I'M KEEPING YOUR WALLET.
...WAR!
WHICH IS WHY I HAVE A SPECIAL UNIT OF ZOMBIES HEADED BY NONE OTHER THAN TUGBOAT.
HE'S PERFECT FOR THE JOB!
PAT PAT
TUGBOAT!
BECAUSE AT THIS STAGE OF A PLAN, ALL THE ZOMBIE FIGHTERS ARE COMPLETELY DISPOSABLE!
MERE PAWNS! NOTHING MORE THAN FODDER!
AND, AGAIN, SOMETHING THAT I CANNOT STRESS ENOUGH, IS THAT TUGBOAT IS PERFECT FOR THE ROLE.
PAT
PAT
TUGBOOOAT.
FOR MY CHEW CHEW TRAIN PLAN, I NEEDED TO MOVE ALL THE PLANTS AWAY FROM ONE SECTION OF TOWN, AND THE OBVIOUS METHOD WAS TO START A WAR IN ANOTHER PART OF TOWN!
HERE
NOT HERE
TAP
TAP
LUCKILY, STARTING WARS IS ONE OF MY SPECIALTIES!
ALONG WITH EATING POP SMARTS AND COMPETITIVE TOE-NAIL CLIPPING!

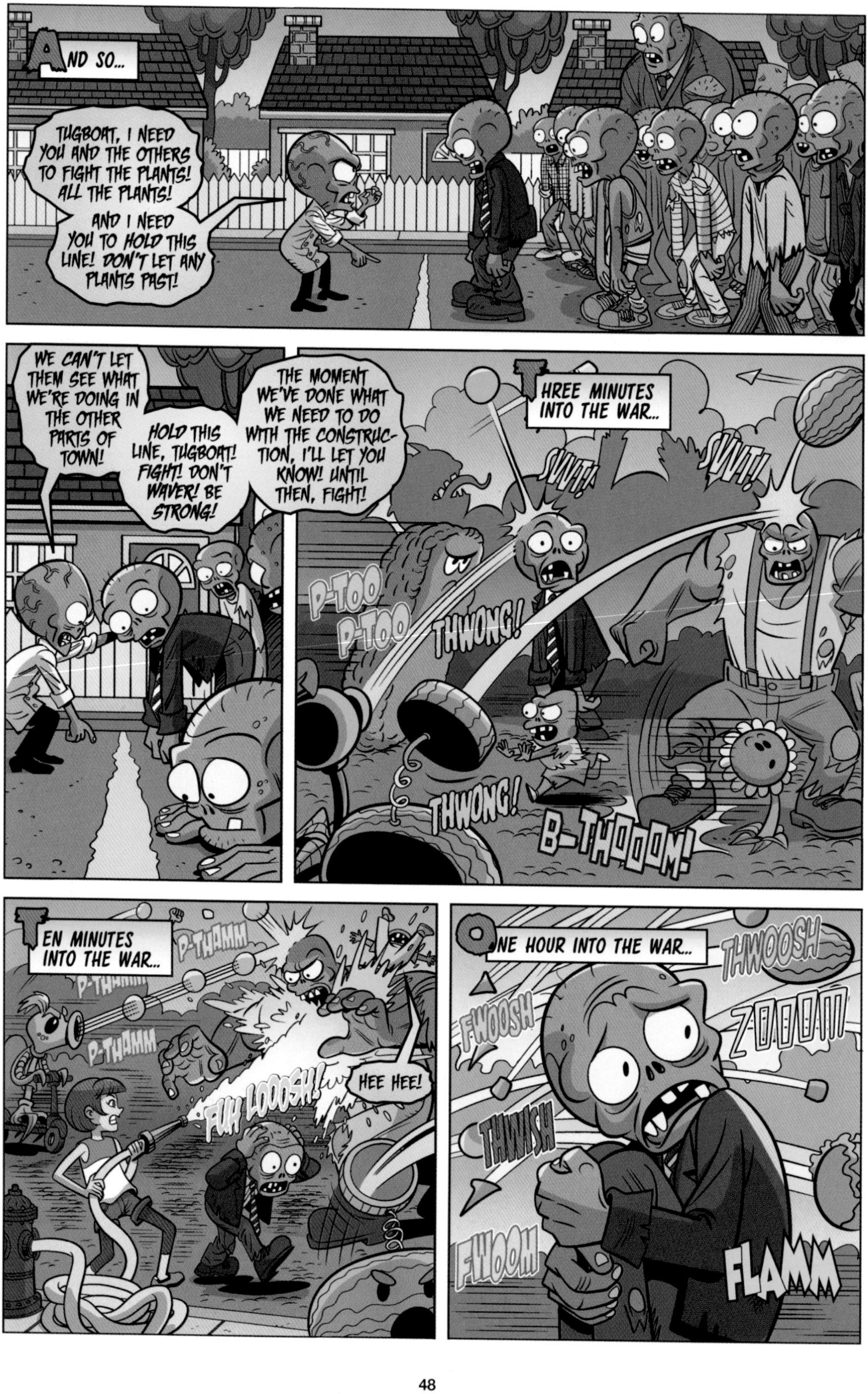
AND SO...
TUGBOAT, I NEED YOU AND THE OTHERS TO FIGHT THE PLANTS! ALL THE PLANTS!
AND I NEED YOU TO HOLD THIS LINE! DON'T LET ANY PLANTS PAST!
WE CAN'T LET THEM SEE WHAT WE'RE DOING IN THE OTHER PARTS OF TOWN!
HOLD THIS LINE, TUGBOAT! FIGHT! DON'T WAVER! BE STRONG!
THE MOMENT WE'VE DONE WHAT WE NEED TO DO WITH THE CONSTRUCTION, I'LL LET YOU KNOW! UNTIL THEN, FIGHT!
THREE MINUTES INTO THE WAR...
SVVT!
SVVT!
P-TOO P-TOO
THWONG!
THWONG!
B-THOOOM!
TEN MINUTES INTO THE WAR...
P-THAMM
P-THAMM
P-THAMM
FUH LOOOSH!
HEE HEE!
ONE HOUR INTO THE WAR...
THWOOSH
FWOOSH
ZOOOM
THWISH
FWOOM
FLAMM

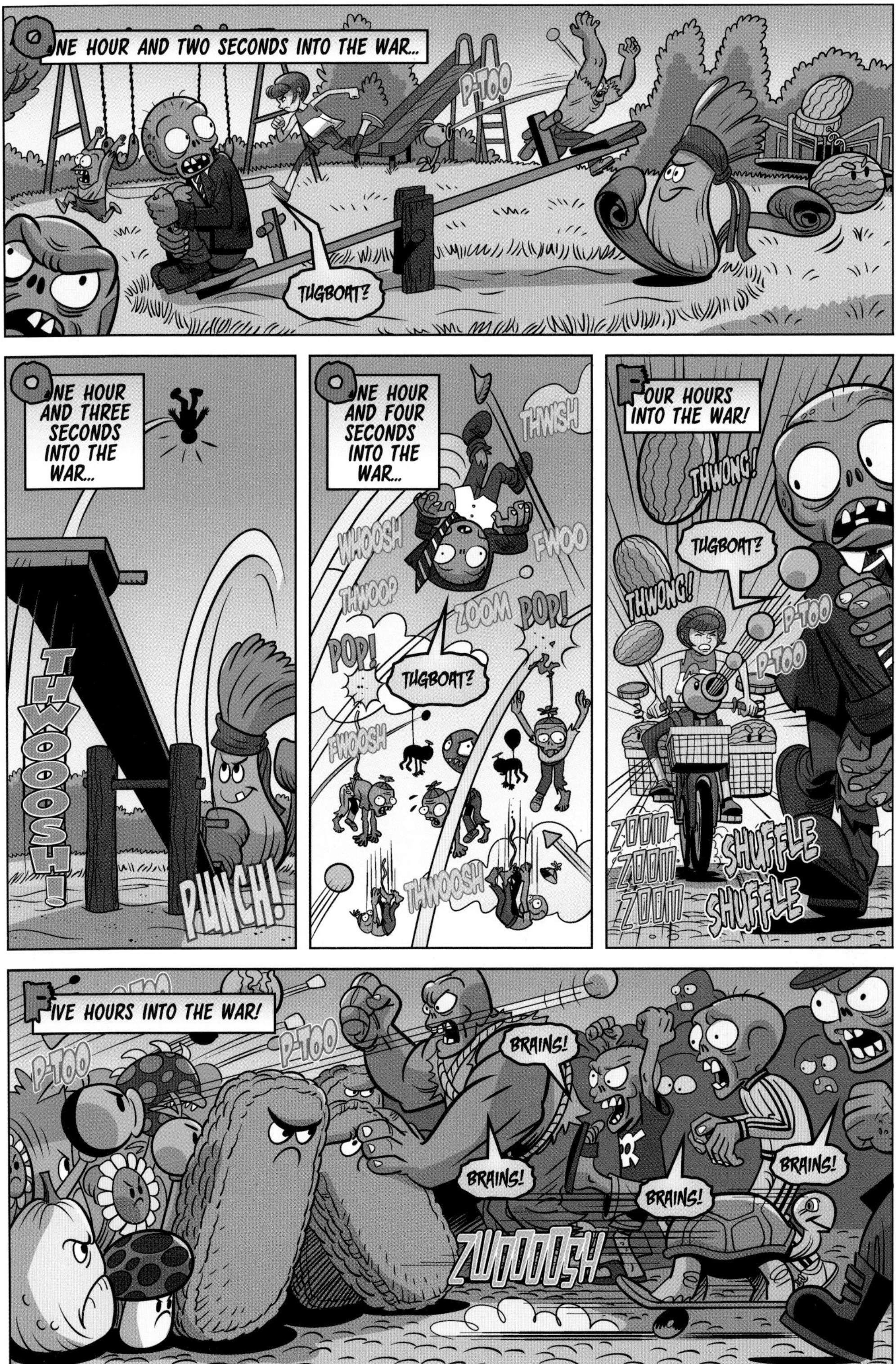
ONE HOUR AND TWO SECONDS INTO THE WAR...
P-TOO
TUGBOAT?
ONE HOUR AND THREE SECONDS INTO THE WAR...
THWOOOSH!
PUNCH!
ONE HOUR AND FOUR SECONDS INTO THE WAR...
THWISH
WHOOSH
FWOO
THWOOP
ZOOM
POP!
POP!
TUGBOAT?
FWOOSH
THWOOSH
FOUR HOURS INTO THE WAR!
THWONG!
TUGBOAT?
THWONG!
P-TOO
P-TOO
ZOOM ZOOM ZOOM
SHUFFLE SHUFFLE
FIVE HOURS INTO THE WAR!
P-TOO
P-TOO
BRAINS!
BRAINS!
BRAINS!
BRAINS!
ZWOOOOSH

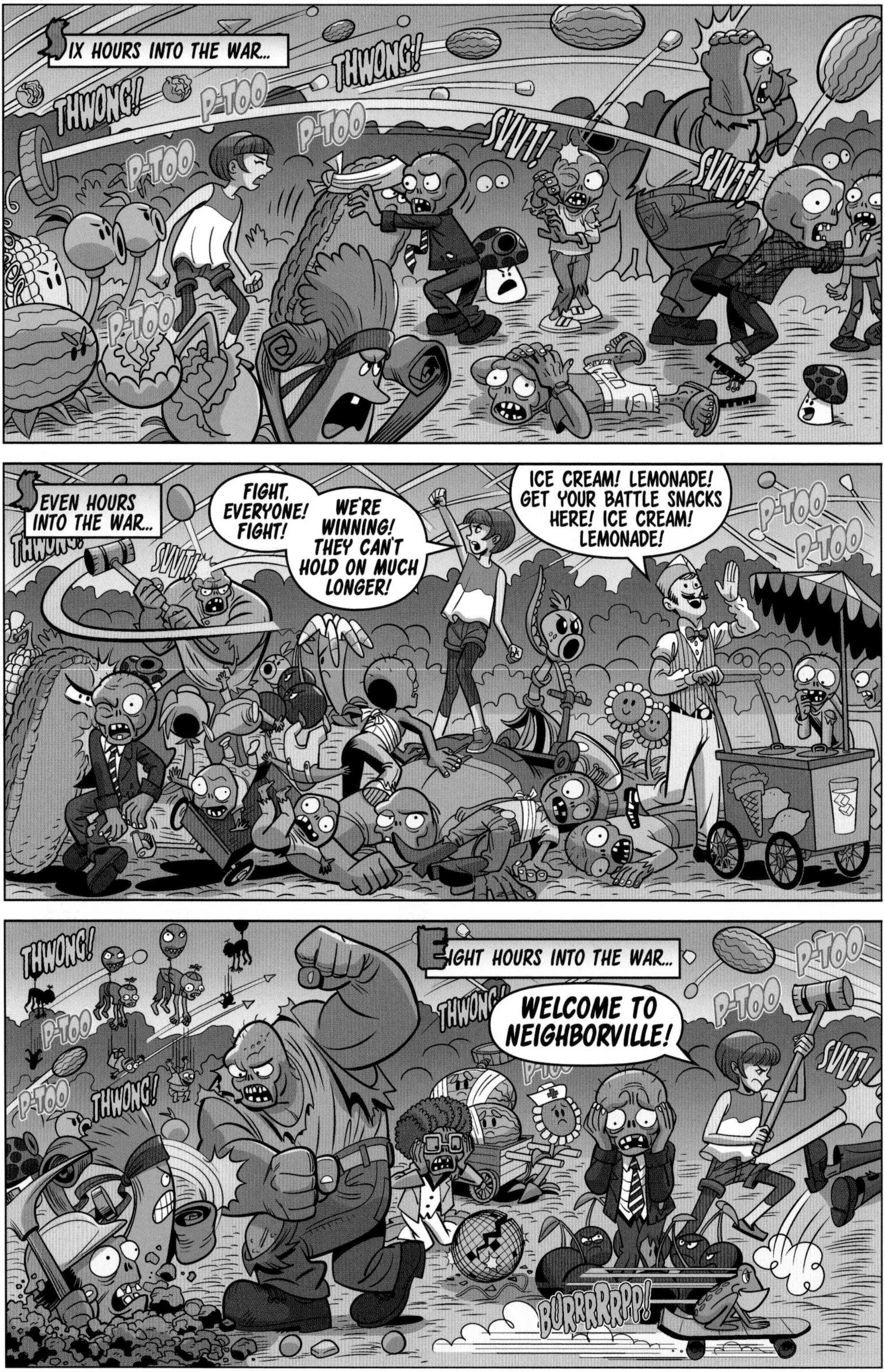
SIX HOURS INTO THE WAR...
THWONG!
P-TOO
THWONG!
P-TOO
P-TOO
SVVT!
SVVT!
P-TOO
P-TOO
SEVEN HOURS INTO THE WAR...
SVVT!
FIGHT, EVERYONE! FIGHT!
WE'RE WINNING! THEY CAN'T HOLD ON MUCH LONGER!
ICE CREAM! LEMONADE! GET YOUR BATTLE SNACKS HERE! ICE CREAM! LEMONADE!
P-TOO
P-TOO
THWONG!
P-TOO
P-TOO
THWONG!
EIGHT HOURS INTO THE WAR...
WELCOME TO NEIGHBORVILLE!
P-TOO
P-TOO
SVVT!
BURRRRRPP!

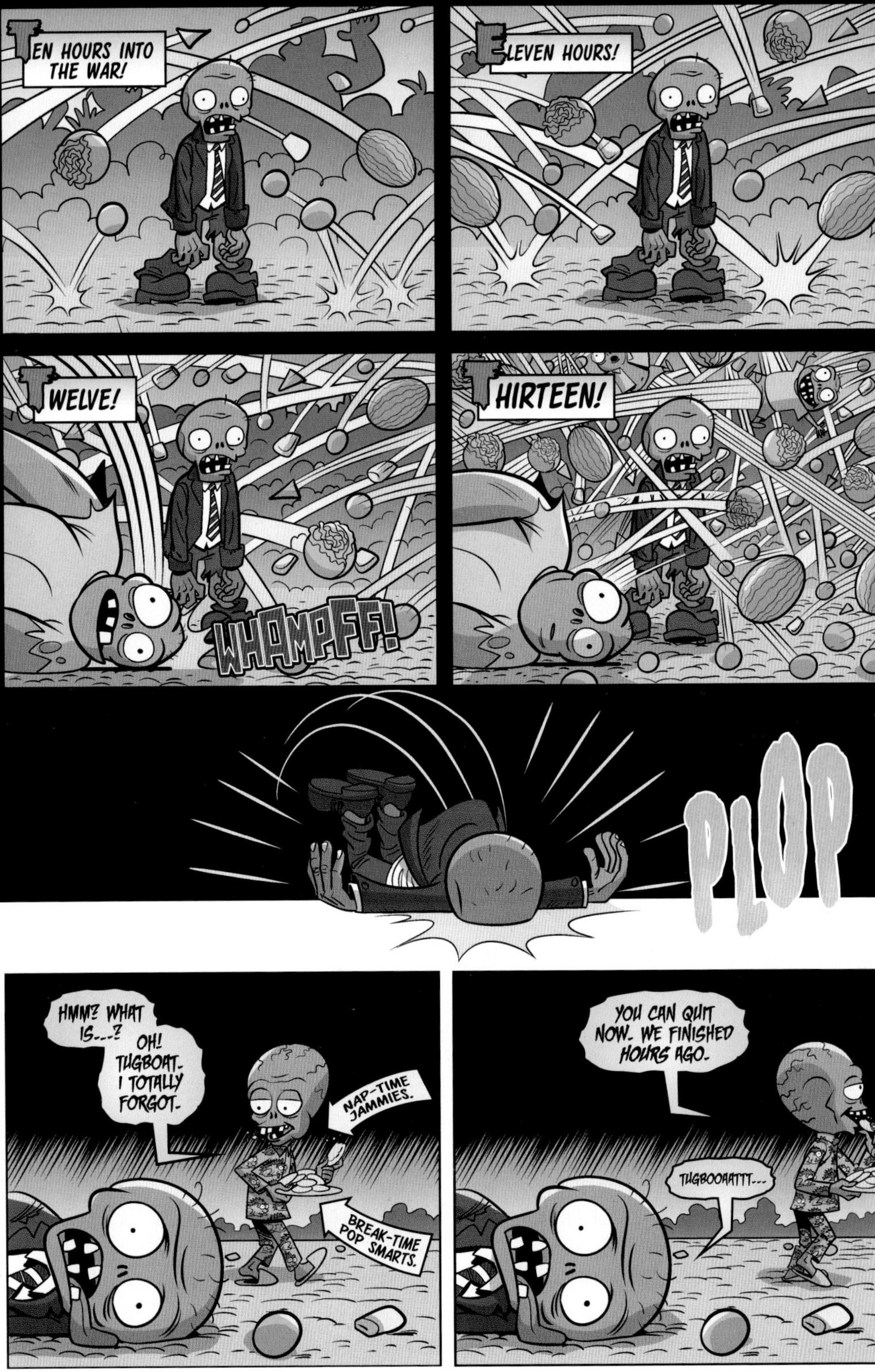
TEN HOURS INTO THE WAR!
ELEVEN HOURS!
TWELVE!
WHAMPFF!
THIRTEEN!
PLOP
HMM? WHAT IS...?
OH! TUGBOAT. I TOTALLY FORGOT.
NAP-TIME JAMMIES.
BREAK-TIME POP SMARTS.
YOU CAN QUIT NOW. WE FINISHED HOURS AGO.
TUGBOOAATTT...

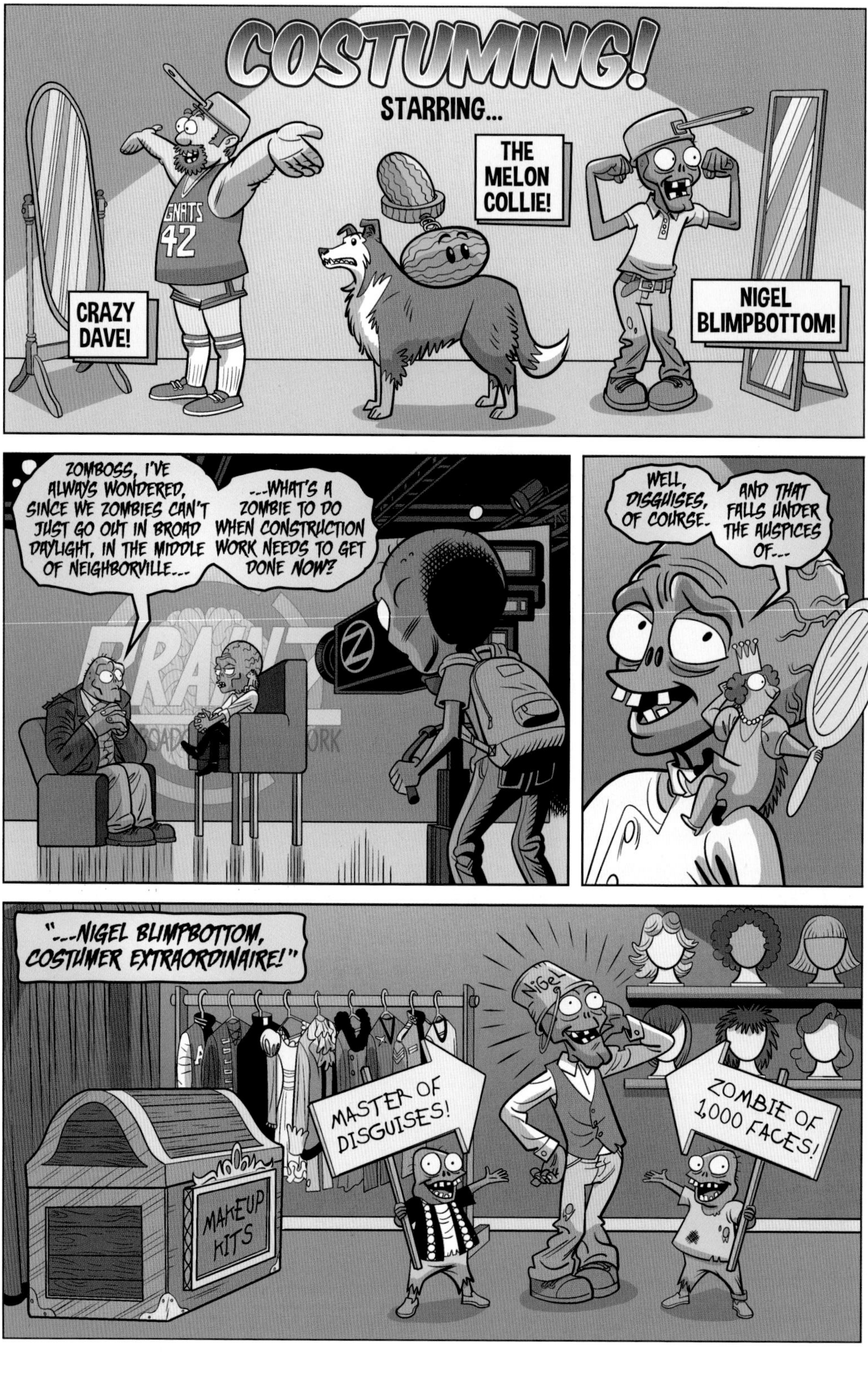

COSTUMING!
STARRING...
CRAZY DAVE!
GNATS 42
THE MELON COLLIE!
NIGEL BLIMPBOTTOM!
ZOMBOSS, I'VE ALWAYS WONDERED, SINCE WE ZOMBIES CAN'T JUST GO OUT IN BROAD DAYLIGHT, IN THE MIDDLE OF NEIGHBORVILLE...
...WHAT'S A ZOMBIE TO DO WHEN CONSTRUCTION WORK NEEDS TO GET DONE NOW?
WELL, DISGUISES, OF COURSE.
AND THAT FALLS UNDER THE AUSPICES OF...
"...NIGEL BLIMPBOTTOM, COSTUMER EXTRAORDINAIRE!"
NiGeL
MASTER OF DISGUISES!
ZOMBIE OF 1,000 FACES!
MAKEUP KITS

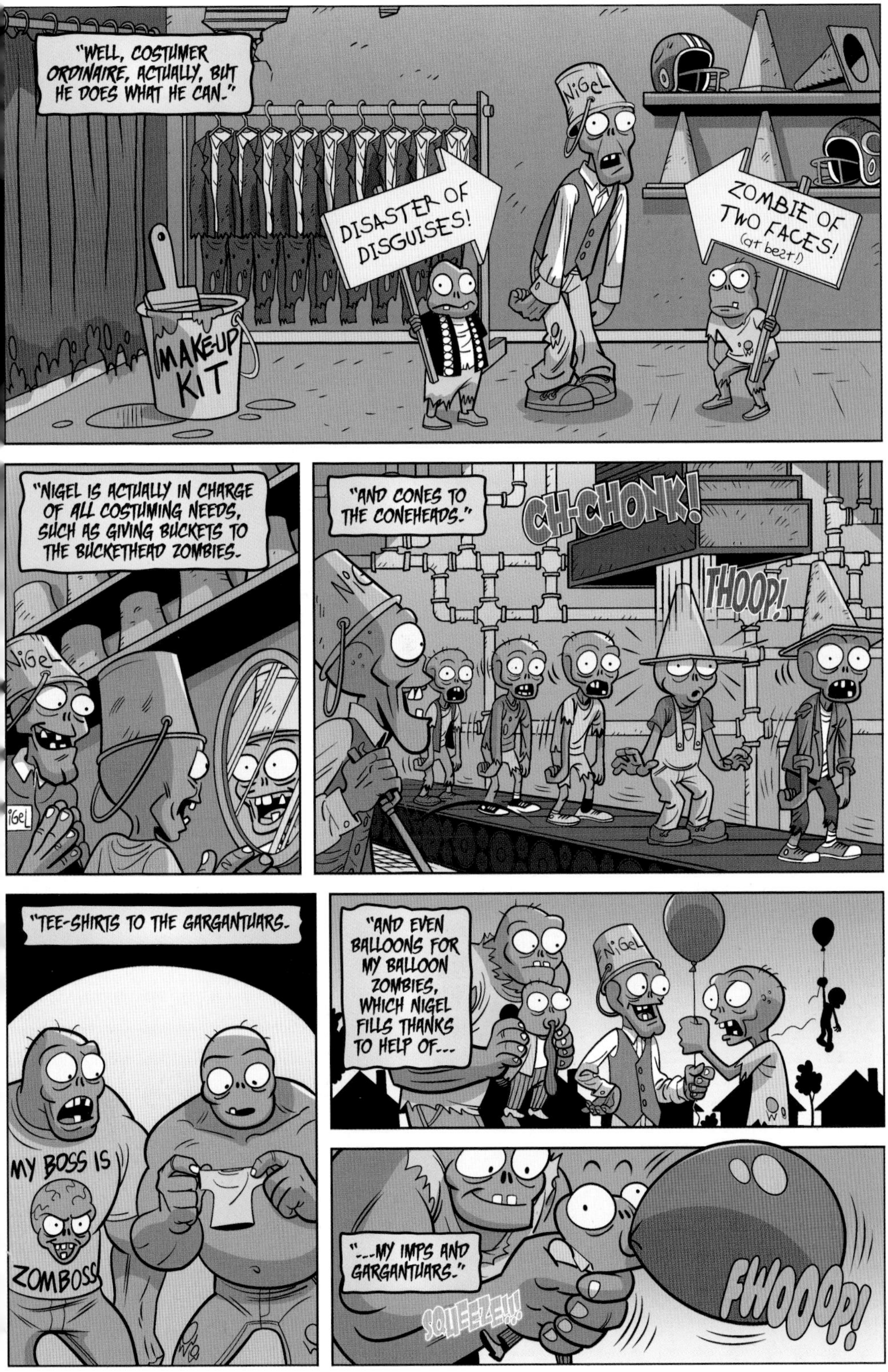
"WELL, COSTUMER ORDINAIRE, ACTUALLY, BUT HE DOES WHAT HE CAN."
NiGeL
DISASTER OF DISGUISES!
ZOMBIE OF TWO FACES! (at best!)
MAKE-UP KIT
"NIGEL IS ACTUALLY IN CHARGE OF ALL COSTUMING NEEDS, SUCH AS GIVING BUCKETS TO THE BUCKETHEAD ZOMBIES.
NiGeL
"AND CONES TO THE CONEHEADS."
CH-CHONK!
THOOP!
"TEE-SHIRTS TO THE GARGANTUARS.
MY BOSS IS
ZOMBOSS
"AND EVEN BALLOONS FOR MY BALLOON ZOMBIES, WHICH NIGEL FILLS THANKS TO HELP OF...
NiGeL
"...MY IMPS AND GARGANTUARS."
SQUEEZE!!!
FWOOOP!

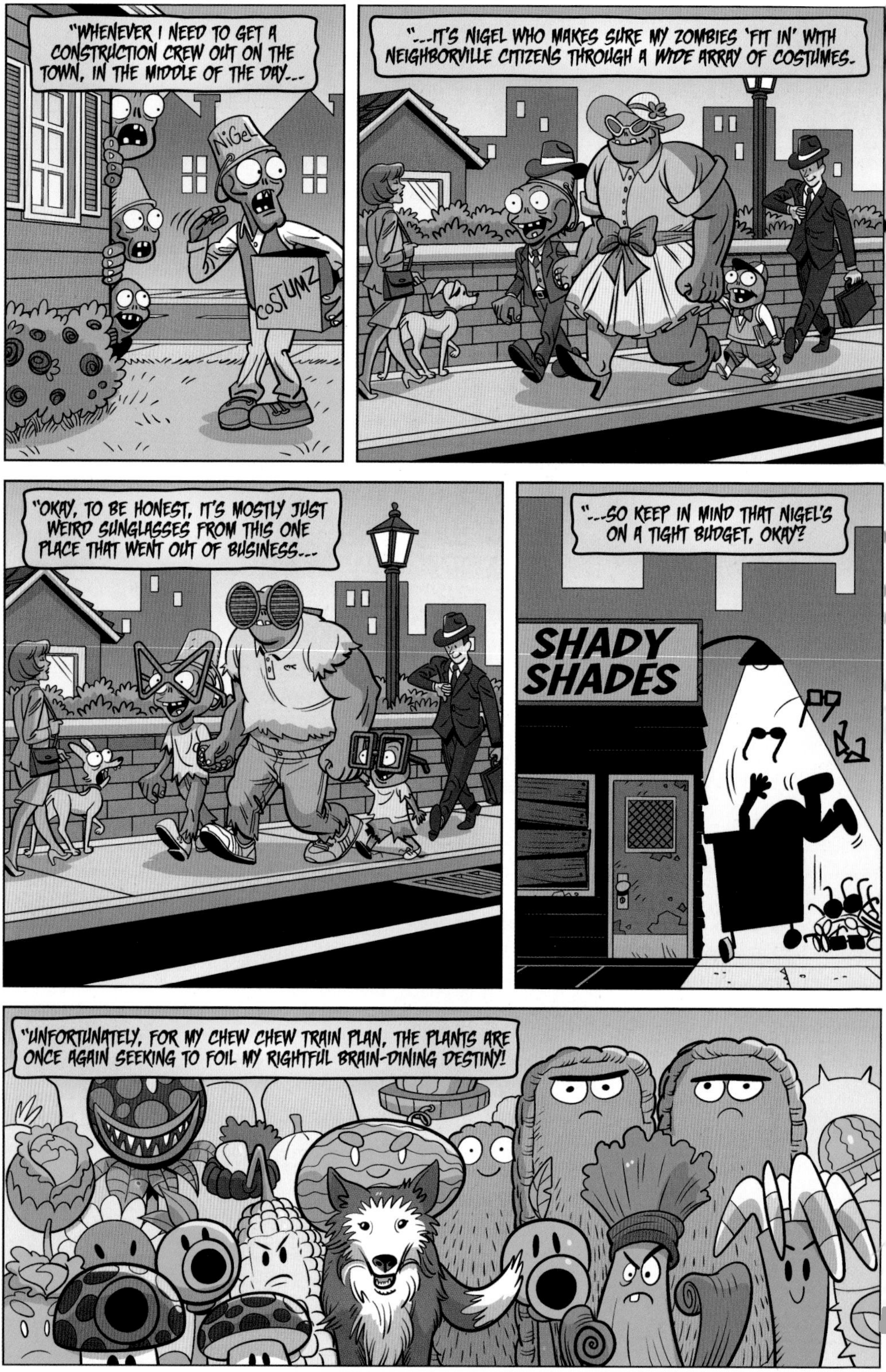
"WHENEVER I NEED TO GET A CONSTRUCTION CREW OUT ON THE TOWN, IN THE MIDDLE OF THE DAY...
NiGeL
CoSTUMZ
"...IT'S NIGEL WHO MAKES SURE MY ZOMBIES 'FIT IN' WITH NEIGHBORVILLE CITIZENS THROUGH A WIDE ARRAY OF COSTUMES.
"OKAY, TO BE HONEST, IT'S MOSTLY JUST WEIRD SUNGLASSES FROM THIS ONE PLACE THAT WENT OUT OF BUSINESS...
"...SO KEEP IN MIND THAT NIGEL'S ON A TIGHT BUDGET, OKAY?
SHADY SHADES
"UNFORTUNATELY, FOR MY CHEW CHEW TRAIN PLAN, THE PLANTS ARE ONCE AGAIN SEEKING TO FOIL MY RIGHTFUL BRAIN-DINING DESTINY!

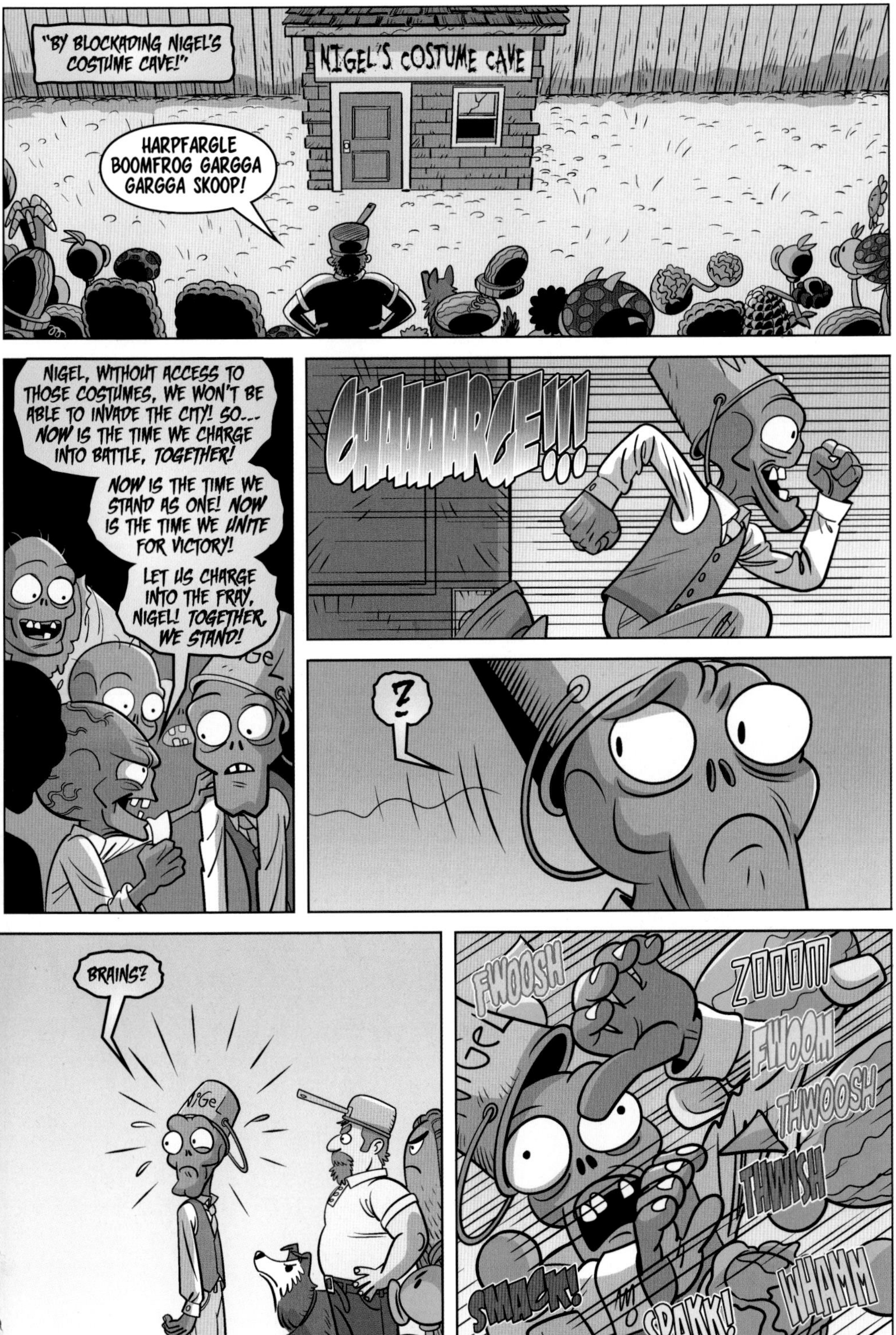
"BY BLOCKADING NIGEL'S COSTUME CAVE!"
NIGEL'S COSTUME CAVE
HARPFARGLE BOOMFROG GARGGA GARGGA SKOOP!
NIGEL, WITHOUT ACCESS TO THOSE COSTUMES, WE WON'T BE ABLE TO INVADE THE CITY! SO... NOW IS THE TIME WE CHARGE INTO BATTLE, TOGETHER!
NOW IS THE TIME WE STAND AS ONE! NOW IS THE TIME WE UNITE FOR VICTORY!
LET US CHARGE INTO THE FRAY, NIGEL! TOGETHER, WE STAND!
CHAAAARGE!!!
?
BRAINS?
NIGEL
FWOOSH
ZOOOM
FWOOM
THWOOSH
THWISH
SMACK!
SPAKK!
WHAMM

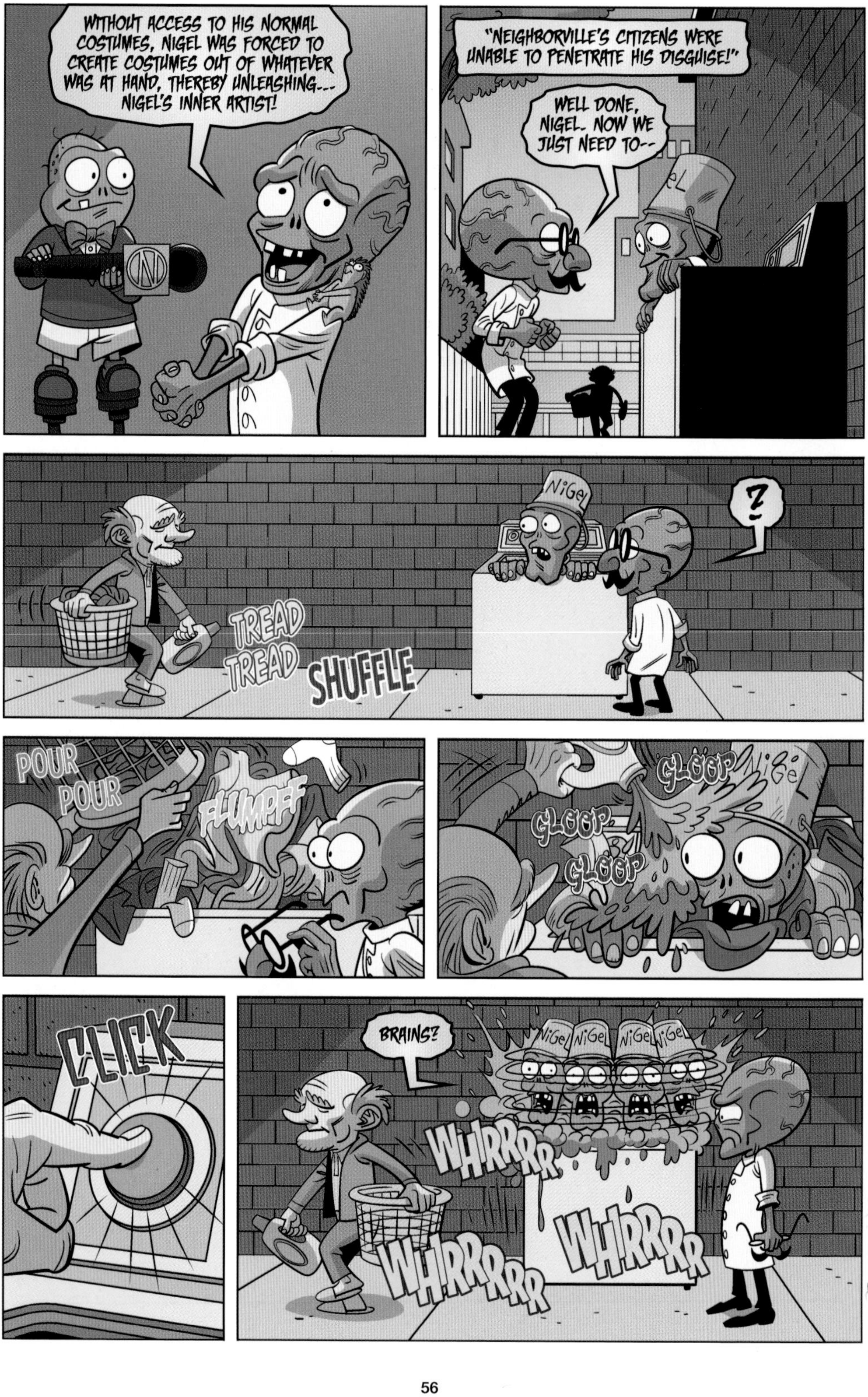
WITHOUT ACCESS TO HIS NORMAL COSTUMES, NIGEL WAS FORCED TO CREATE COSTUMES OUT OF WHATEVER WAS AT HAND, THEREBY UNLEASHING... NIGEL'S INNER ARTIST!
"NEIGHBORVILLE'S CITIZENS WERE UNABLE TO PENETRATE HIS DISGUISE!"
WELL DONE, NIGEL. NOW WE JUST NEED TO--
NiGeL
TREAD TREAD
SHUFFLE
?
POUR POUR
FLUMPFF
GLOOP
GLOOP
GLOOP
CLICK
BRAINS?
WHRRRRR
WHRRRRR
WHRRRRR

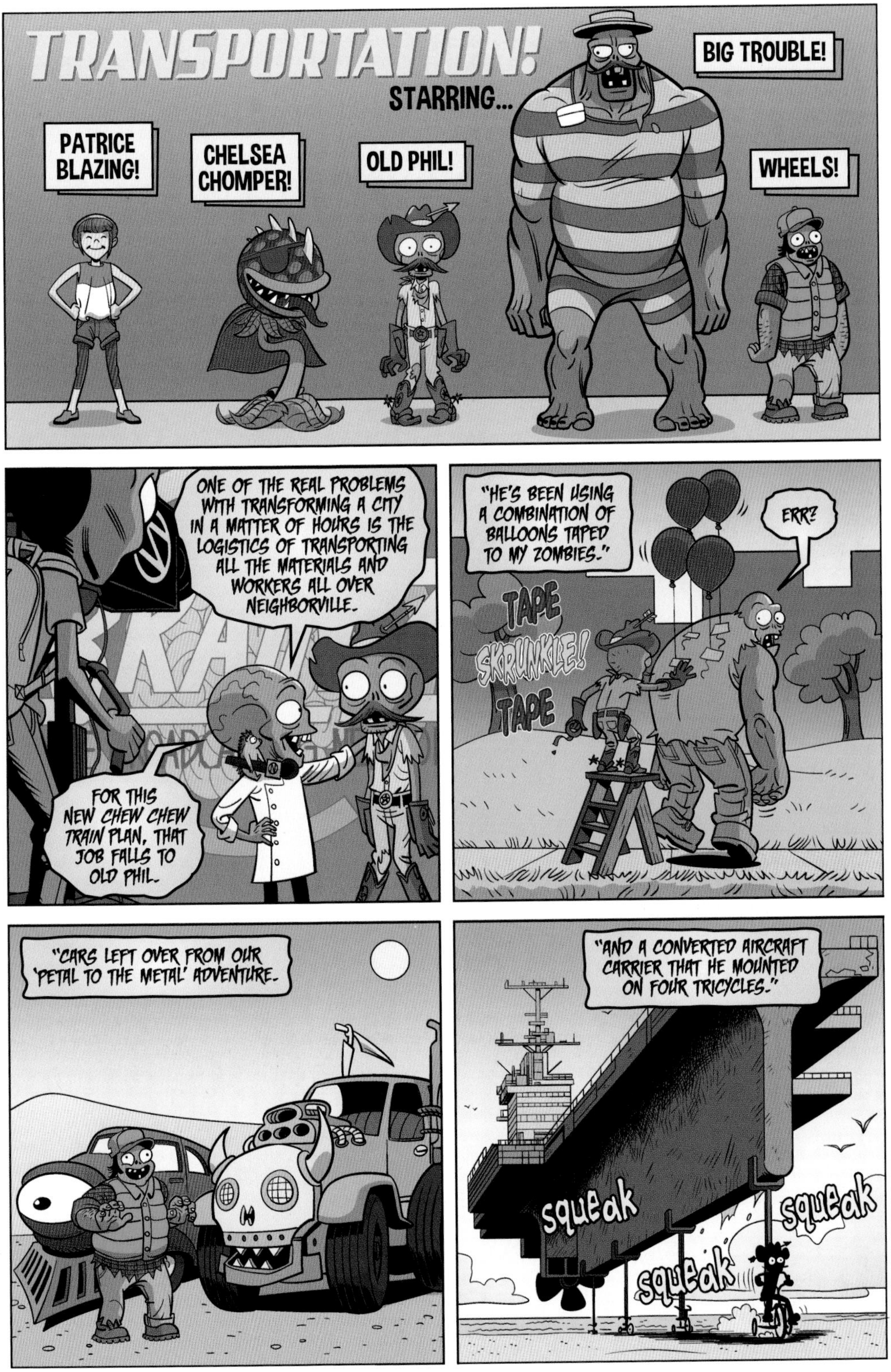
TRANSPORTATION!
STARRING...
PATRICE BLAZING!
CHELSEA CHOMPER!
OLD PHIL!
BIG TROUBLE!
WHEELS!
ONE OF THE REAL PROBLEMS WITH TRANSFORMING A CITY IN A MATTER OF HOURS IS THE LOGISTICS OF TRANSPORTING ALL THE MATERIALS AND WORKERS ALL OVER NEIGHBORVILLE.
FOR THIS NEW CHEW CHEW TRAIN PLAN, THAT JOB FALLS TO OLD PHIL.
"HE'S BEEN USING A COMBINATION OF BALLOONS TAPED TO MY ZOMBIES."
ERR?
TAPE
SKRUNKLE!
TAPE
"CARS LEFT OVER FROM OUR 'PETAL TO THE METAL' ADVENTURE.
"AND A CONVERTED AIRCRAFT CARRIER THAT HE MOUNTED ON FOUR TRICYCLES."
squeak
squeak
squeak

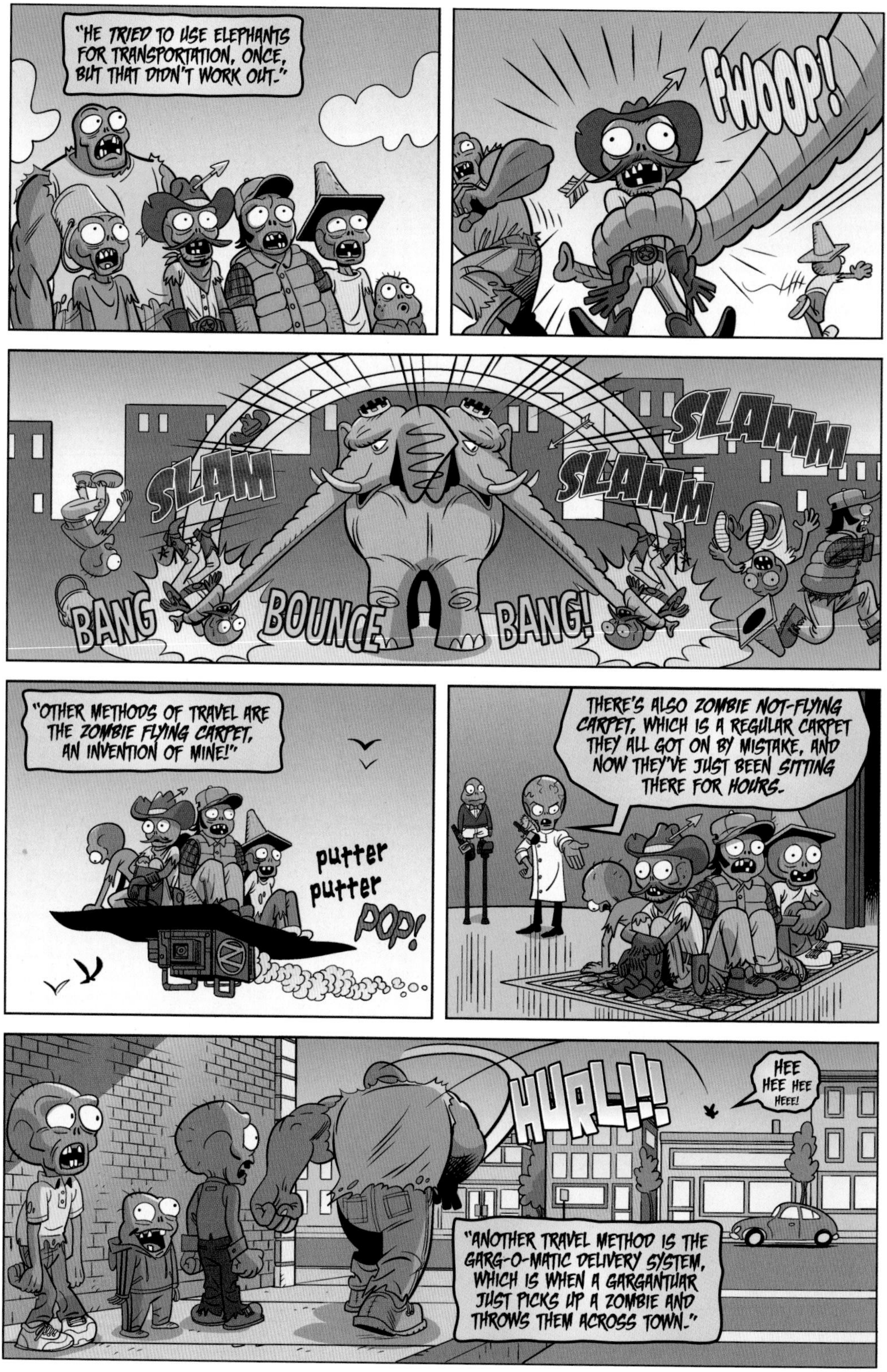
"HE TRIED TO USE ELEPHANTS FOR TRANSPORTATION, ONCE, BUT THAT DIDN'T WORK OUT."
FWOOP!
SLAM
SLAMM
SLAMM
BANG
BOUNCE
BANG!
"OTHER METHODS OF TRAVEL ARE THE ZOMBIE FLYING CARPET, AN INVENTION OF MINE!"
putter
putter
POP!
THERE'S ALSO ZOMBIE NOT-FLYING CARPET, WHICH IS A REGULAR CARPET THEY ALL GOT ON BY MISTAKE, AND NOW THEY'VE JUST BEEN SITTING THERE FOR HOURS.
HURL!!!
HEE HEE HEE HEEE!
"ANOTHER TRAVEL METHOD IS THE GARG-O-MATIC DELIVERY SYSTEM, WHICH IS WHEN A GARGANTUAR JUST PICKS UP A ZOMBIE AND THROWS THEM ACROSS TOWN."

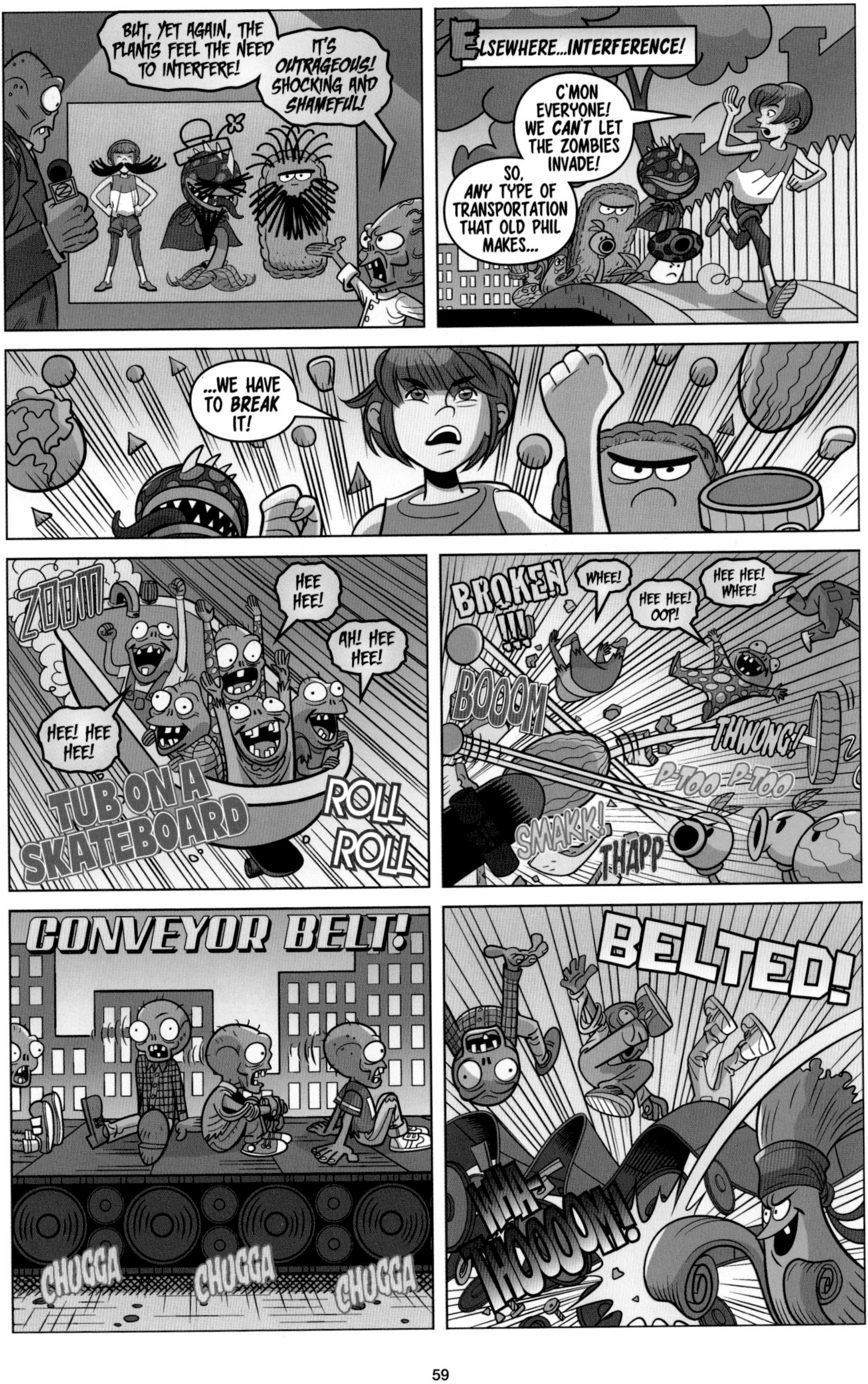
BUT, YET AGAIN, THE PLANTS FEEL THE NEED TO INTERFERE!
IT'S OUTRAGEOUS! SHOCKING AND SHAMEFUL!
ELSEWHERE...INTERFERENCE!
C'MON EVERYONE! WE CAN'T LET THE ZOMBIES INVADE!
SO, ANY TYPE OF TRANSPORTATION THAT OLD PHIL MAKES...
...WE HAVE TO BREAK IT!
ZOOM
HEE HEE!
AH! HEE HEE!
HEE! HEE HEE!
TUB ON A SKATEBOARD
ROLL ROLL
BROKEN!!!
WHEE!
HEE HEE! OOP!
HEE HEE! WHEE!
BOOOM
THWONG!
P-TOO P-TOO
SMAKK!
THAPP
CONVEYOR BELT!
CHUGGA CHUGGA CHUGGA
BELTED!
WHA-THOOOM!

ELECTRIC HORSES!
UNPLUGGED!
PNEUMATIC TUBES!
PHWOOMP!
FLOOOP!
FOOOFF!
THUUUBB!
CORKED!
HITCHING A RIDE!
FREE RIDE!

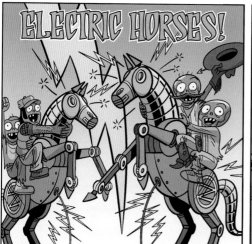

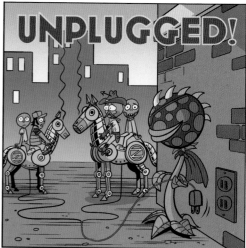

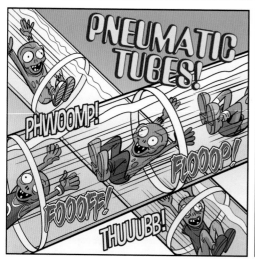

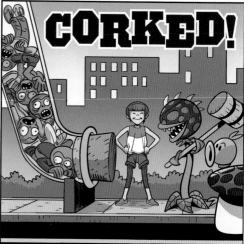

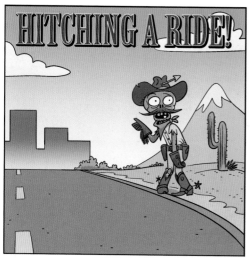

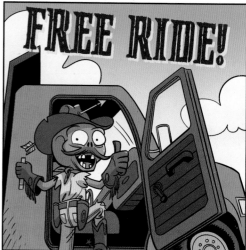

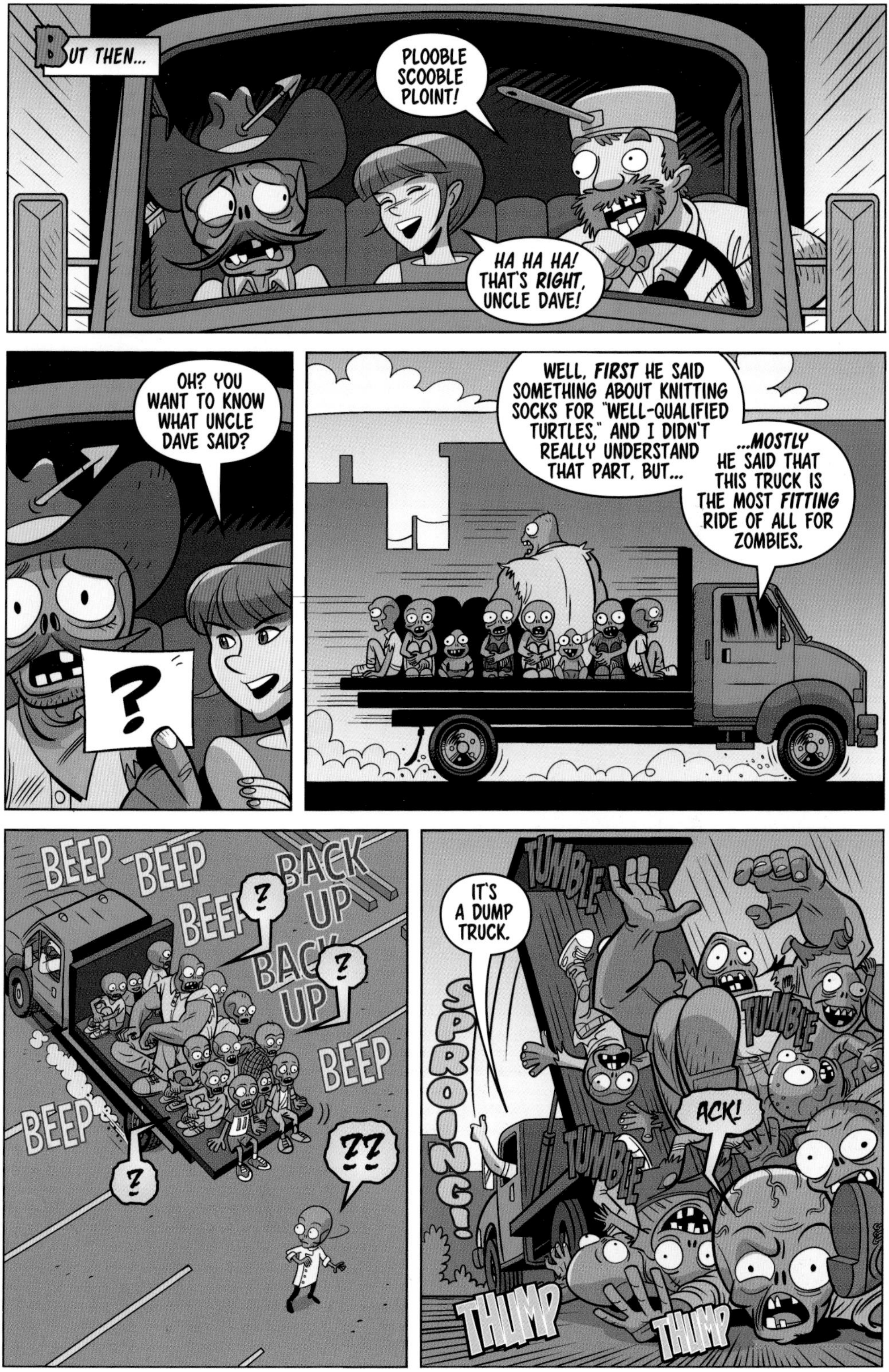
BUT THEN...
PLOOBLE SCOOBLE PLOINT!
HA HA HA! THAT'S RIGHT, UNCLE DAVE!
OH? YOU WANT TO KNOW WHAT UNCLE DAVE SAID?
?
WELL, FIRST HE SAID SOMETHING ABOUT KNITTING SOCKS FOR "WELL-QUALIFIED TURTLES," AND I DIDN'T REALLY UNDERSTAND THAT PART, BUT...
...MOSTLY HE SAID THAT THIS TRUCK IS THE MOST FITTING RIDE OF ALL FOR ZOMBIES.
BEEP BEEP BEEP
BACK UP BACK UP
?
?
BEEP
BEEP
?
??
IT'S A DUMP TRUCK.
TUMBLE
SPROING!
TUMBLE
TUMBLE
ACK!
THUMP
THUMP

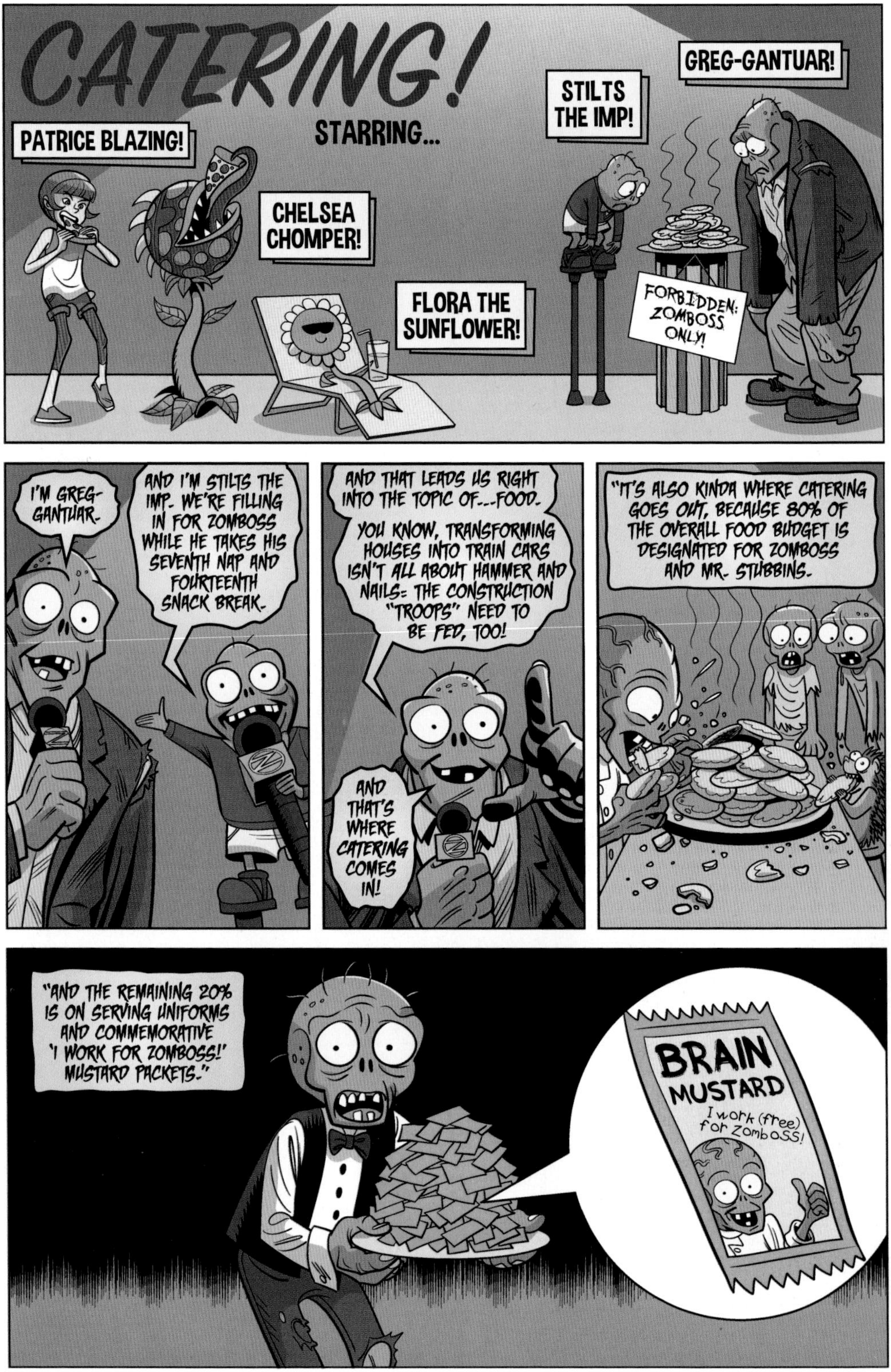
CATERING!
STARRING...
PATRICE BLAZING!
CHELSEA CHOMPER!
FLORA THE SUNFLOWER!
STILTS THE IMP!
GREG-GANTUAR!
FORBIDDEN: ZOMBOSS ONLY!
I'M GREG-GANTUAR.
AND I'M STILTS THE IMP. WE'RE FILLING IN FOR ZOMBOSS WHILE HE TAKES HIS SEVENTH NAP AND FOURTEENTH SNACK BREAK.
AND THAT LEADS US RIGHT INTO THE TOPIC OF...FOOD.
YOU KNOW, TRANSFORMING HOUSES INTO TRAIN CARS ISN'T ALL ABOUT HAMMER AND NAILS: THE CONSTRUCTION "TROOPS" NEED TO BE FED, TOO!
AND THAT'S WHERE CATERING COMES IN!
"IT'S ALSO KINDA WHERE CATERING GOES OUT, BECAUSE 80% OF THE OVERALL FOOD BUDGET IS DESIGNATED FOR ZOMBOSS AND MR. STUBBINS.
"AND THE REMAINING 20% IS ON SERVING UNIFORMS AND COMMEMORATIVE 'I WORK FOR ZOMBOSS!' MUSTARD PACKETS."
BRAIN MUSTARD
I work (free) for Zomboss!

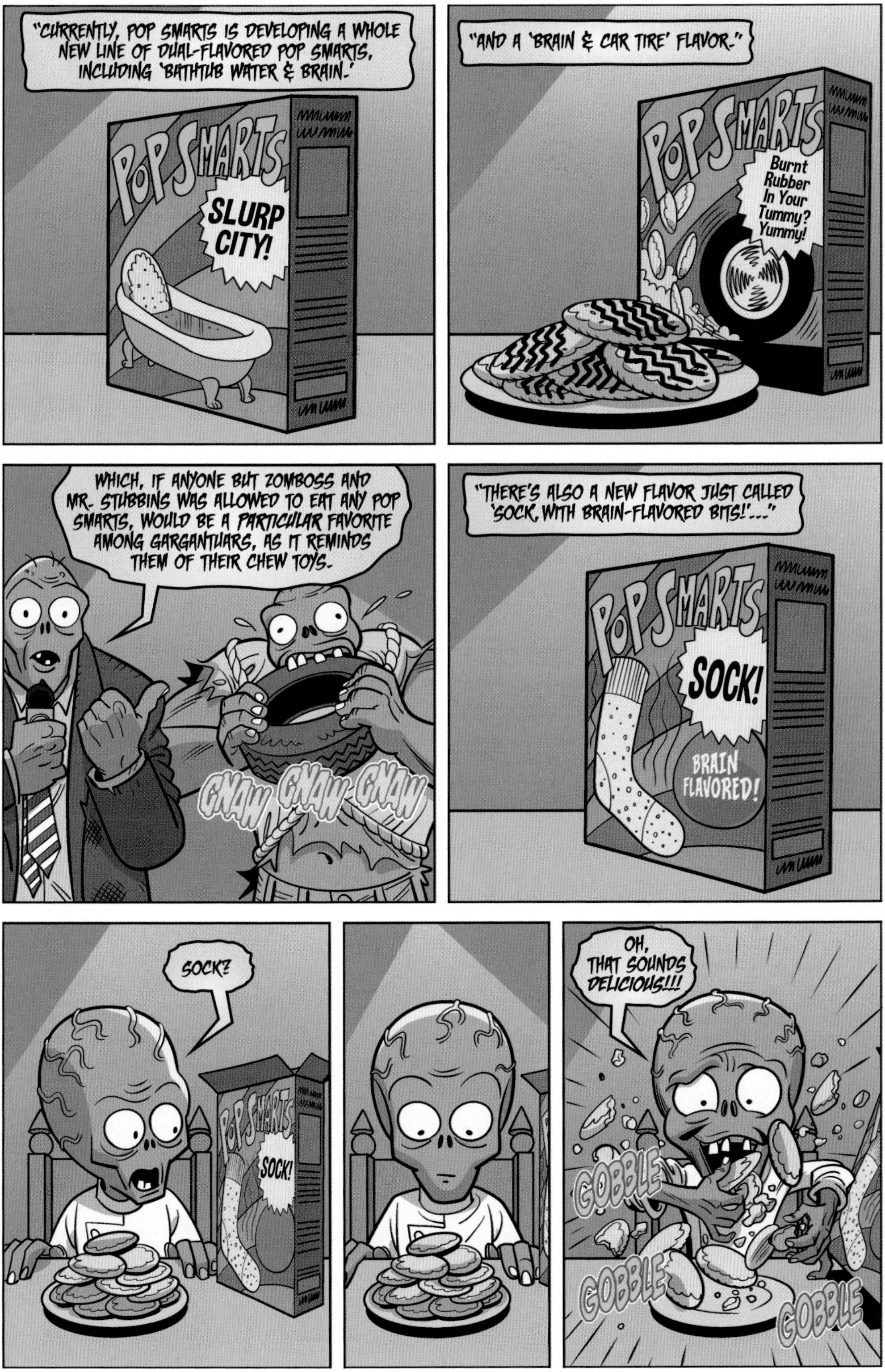
"CURRENTLY, POP SMARTS IS DEVELOPING A WHOLE NEW LINE OF DUAL-FLAVORED POP SMARTS, INCLUDING 'BATHTUB WATER & BRAIN.'
POP SMARTS
SLURP CITY!
"AND A 'BRAIN & CAR TIRE' FLAVOR."
POP SMARTS
Burnt Rubber In Your Tummy? Yummy!
WHICH, IF ANYONE BUT ZOMBOSS AND MR. STUBBINS WAS ALLOWED TO EAT ANY POP SMARTS, WOULD BE A PARTICULAR FAVORITE AMONG GARGANTUARS, AS IT REMINDS THEM OF THEIR CHEW TOYS.
GNAW GNAW GNAW
"THERE'S ALSO A NEW FLAVOR JUST CALLED 'SOCK, WITH BRAIN-FLAVORED BITS!'..."
POP SMARTS
SOCK!
BRAIN FLAVORED!
SOCK?
POP SMARTS
SOCK!
OH, THAT SOUNDS DELICIOUS!!!
GOBBLE
GOBBLE
GOBBLE

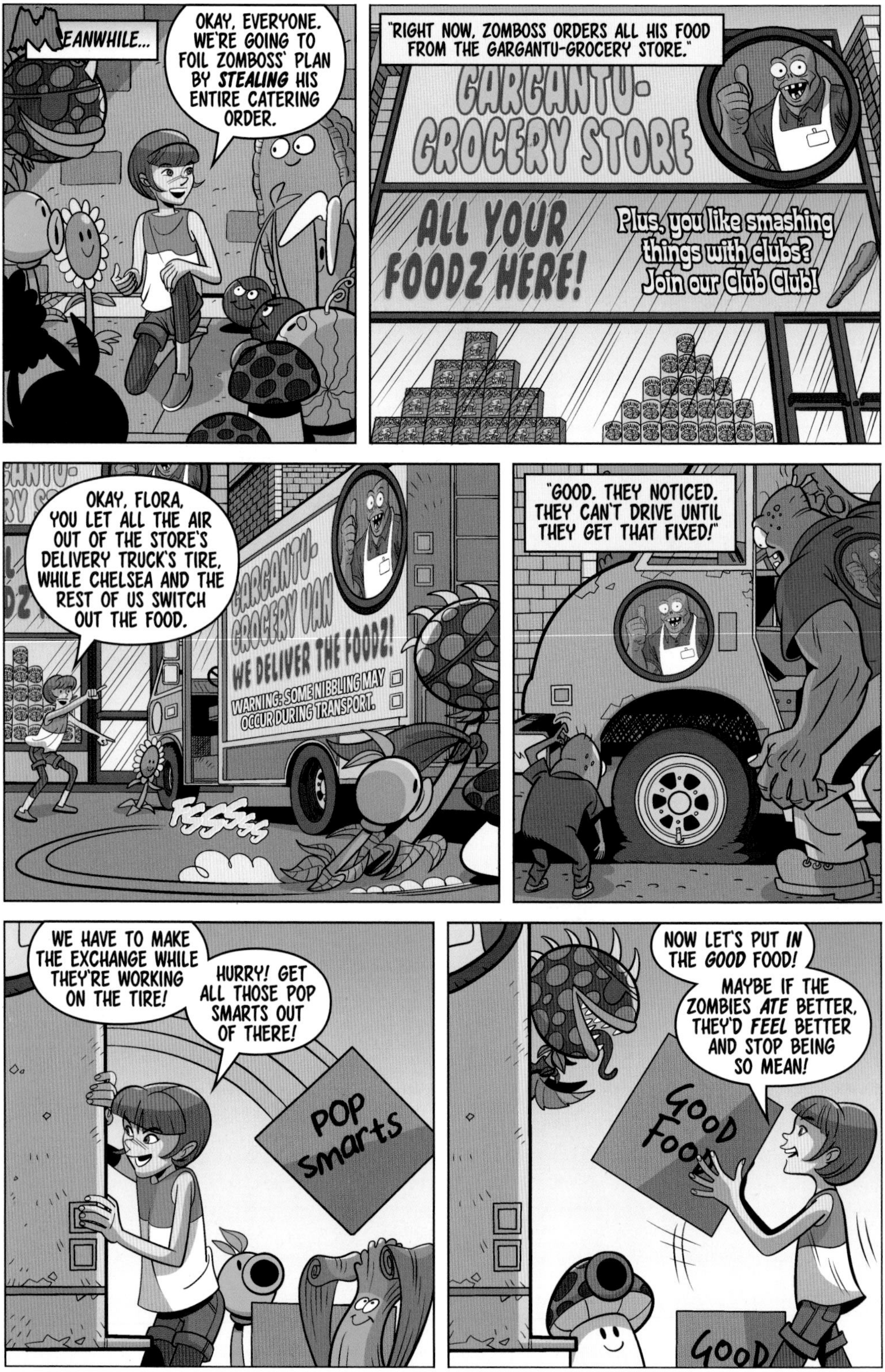
MEANWHILE...
OKAY, EVERYONE. WE'RE GOING TO FOIL ZOMBOSS' PLAN BY *STEALING* HIS ENTIRE CATERING ORDER.
"RIGHT NOW, ZOMBOSS ORDERS ALL HIS FOOD FROM THE GARGANTU-GROCERY STORE."
GARGANTU-GROCERY STORE
ALL YOUR FOODZ HERE!
Plus, you like smashing things with clubs? Join our Club Club!
OKAY, FLORA, YOU LET ALL THE AIR OUT OF THE STORE'S DELIVERY TRUCK'S TIRE, WHILE CHELSEA AND THE REST OF US SWITCH OUT THE FOOD.
GARGANTU-GROCERY VAN
WE DELIVER THE FOODZ!
WARNING: SOME NIBBLING MAY OCCUR DURING TRANSPORT.
FSSSSS
"GOOD. THEY NOTICED. THEY CAN'T DRIVE UNTIL THEY GET THAT FIXED!"
WE HAVE TO MAKE THE EXCHANGE WHILE THEY'RE WORKING ON THE TIRE!
HURRY! GET ALL THOSE POP SMARTS OUT OF THERE!
POP Smarts
NOW LET'S PUT *IN* THE *GOOD* FOOD!
MAYBE IF THE ZOMBIES *ATE* BETTER, THEY'D *FEEL* BETTER AND STOP BEING SO MEAN!
GOOD FOOD
GOOD

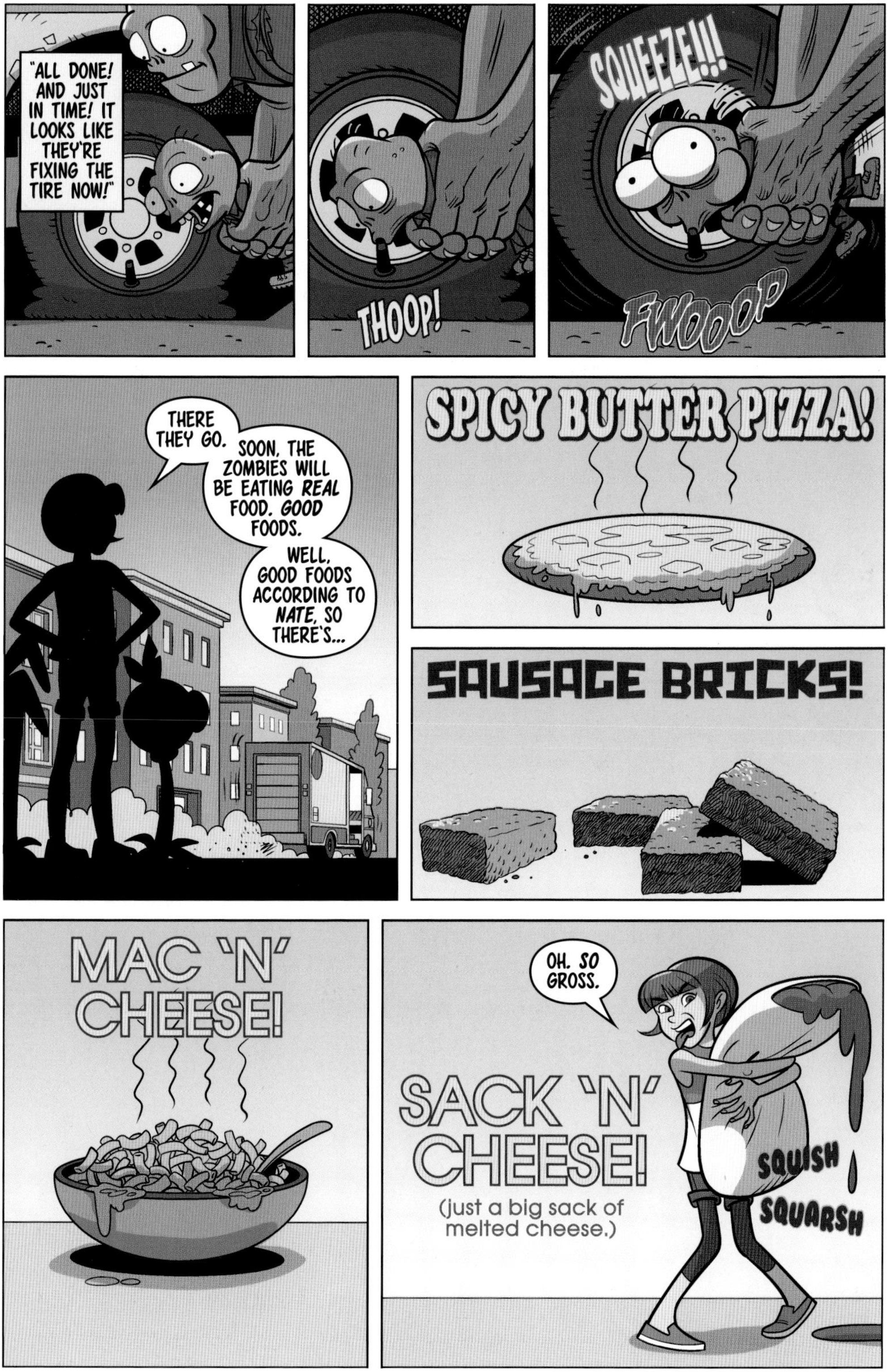
"ALL DONE! AND JUST IN TIME! IT LOOKS LIKE THEY'RE FIXING THE TIRE NOW!"
THOOP!
SQUEEZE!!!
FWOOOP
THERE THEY GO.
SOON, THE ZOMBIES WILL BE EATING REAL FOOD. GOOD FOODS.
WELL, GOOD FOODS ACCORDING TO NATE, SO THERE'S...
SPICY BUTTER PIZZA!
SAUSAGE BRICKS!
MAC 'N' CHEESE!
OH. SO GROSS.
SACK 'N' CHEESE!
(just a big sack of melted cheese.)
SQUISH
SQUARSH

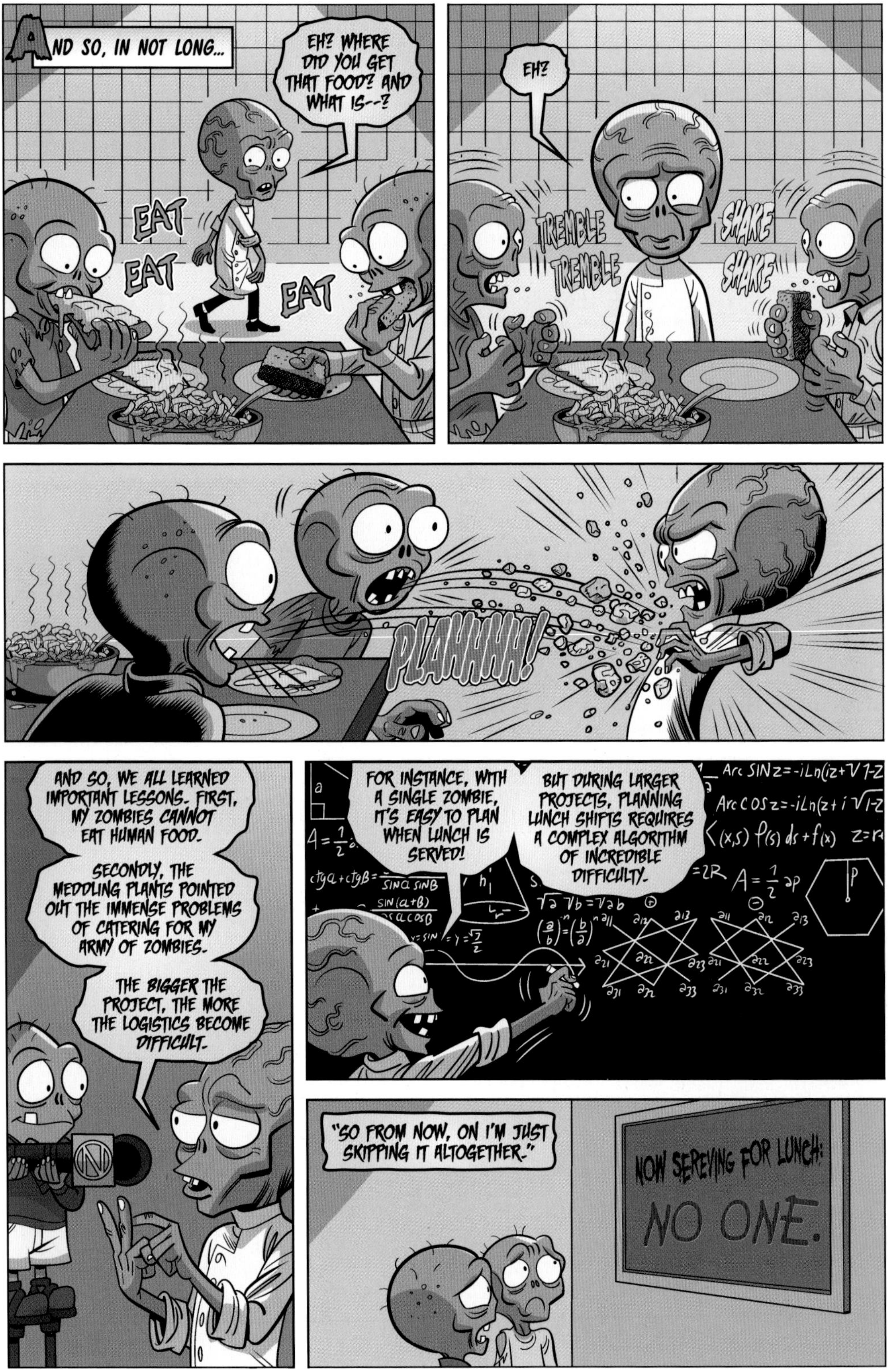
AND SO, IN NOT LONG...
EH? WHERE DID YOU GET THAT FOOD? AND WHAT IS--?
EAT
EAT
EAT
EH?
TREMBLE
TREMBLE
SHAKE
SHAKE
PLAHHHH!
AND SO, WE ALL LEARNED IMPORTANT LESSONS. FIRST, MY ZOMBIES CANNOT EAT HUMAN FOOD.
SECONDLY, THE MEDDLING PLANTS POINTED OUT THE IMMENSE PROBLEMS OF CATERING FOR MY ARMY OF ZOMBIES.
THE BIGGER THE PROJECT, THE MORE THE LOGISTICS BECOME DIFFICULT.
FOR INSTANCE, WITH A SINGLE ZOMBIE, IT'S EASY TO PLAN WHEN LUNCH IS SERVED!
BUT DURING LARGER PROJECTS, PLANNING LUNCH SHIFTS REQUIRES A COMPLEX ALGORITHM OF INCREDIBLE DIFFICULTY.
"SO FROM NOW, ON I'M JUST SKIPPING IT ALTOGETHER."
NOW SEREVING FOR LUNCH:
NO ONE.

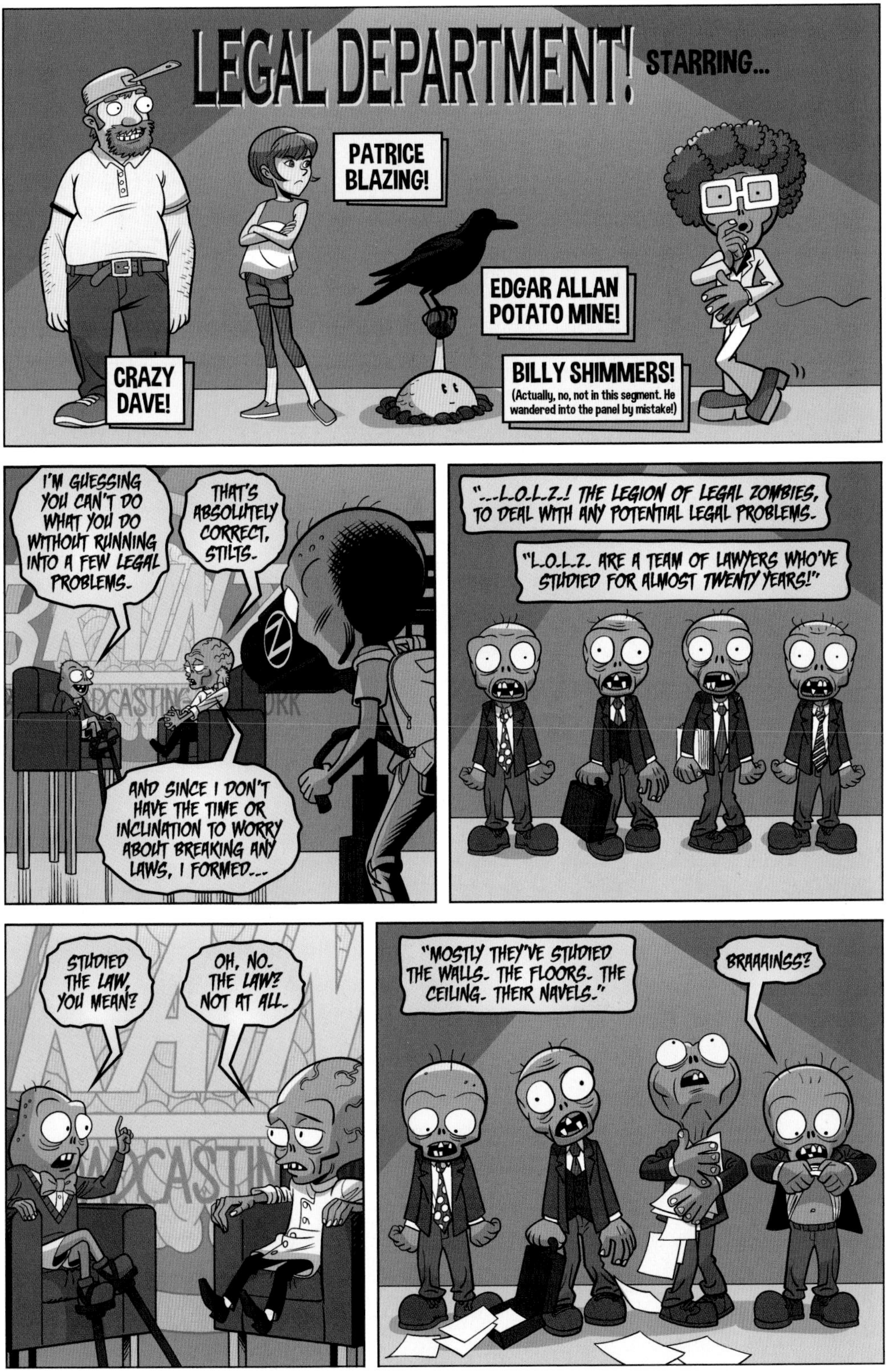
LEGAL DEPARTMENT! STARRING...
CRAZY DAVE!
PATRICE BLAZING!
EDGAR ALLAN POTATO MINE!
BILLY SHIMMERS!
(Actually, no, not in this segment. He wandered into the panel by mistake!)
I'M GUESSING YOU CAN'T DO WHAT YOU DO WITHOUT RUNNING INTO A FEW LEGAL PROBLEMS.
THAT'S ABSOLUTELY CORRECT, STILTS.
AND SINCE I DON'T HAVE THE TIME OR INCLINATION TO WORRY ABOUT BREAKING ANY LAWS, I FORMED...
"...L.O.L.Z.! THE LEGION OF LEGAL ZOMBIES, TO DEAL WITH ANY POTENTIAL LEGAL PROBLEMS.
"L.O.L.Z. ARE A TEAM OF LAWYERS WHO'VE STUDIED FOR ALMOST TWENTY YEARS!"
STUDIED THE LAW, YOU MEAN?
OH, NO. THE LAW? NOT AT ALL.
"MOSTLY THEY'VE STUDIED THE WALLS. THE FLOORS. THE CEILING. THEIR NAVELS."
BRAAAINSS?

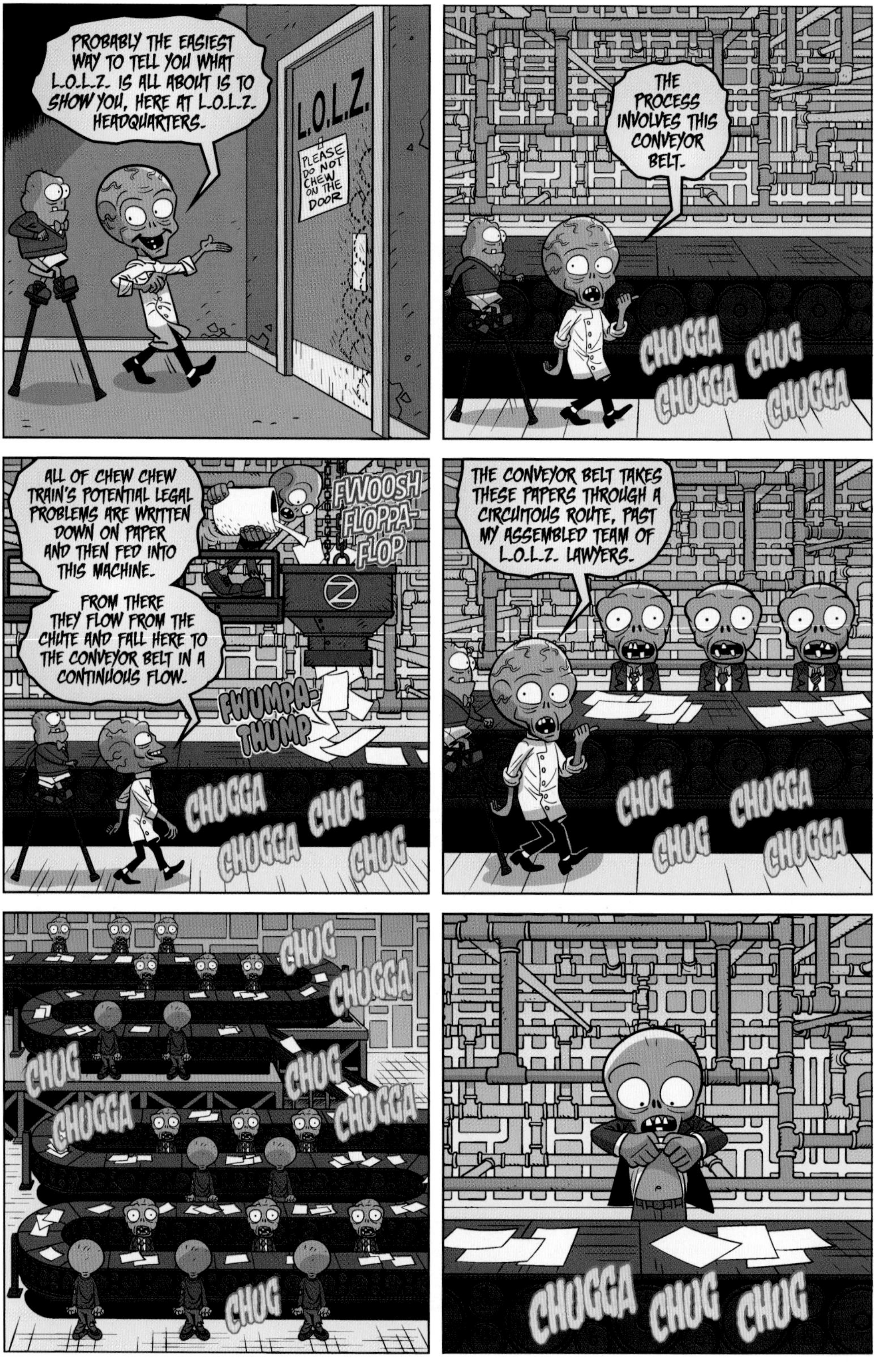
PROBABLY THE EASIEST WAY TO TELL YOU WHAT L.O.L.Z. IS ALL ABOUT IS TO SHOW YOU, HERE AT L.O.L.Z. HEADQUARTERS.
L.O.L.Z.
PLEASE DO NOT CHEW ON THE DOOR
THE PROCESS INVOLVES THIS CONVEYOR BELT.
CHUGGA CHUGGA CHUG CHUGGA
ALL OF CHEW CHEW TRAIN'S POTENTIAL LEGAL PROBLEMS ARE WRITTEN DOWN ON PAPER AND THEN FED INTO THIS MACHINE.
FROM THERE THEY FLOW FROM THE CHUTE AND FALL HERE TO THE CONVEYOR BELT IN A CONTINUOUS FLOW.
FWOOSH FLOPPA-FLOP
FWUMPA-THUMP
CHUGGA CHUGGA CHUG CHUG
THE CONVEYOR BELT TAKES THESE PAPERS THROUGH A CIRCUITOUS ROUTE, PAST MY ASSEMBLED TEAM OF L.O.L.Z. LAWYERS.
CHUG CHUG CHUGGA CHUGGA
CHUG CHUGGA CHUG CHUGGA CHUG CHUGGA CHUG
CHUGGA CHUG CHUG

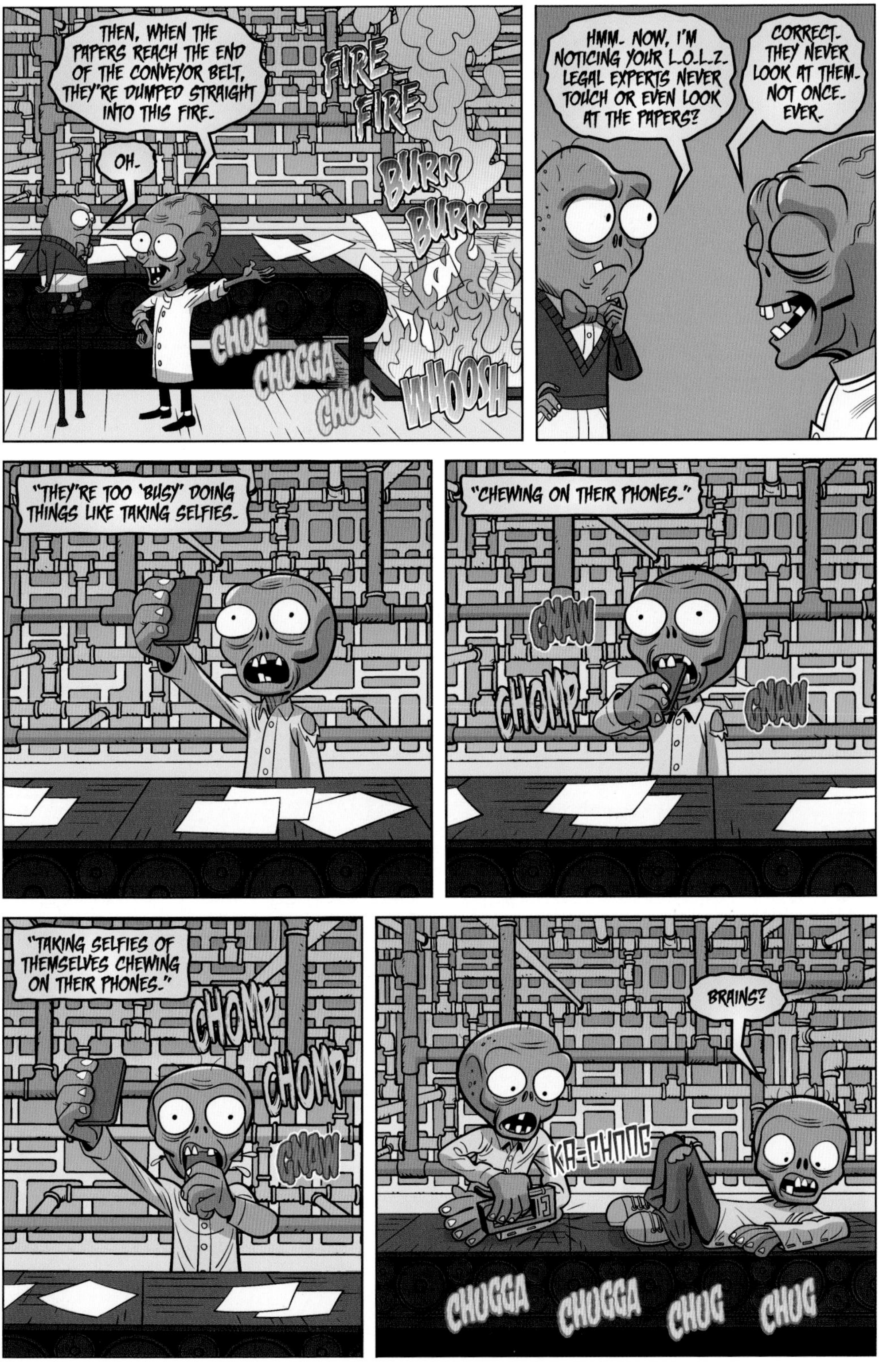
THEN, WHEN THE PAPERS REACH THE END OF THE CONVEYOR BELT, THEY'RE DUMPED STRAIGHT INTO THIS FIRE.
OH.
FIRE
FIRE
BURN
BURN
CHUG
CHUGGA
CHUG
WHOOSH
HMM. NOW, I'M NOTICING YOUR L.O.L.Z. LEGAL EXPERTS NEVER TOUCH OR EVEN LOOK AT THE PAPERS?
CORRECT. THEY NEVER LOOK AT THEM. NOT ONCE. EVER.
"THEY'RE TOO 'BUSY' DOING THINGS LIKE TAKING SELFIES.
"CHEWING ON THEIR PHONES."
GNAW
CHOMP
GNAW
"TAKING SELFIES OF THEMSELVES CHEWING ON THEIR PHONES."
CHOMP
CHOMP
GNAW
BRAINS?
KA-CHNNG
CHUGGA
CHUGGA
CHUG
CHUG

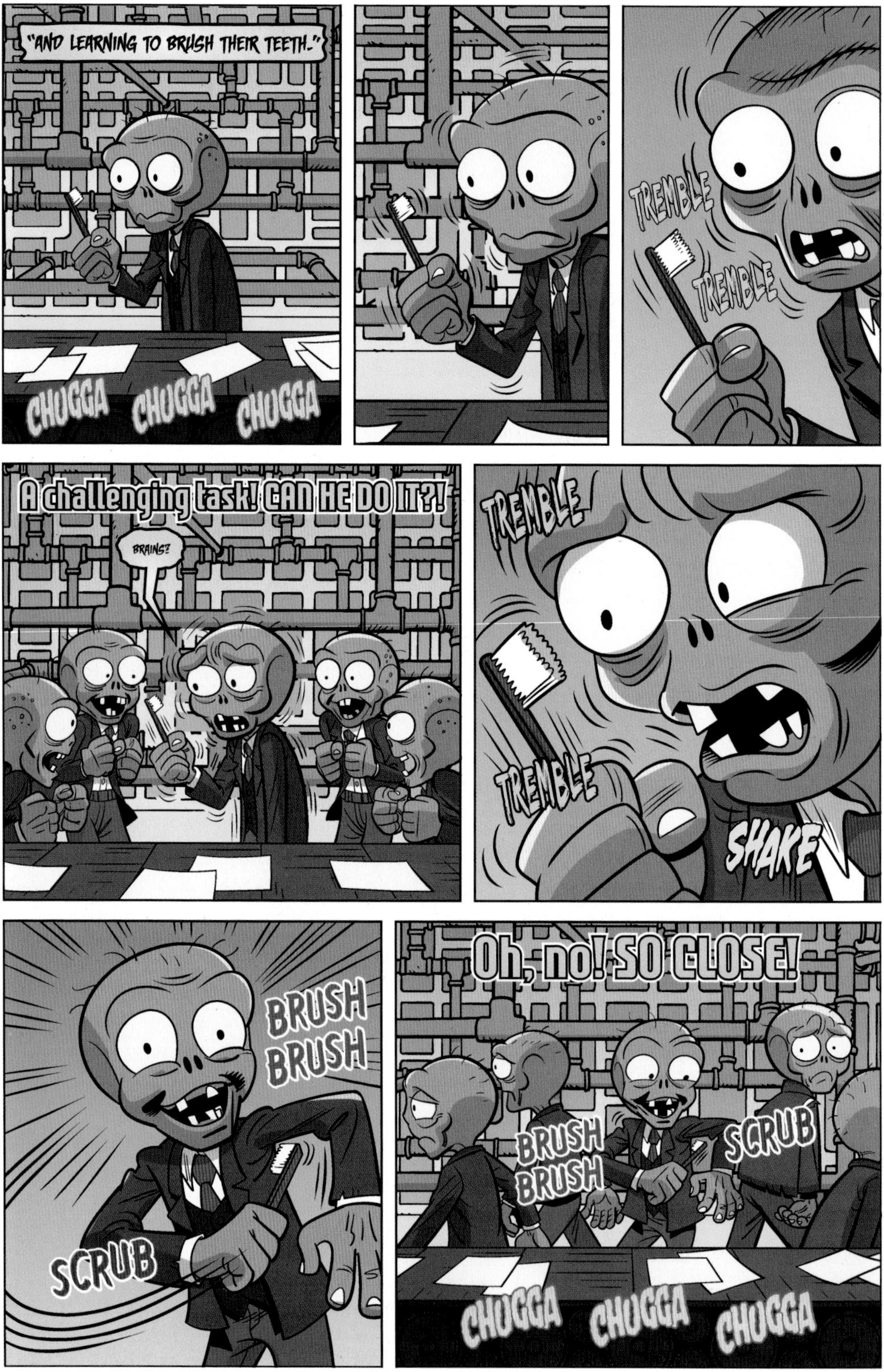
"AND LEARNING TO BRUSH THEIR TEETH."
CHUGGA CHUGGA CHUGGA
TREMBLE
TREMBLE
A challenging task! CAN HE DO IT?!
BRAINS?
TREMBLE
TREMBLE
SHAKE
BRUSH BRUSH
SCRUB
Oh, no! SO CLOSE!
BRUSH BRUSH
SCRUB
CHUGGA CHUGGA CHUGGA

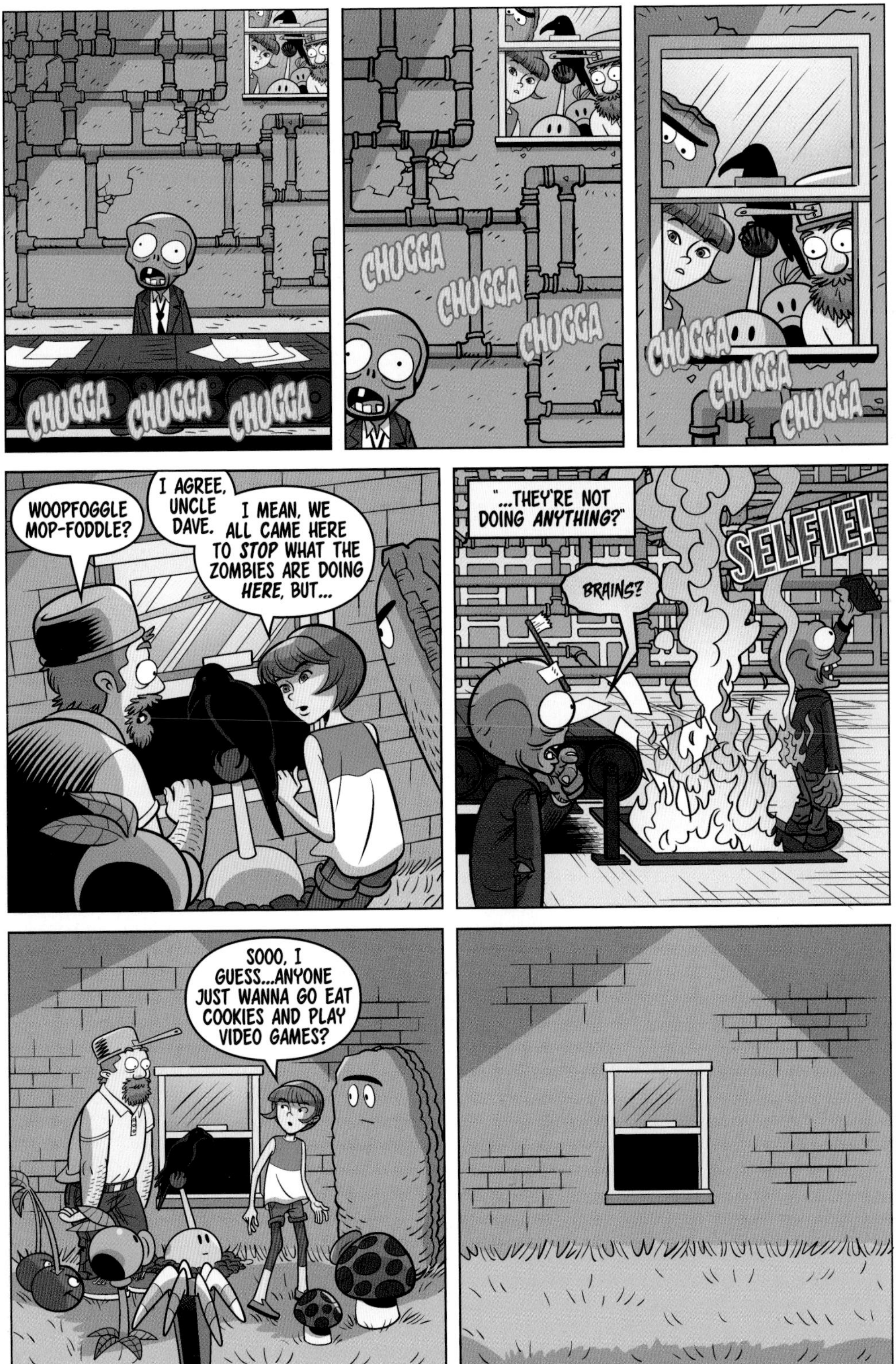
CHUGGA CHUGGA CHUGGA
CHUGGA CHUGGA CHUGGA
CHUGGA CHUGGA CHUGGA
WOOPFOGGLE MOP-FODDLE?
I AGREE, UNCLE DAVE.
I MEAN, WE ALL CAME HERE TO STOP WHAT THE ZOMBIES ARE DOING HERE, BUT...
"...THEY'RE NOT DOING ANYTHING?"
SELFIE!
BRAINS?
SOOO, I GUESS...ANYONE JUST WANNA GO EAT COOKIES AND PLAY VIDEO GAMES?

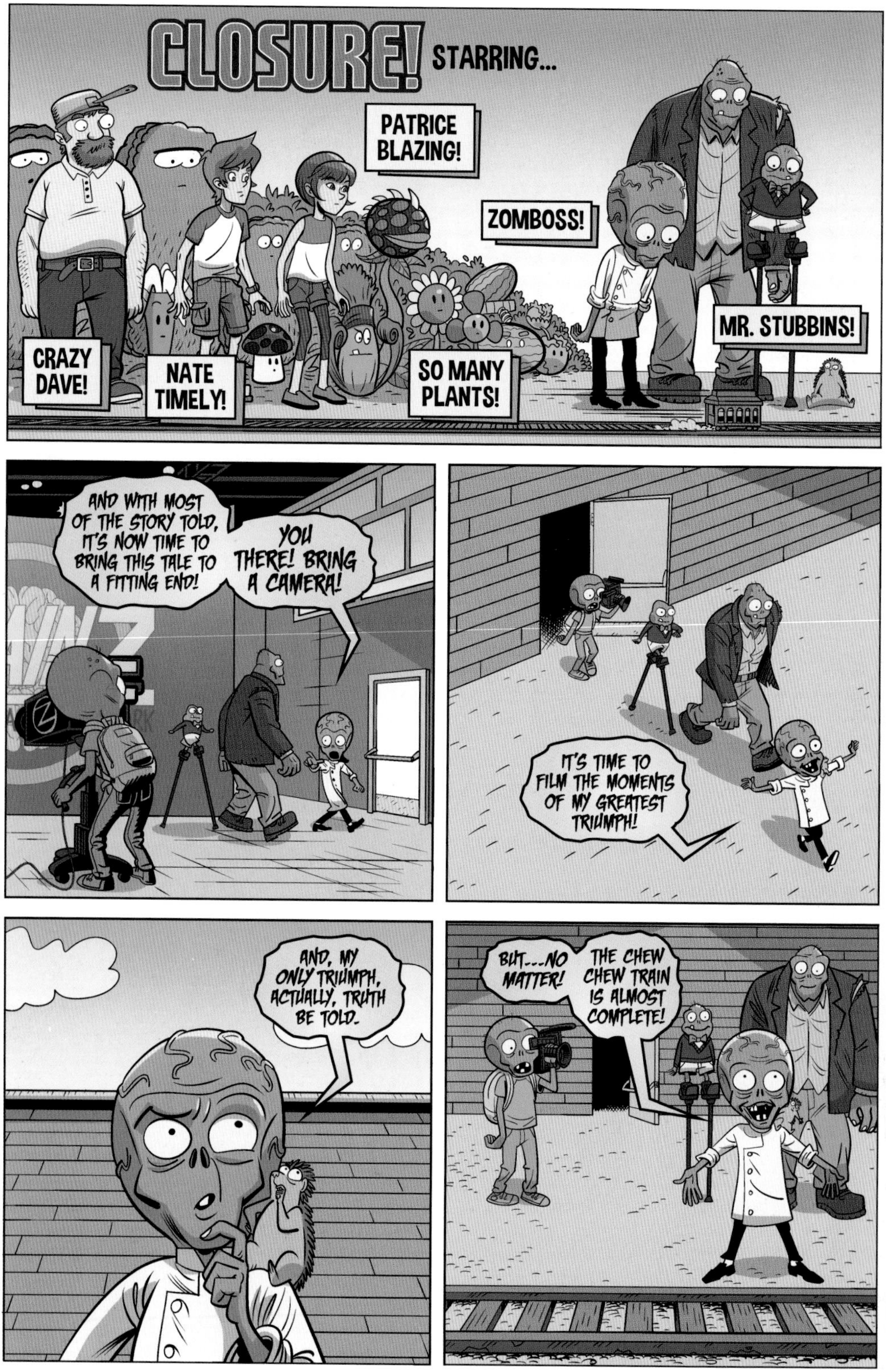
CLOSURE! STARRING...
PATRICE BLAZING!
ZOMBOSS!
MR. STUBBINS!
CRAZY DAVE!
NATE TIMELY!
SO MANY PLANTS!
AND WITH MOST OF THE STORY TOLD, IT'S NOW TIME TO BRING THIS TALE TO A FITTING END!
YOU THERE! BRING A CAMERA!
IT'S TIME TO FILM THE MOMENTS OF MY GREATEST TRIUMPH!
AND, MY ONLY TRIUMPH, ACTUALLY, TRUTH BE TOLD.
BUT...NO MATTER!
THE CHEW CHEW TRAIN IS ALMOST COMPLETE!

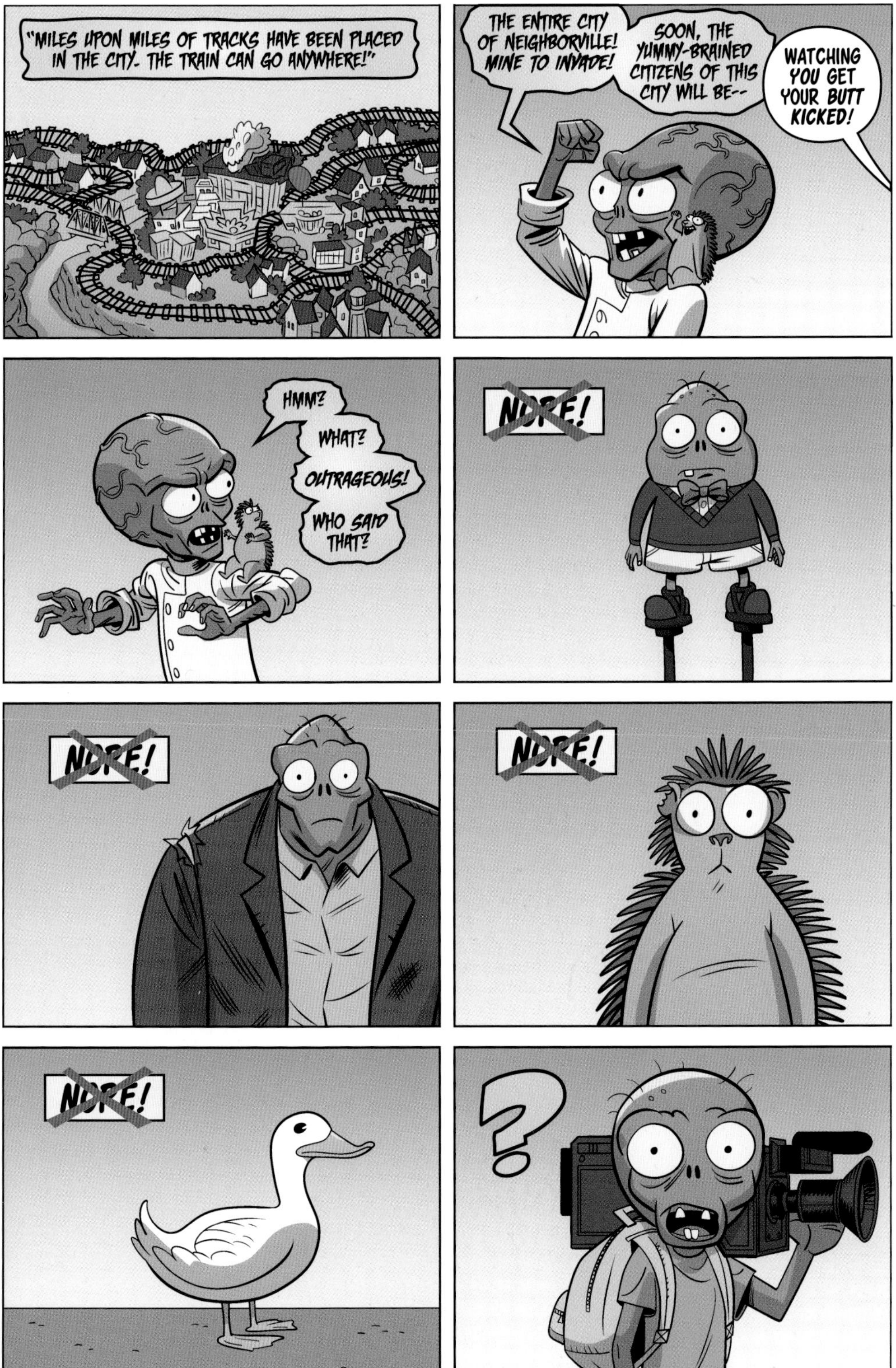
"MILES UPON MILES OF TRACKS HAVE BEEN PLACED IN THE CITY. THE TRAIN CAN GO ANYWHERE!"
THE ENTIRE CITY OF NEIGHBORVILLE! MINE TO INVADE!
SOON, THE YUMMY-BRAINED CITIZENS OF THIS CITY WILL BE--
WATCHING YOU GET YOUR BUTT KICKED!
HMM?
WHAT?
OUTRAGEOUS!
WHO SAID THAT?
NOPE!
NOPE!
NOPE!
NOPE!
?

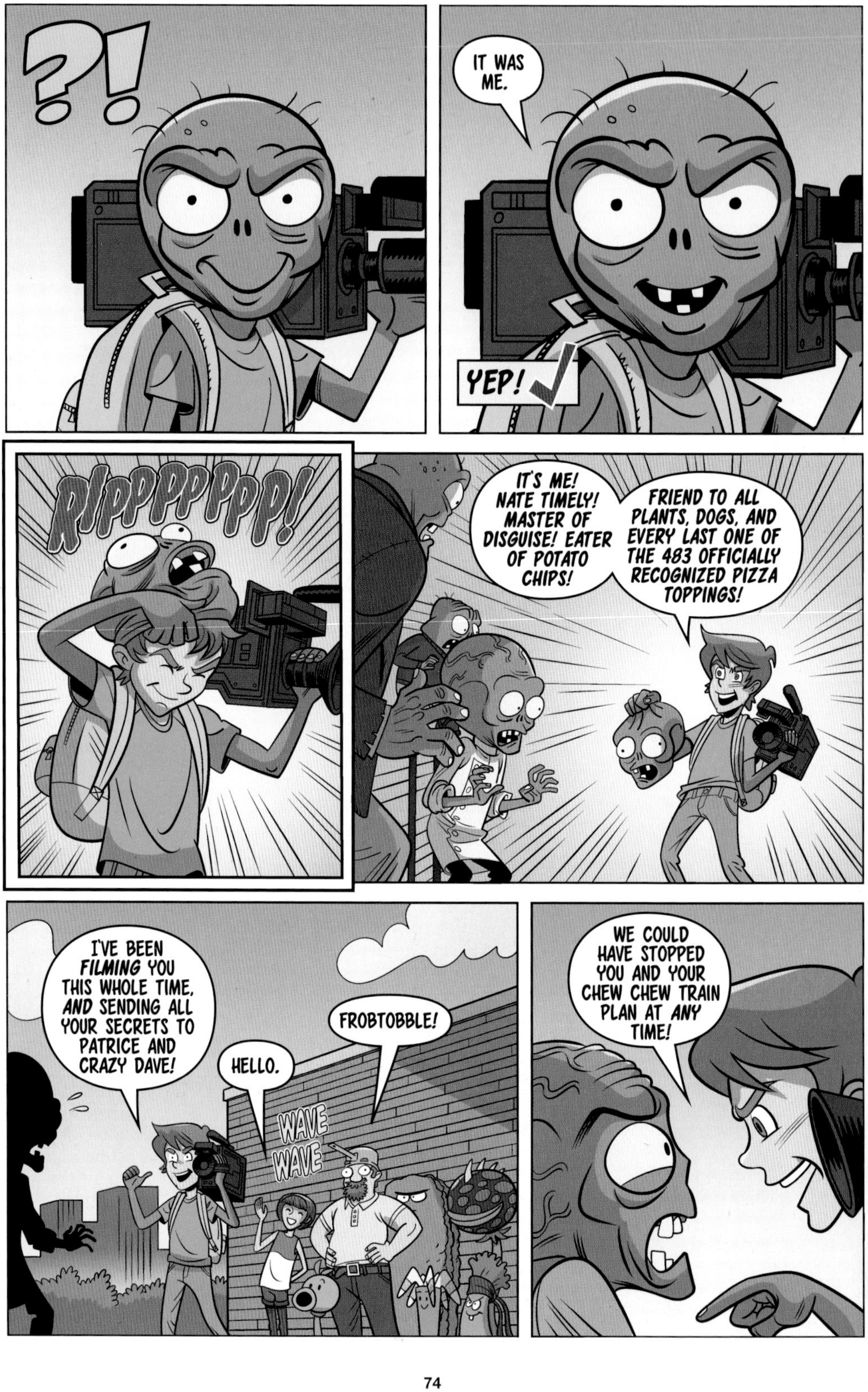
?!
IT WAS ME.
YEP!
RIPPPPPPPP!
IT'S ME! NATE TIMELY! MASTER OF DISGUISE! EATER OF POTATO CHIPS!
FRIEND TO ALL PLANTS, DOGS, AND EVERY LAST ONE OF THE 483 OFFICIALLY RECOGNIZED PIZZA TOPPINGS!
I'VE BEEN FILMING YOU THIS WHOLE TIME, AND SENDING ALL YOUR SECRETS TO PATRICE AND CRAZY DAVE!
HELLO.
FROBTOBBLE!
WAVE
WAVE
WE COULD HAVE STOPPED YOU AND YOUR CHEW CHEW TRAIN PLAN AT ANY TIME!

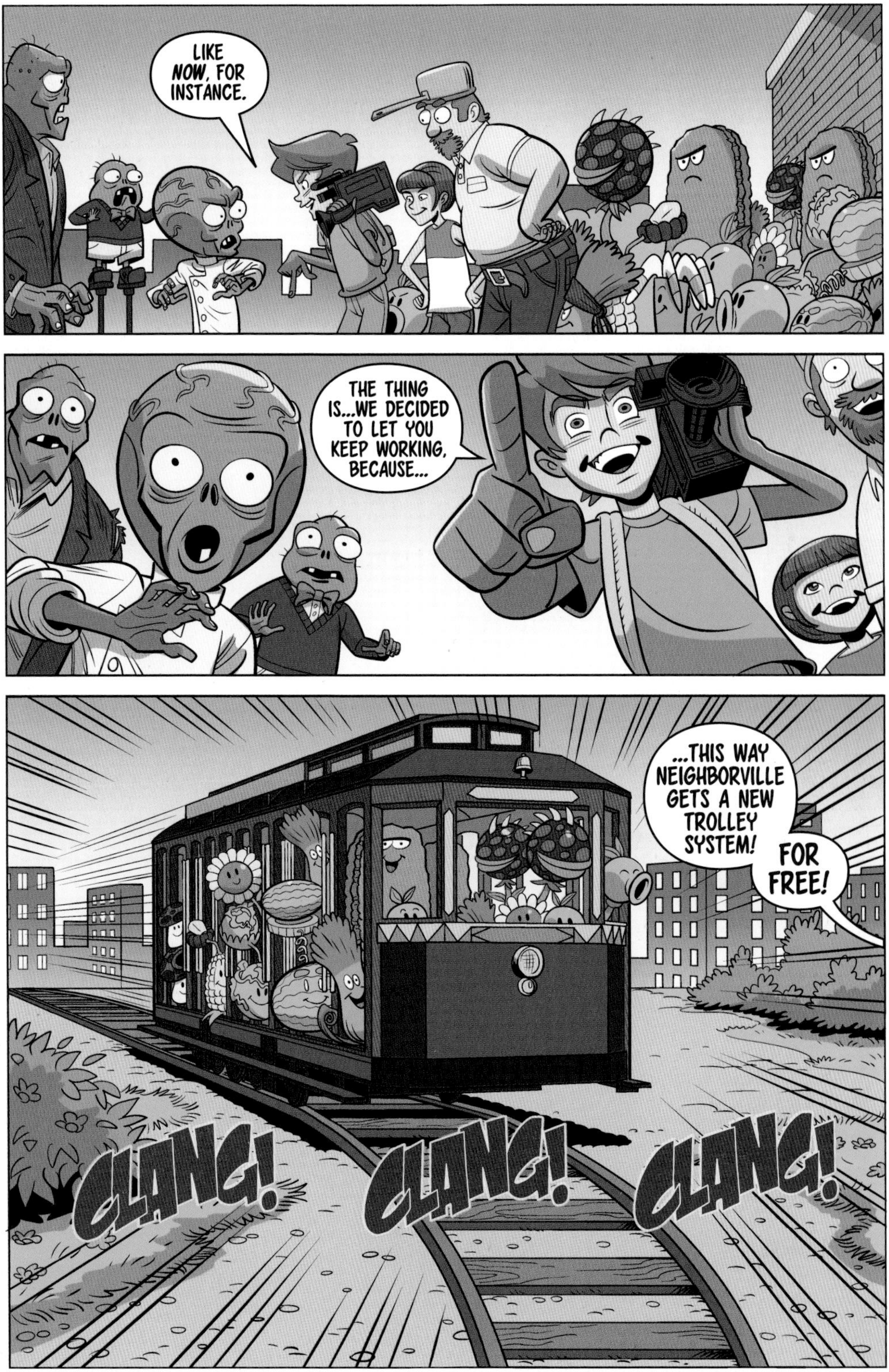
LIKE NOW, FOR INSTANCE.
THE THING IS...WE DECIDED TO LET YOU KEEP WORKING, BECAUSE...
...THIS WAY NEIGHBORVILLE GETS A NEW TROLLEY SYSTEM!
FOR FREE!
CLANG! CLANG! CLANG!

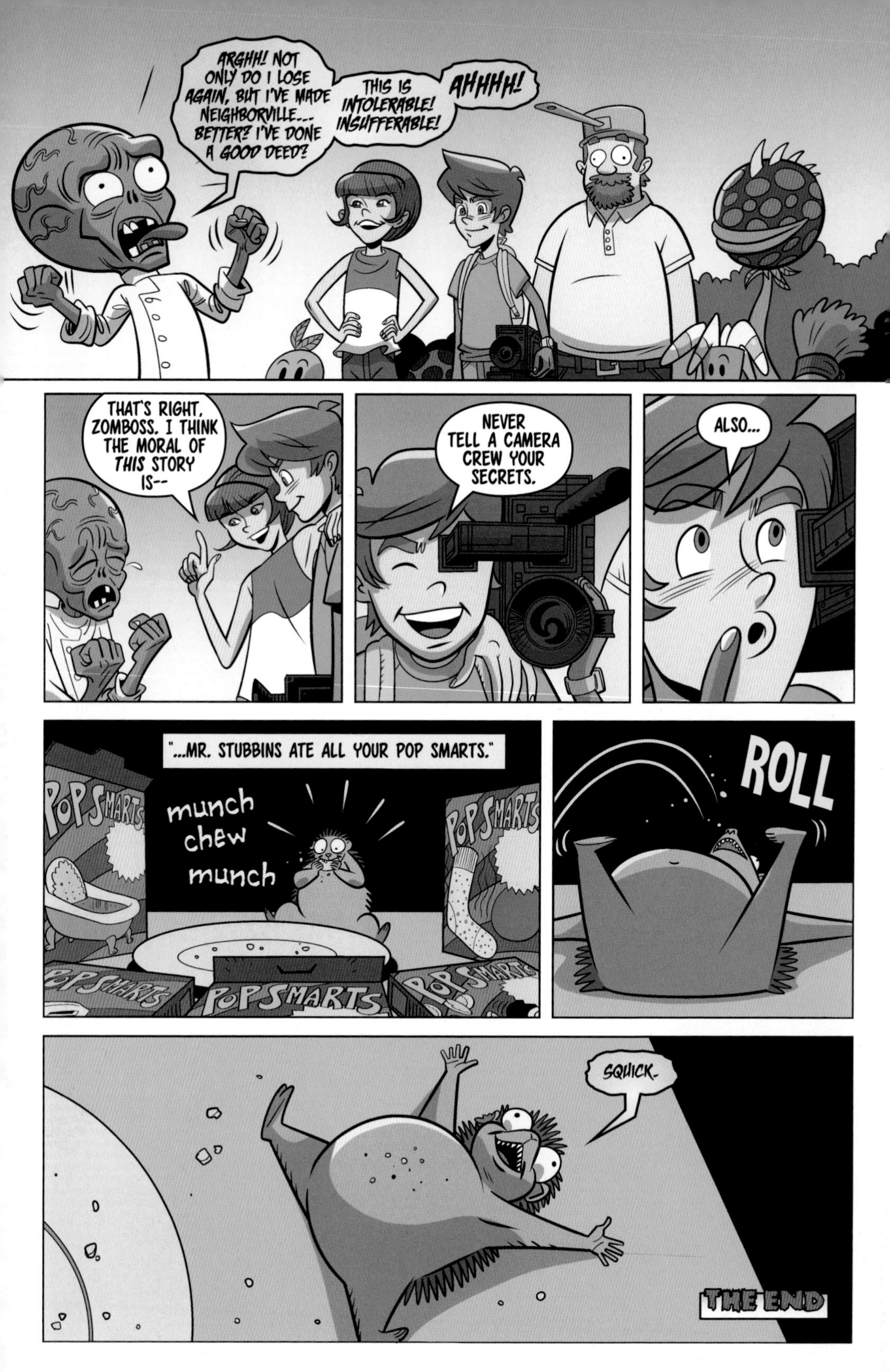
ARGHH! NOT ONLY DO I LOSE AGAIN, BUT I'VE MADE NEIGHBORVILLE... BETTER? I'VE DONE A GOOD DEED?
THIS IS INTOLERABLE! INSUFFERABLE!
AHHHH!
THAT'S RIGHT, ZOMBOSS. I THINK THE MORAL OF THIS STORY IS--
NEVER TELL A CAMERA CREW YOUR SECRETS.
ALSO...
"...MR. STUBBINS ATE ALL YOUR POP SMARTS."
POP SMARTS
munch
chew
munch
ROLL
SQUICK.
THE END

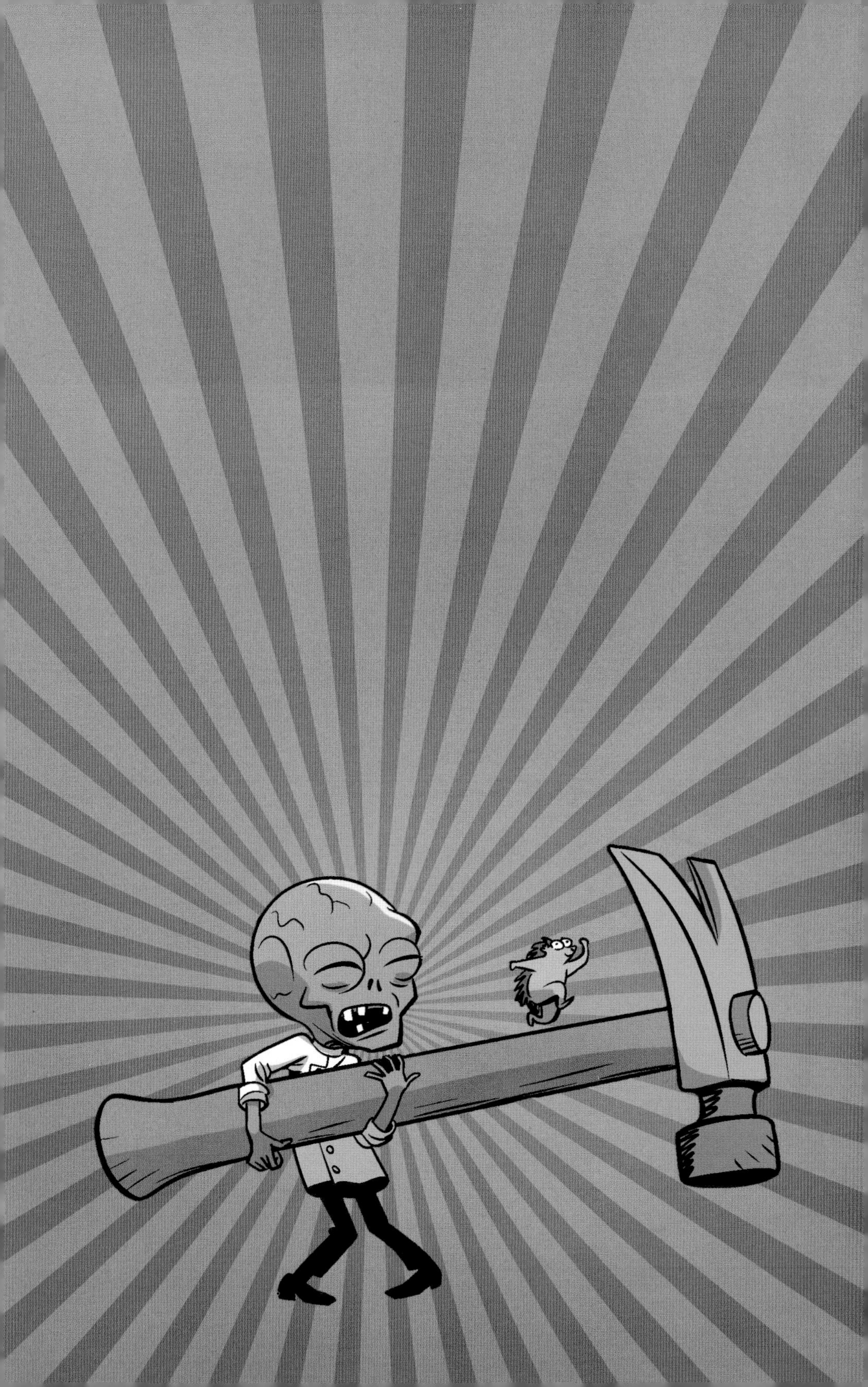

PLANTS VS. ZOMBIES: CONSTRUCTIONARY TALES
COVER PENCILS BY RON CHAN

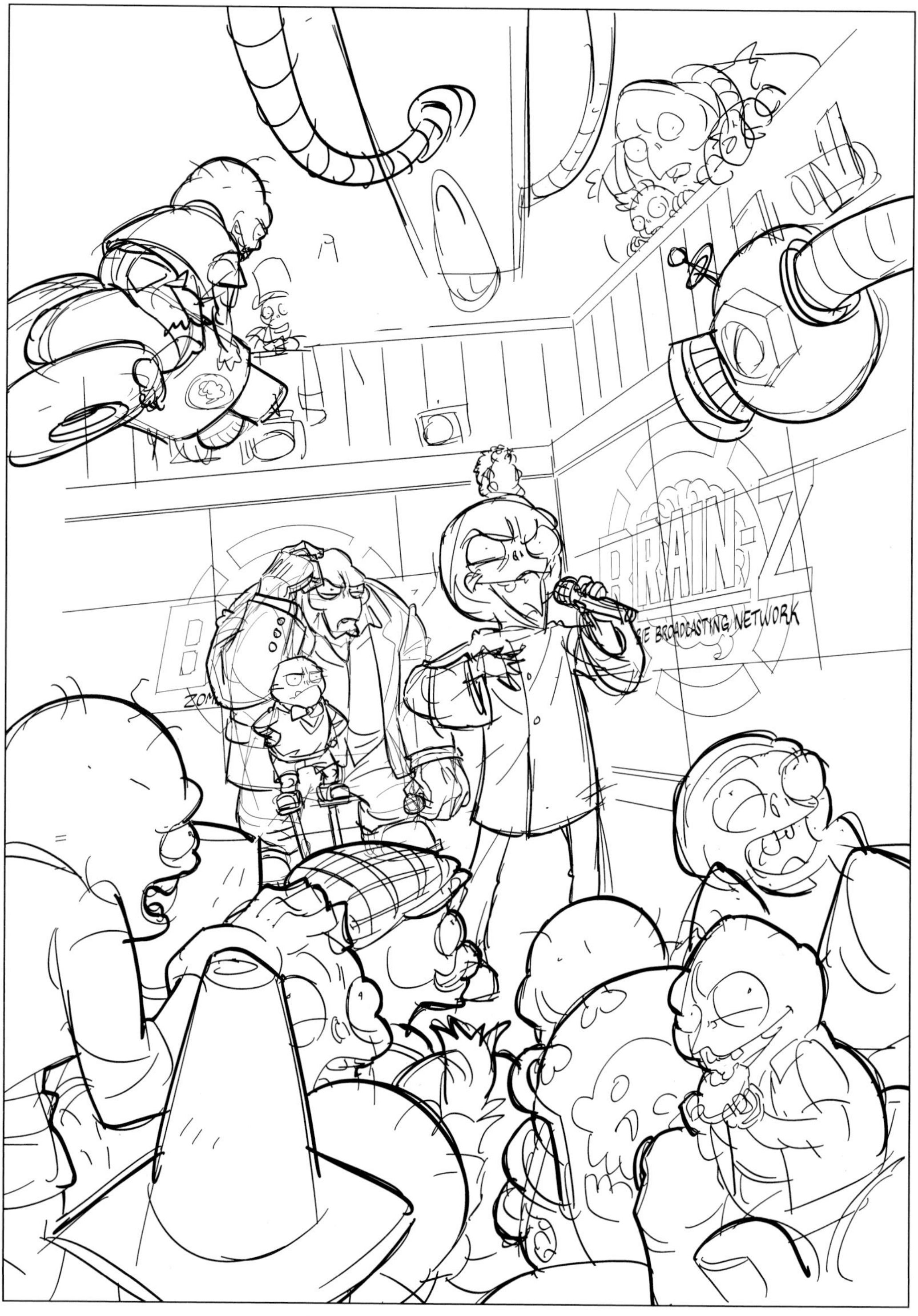
BRAIN-Z
BIE BROADCASTING NETWORK

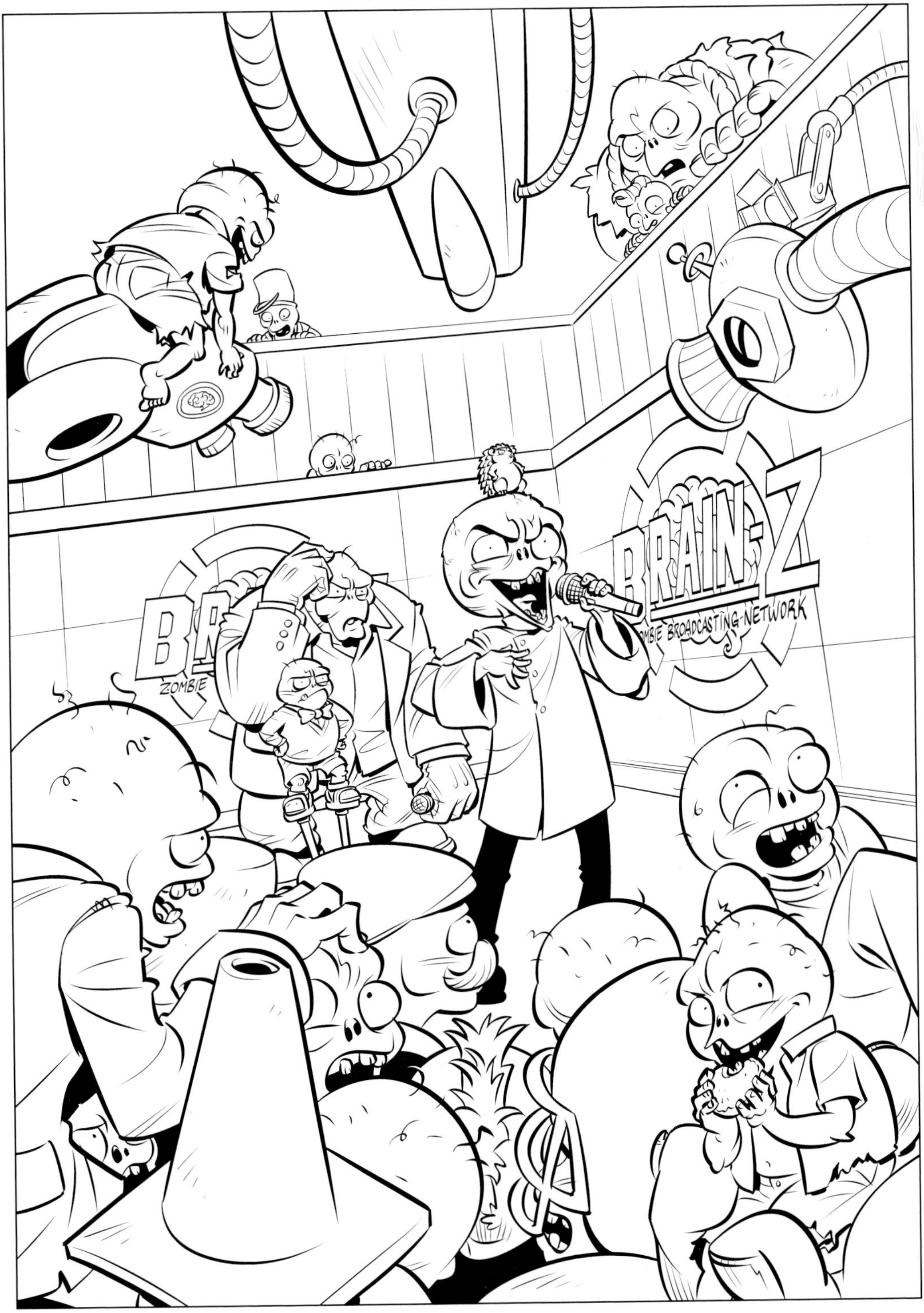
BRAIN-Z
ZOMBIE BROADCASTING NETWORK
BR
ZOMBIE

CONSTRUCTIONARY TALES **PENCIL ART GALLERY!**
ALL PAGES BY ARTIST JESSE HAMM

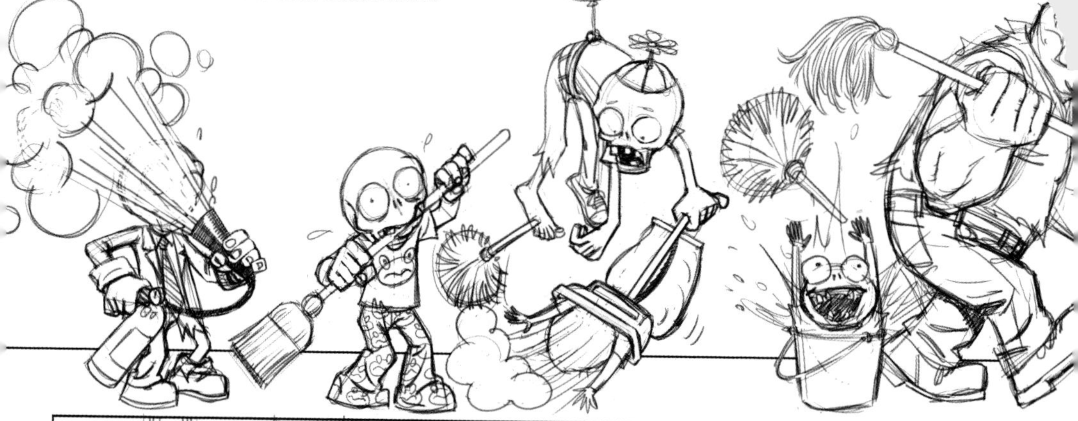

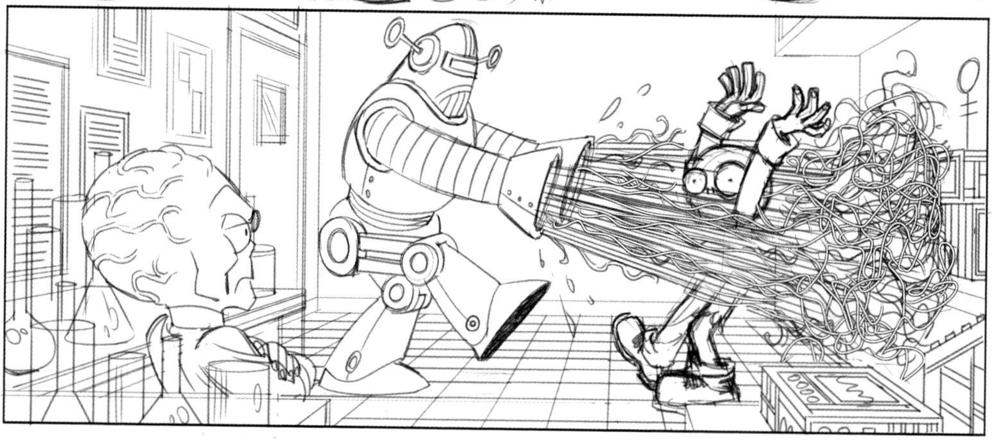

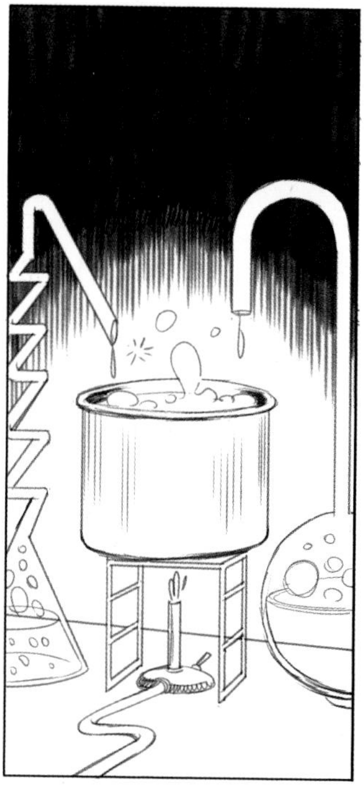

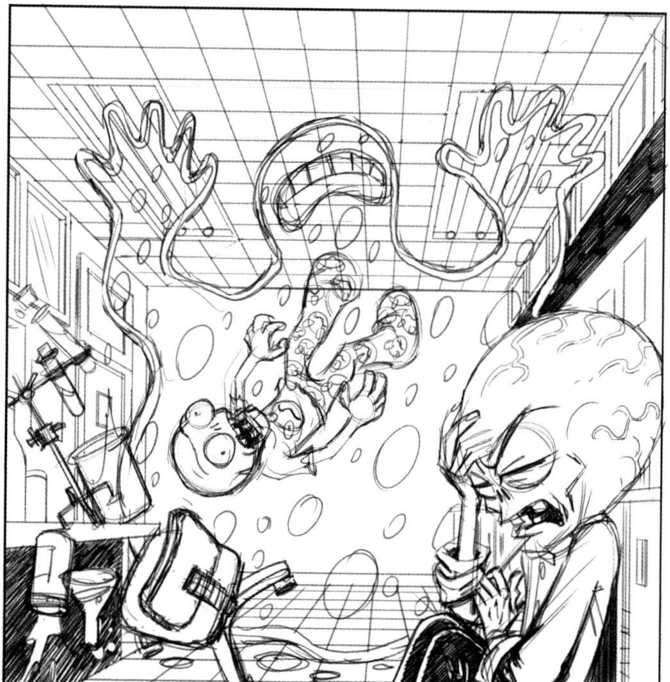

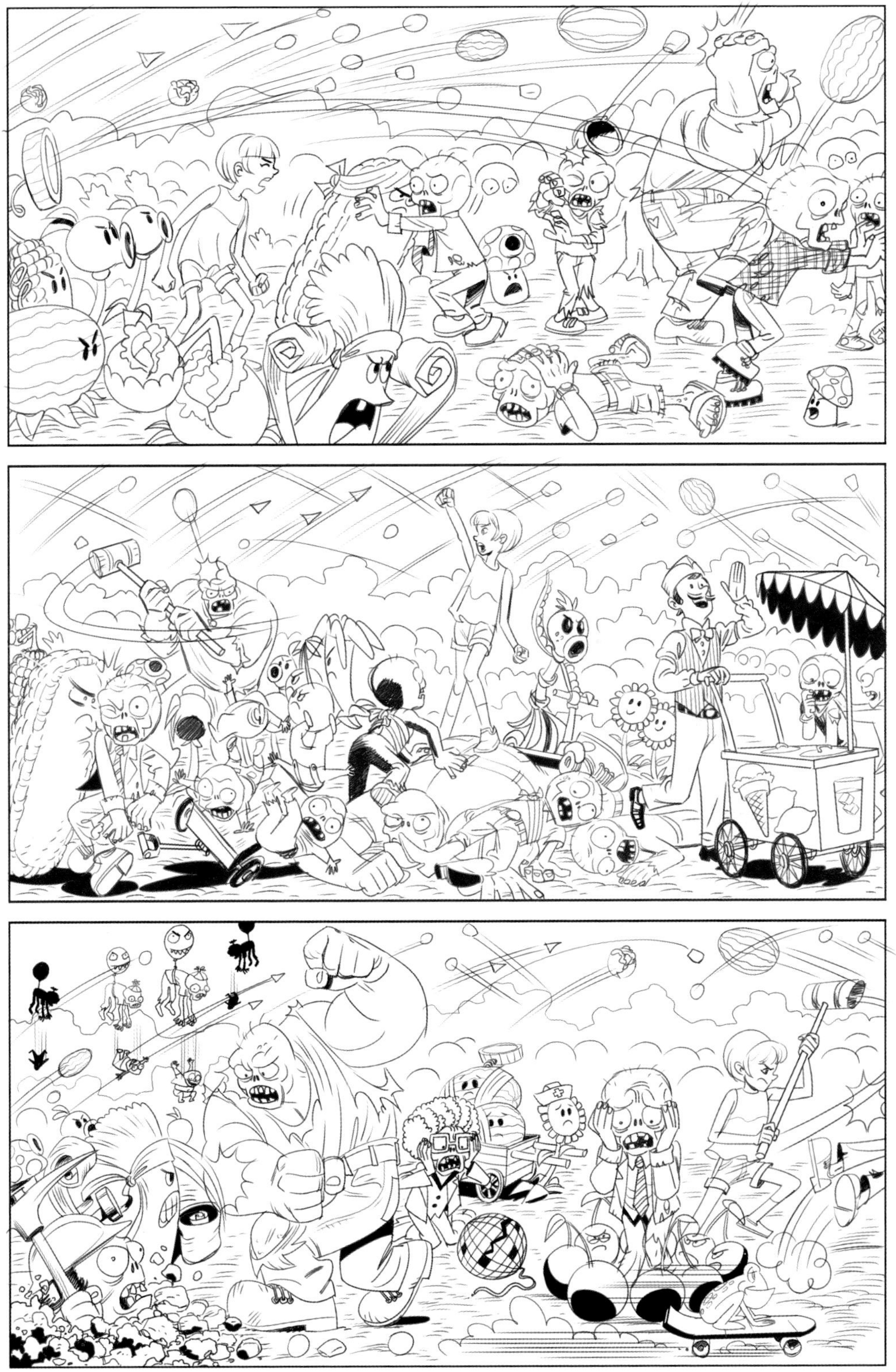

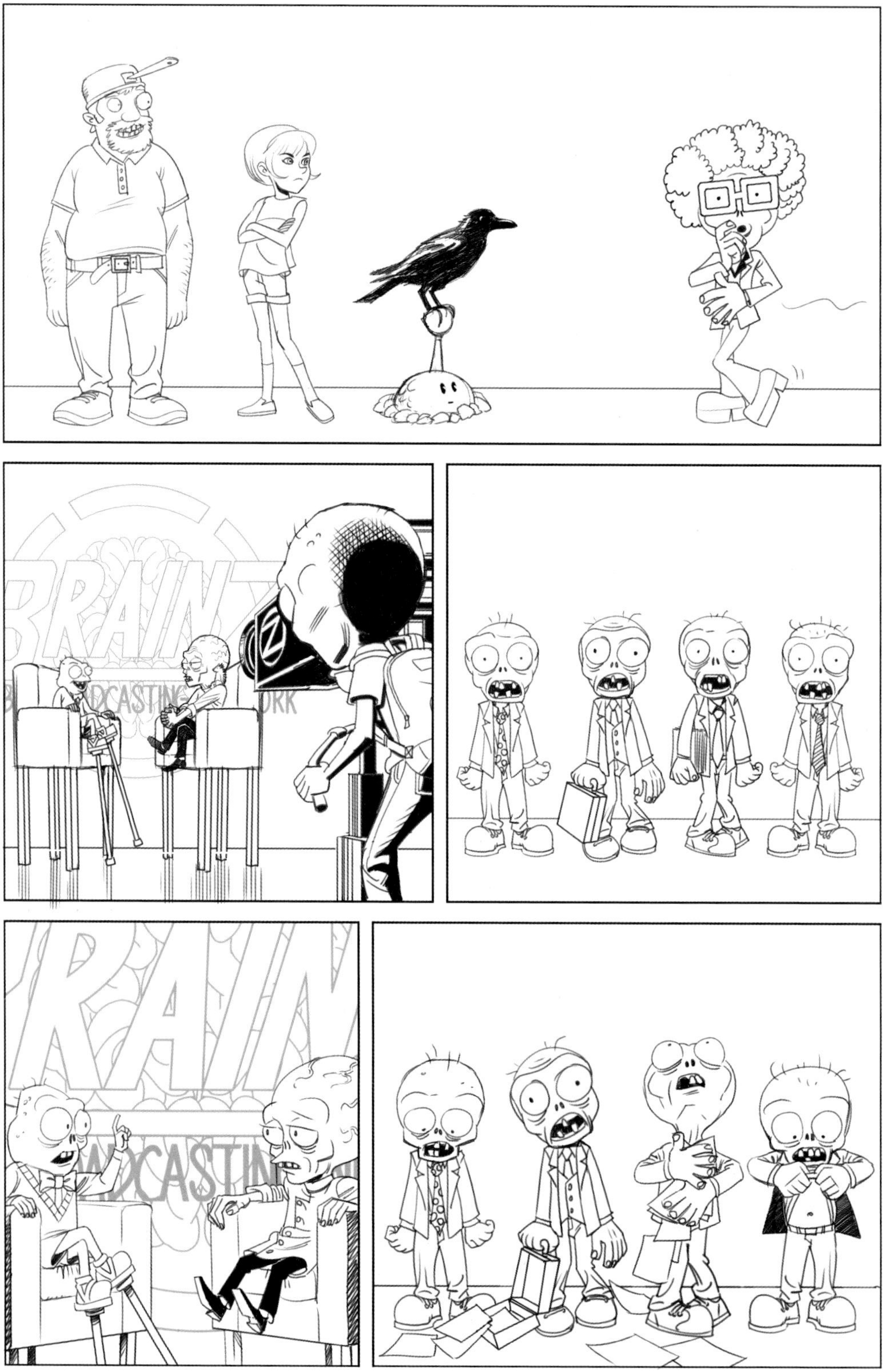

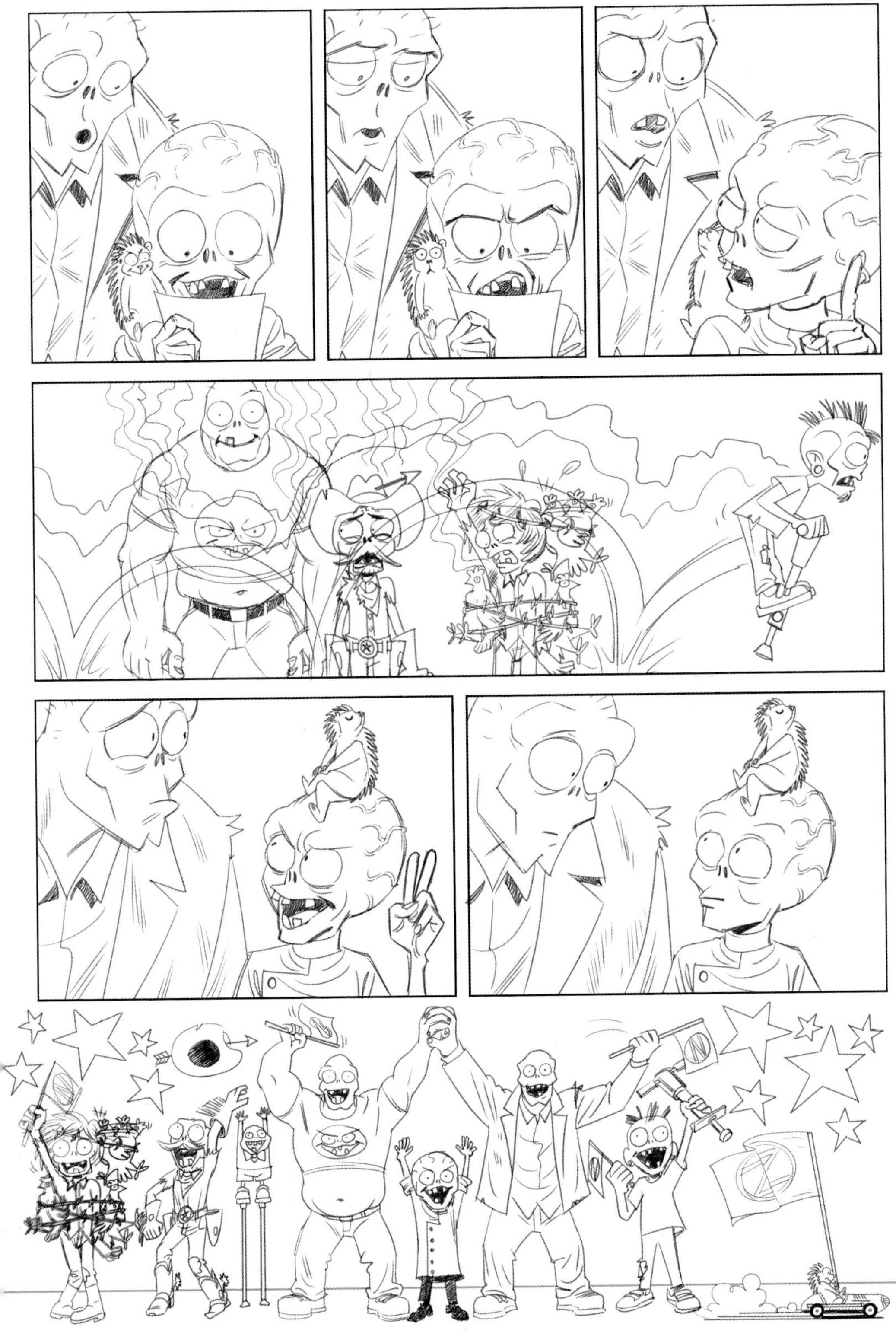

CREATOR BIOS

PAUL TOBIN is a 12th level writer and a 15th level cookie eater. He begins each morning in the manner we all do, by battling those zombies that have strayed too close to his pillow fort. Between writing all the *Plants vs. Zombies* comics and taking four naps a day, he's also found time to write the *Genius Factor* series of novels, the ape-filled *Banana Sunday* graphic novel, the award-winning *Bandette* series, the upcoming *Wrassle Castle* and *Earth Boy* graphic novels, and many other works. He has ridden a giant turtle and an elephant on purpose, and a tornado by accident.

Paul Tobin

JESSE HAMM lives with his wife and three cats near the Columbia River Gorge. He is a member of Helioscope, a comic art studio in Portland, Oregon, and has been drawing comics professionally for over fifteen years. Characters whose adventures he's drawn include Batman, Hawkeye, Flash Gordon, Prince Valiant, and The Phantom. When he is not drawing comics, Jesse busies himself sharing cartooning tips on Twitter and writing online articles about how to draw. He also enjoys watching old movies, taking long walks with his wife, and reading books about theology.

Jesse Hamm

Heather Breckel

HEATHER BRECKEL went to the Columbus College of Art and Design for animation. She decided animation wasn't for her, so she switched to comics. She's been working as a colorist for nearly ten years and has worked for nearly every major comics publisher out there. When she's not burning the midnight oil in a deadline crunch, she's either dying a bunch in videogames or telling her cats to stop running around at two in the morning.

Steve Dutro

STEVE DUTRO is a pinball fan and an Eisner Award-nominated comic book letterer from Redding, California, who can also drive a tractor. He graduated from the Kubert School and has been lettering comics since the days when foil-embossed covers were cool, working for Dark Horse (*The Fifth Beatle*, *I Am a Hero*, *StarCraft*, *Star Wars*, *Witcher*), Viz, Marvel, and DC Comics. He has submitted a request to the Department of Homeland Security that in the event of a zombie apocalypse he be put in charge of all digital freeway signs so citizens can be alerted to avoid nearby brain-eatings and the like. He finds the *Plants vs. Zombies* game to be a real stress-fest, but highly recommends the *Plants vs. Zombies* table on *Pinball FX2* for game-room hipsters.

ALSO AVAILABLE FROM DARK HORSE!

THE HIT VIDEO GAME CONTINUES ITS COMIC BOOK INVASION!

THE ART OF PLANTS VS. ZOMBIES
Part zombie memoir, part celebration of zombie triumphs, and part anti-plant screed, *The Art of Plants vs. Zombies* is a treasure trove of never-before-seen concept art, character sketches, and surprises from PopCap's popular *Plants vs. Zombies* games!
ISBN 978-1-61655-331-9 | $10.99

PLANTS VS. ZOMBIES: LAWNMAGEDDON
Crazy Dave—the babbling-yet-brilliant inventor and top-notch neighborhood defender—helps young adventurer Nate fend off a zombie invasion that threatens to overrun the peaceful town of Neighborville in *Plants vs. Zombies: Lawnmageddon*! Their only hope is a brave army of chomping, squashing, and pea-shooting plants! A wacky adventure for zombie zappers young and old!
ISBN 978-1-61655-192-6 | $10.99

PLANTS VS. ZOMBIES: TIMEPOCALYPSE
Crazy Dave helps Patrice and Nate Timely fend off Zomboss' latest attack in *Plants vs. Zombies: Timepocalypse*! This new standalone tale will tickle your funny bones and thrill your brains through any timeline!
ISBN 978-1-61655-621-1 | $10.99

PLANTS VS. ZOMBIES: BULLY FOR YOU
Patrice and Nate are ready to investigate a strange college campus to keep the streets safe from zombies!
ISBN 978-1-61655-889-5 | $10.99

PLANTS VS. ZOMBIES: GARDEN WARFARE VOLUME 1
Based on the hit video game, this comic tells the story leading up to the events in *Plants vs. Zombies: Garden Warfare 2*!
ISBN 978-1-61655-946-5 | $10.99

VOLUME 2 ISBN 978-1-50670-548-4 | $10.99

VOLUME 3 ISBN 978-1-50670-837-9 | $10.99

PLANTS VS. ZOMBIES: GROWN SWEET HOME
With newfound knowledge of humanity, Dr. Zomboss strikes at the heart of Neighborville . . . sparking a series of plant-versus-zombie brawls!
ISBN 978-1-61655-971-7 | $10.99

PLANTS VS. ZOMBIES: PETAL TO THE METAL
Crazy Dave takes on the tough *Don't Blink* video game—and challenges Dr. Zomboss to a race to determine the future of Neighborville!
ISBN 978-1-61655-999-1 | $10.99

PLANTS VS. ZOMBIES: BOOM BOOM MUSHROOM
The gang discover Zomboss' secret plan for swallowing the city of Neighborville whole! A rare mushroom must be found in order to save the humans aboveground!
ISBN 978-1-50670-037-3 | $10.99

PLANTS VS. ZOMBIES: BATTLE EXTRAVAGONZO
Zomboss is back, hoping to buy the same factory that Crazy Dave is eyeing! Will Crazy Dave and his intelligent plants beat Zomboss and his zombie army to the punch?
ISBN 978-1-50670-189-9 | $10.99

PLANTS VS. ZOMBIES: LAWN OF DOOM
With Zomboss filling everyone's yards with traps and special soldiers, will he and his zombie army turn Halloween into their zanier Lawn of Doom celebration?!
ISBN 978-1-50670-204-9 | $10.99

**PLANTS VS. ZOMBIES:
THE GREATEST SHOW UNEARTHED**
Dr. Zomboss believes that all humans hold a secret desire to run away and join the circus, so he aims to use his "Big Z's Adequately Amazing Flytrap Circus" to lure Neighborville's citizens to their doom!
ISBN 978-1-50670-298-8 | $10.99

PLANTS VS. ZOMBIES: RUMBLE AT LAKE GUMBO
The battle for clean water begins! Nate, Patrice, and Crazy Dave spot trouble and grab all the Tangle Kelp and Party Crabs they can to quell another zombie attack!
ISBN 978-1-50670-497-5 | $10.99

PLANTS VS. ZOMBIES: WAR AND PEAS
When Dr. Zomboss and Crazy Dave find themselves members of the same book club, a literary war is inevitable! The position of leader of the book club opens up and Zomboss and Crazy Dave compete for the top spot in a scholarly scuffle for the ages!
ISBN 978-1-50670-677-1 | $10.99

PLANTS VS. ZOMBIES: DINO-MIGHT
Dr. Zomboss sets his sights on destroying the yards in town and rendering the plants homeless—and his plans include dogs, cats, rabbits, hammock sloths, and, somehow, dinosaurs . . . !
ISBN 978-1-50670-838-6 | $10.99

PLANTS VS. ZOMBIES: SNOW THANKS
Dr. Zomboss invents a Cold Crystal capable of freezing Neighborville, burying the town in snow and ice! It's up to the humans and the fieriest plants to save Neighborville—with the help of pirates!
ISBN 978-1-50670-839-3 | $10.99

PLANTS VS. ZOMBIES: A LITTLE PROBLEM
Will an invasion of teeny-tiny miniature zombies mean the party for Crazy Dave's two-hundred-year-old pants gets canceled?
ISBN 978-1-50670-840-9 | $10.99

**PLANTS VS. ZOMBIES:
BETTER HOMES AND GUARDENS**
Nate and Patrice try thwarting zombie attacks by putting defending "Guardens" plants *inside* homes as well as in yards! But as soon as Dr. Zomboss finds out, he's determined to circumvent this plan with an epically evil one of his own . . .
ISBN 978-1-50671-305-2 | $10.99

PLANTS VS. ZOMBIES: MULTI-BALL-ISTIC
Dr. Zomboss turns the entirety of Neighborville into a giant, fully functional pinball machine! Nate, Patrice, and their plant posse must find a way to halt this uniquely horrifying zombie invasion. Will the battle go full-tilt zombies?!
ISBN 978-1-50671-307-6 | $10.99

PLANTS VS. ZOMBIES: CONSTRUCTIONARY TALES
A behind-the-scenes look at the secret schemes and craziest contraptions concocted by Zomboss, as he proudly leads around a film crew from the Zombie Broadcasting Network!
ISBN 978-1-50672-091-3 | $10.99

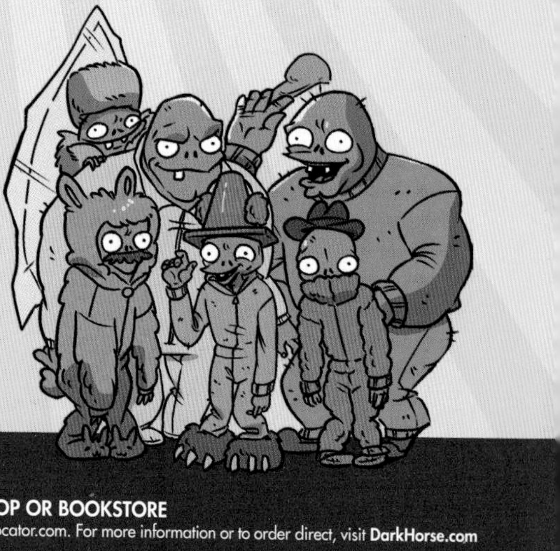

DARK HORSE BOOKS · EA · PopCap

AVAILABLE AT YOUR LOCAL COMICS SHOP OR BOOKSTORE
To find a comics shop in your area, visit comicshoplocator.com. For more information or to order direct, visit **DarkHorse.com**